The Place You Belong

The Place You Belong

Marcia Harrison Carpenter

Carpenter's Son Publishing

The Place You Belong

© 2020 Marcia Harrison Carpenter

Published by Carpenter's Son Publishing, Franklin, Tennessee

Published in association with Larry Carpenter of Christian Book Services, LLC
www.christianbookservices.com

Cover and Interior Design by Suzanne Lawing

Edited by Lapiz Digital Services

Printed in the United States of America

978-1-949572-71-1

Chapter 1

Joselene Matthews's heart raced. She swallowed hard against the cottony dryness of her mouth. What if he didn't want her here? Where would she go? All the money and time spent on this single trip to Terre Haute. It had to work out. It just had to.

She sucked in a deep breath and held it. Was she at the right house? Hands shaking, palms sweating, she lifted the scrap of paper with the address scribbled on it to check. The number above the front door indicated she was at the correct place. Her heart pounded as she released the air through her teeth. She'd dreamed of this moment for weeks.

She marched up the steps to the porch of the blue-and-yellow Victorian house, plunked down her suitcase, and flexed her fingers while she gazed about. Pretentious houses and spacious lawns indicated to her that money lived in this neighborhood. Her thoughts whirled. Would she fit in with highfalutin people—a mere country girl from a small town with unpaved streets? Josie shook her head. She couldn't go back to Bradford. It was now or never for a future here.

The wind whipped across the porch making the swing sway. Josie tucked in a wisp of hair the breeze wrested from her cloche and clutched the edges of her woolen coat to hug it against her chest. She repositioned her pocketbook on her arm and stepped up to the massive front door. Her hand trembling, she raised the polished brass doorknocker. "Please, *please*, Lord, let him be here."

Before she could release it, the door opened abruptly and a young man stormed out. Startled, Josie jumped backward, losing her balance. Flapping her arms, she dropped her purse.

"Sorry, miss." The man caught her, grabbed her elbows to steady her, and kept her from tumbling head-first into the house. "You all right?"

"I . . . I think so." Josie's face burned as she worked to straighten her hat, pushed askew in the struggle.

He bent over to retrieve her pocketbook and handed it to her.

"Oh, thank you."

His mouth curled into a lopsided grin as he doffed his fedora with a flourish and hurried down the front walk. He climbed into the spit-polished Studebaker parked at the curb, started the engine, and pulled away.

Josie remained where she was with her mouth open.

"May I help you?"

Josie jumped and spun around to face a woman of average height and build, and whose salt-and-pepper hair was severely pulled back to form a proper, coiled-up bun. "Oh! Hello. Is this the residence of Landon Matthews?"

The woman stood ramrod straight, folded her arms across her chest, and looked down out of the bottom of her wire-rimmed spectacles at Josie. "Yes."

"Is he home?" Please, *please* say yes.

"Do you have an appointment with him today?"

Josie tensed, forcing her shoulders to straighten. "Um . . . not exactly." She scrutinized the woman in the doorway. A gatekeeper's stern expression. Simple blue cotton dress. Sturdy shoes.

"Saturday is Mr. Matthews's day off. I'm his housekeeper. Perhaps I can help you. What do you want?"

"I need to see *him*." Hopefully, her words sounded compelling.

"HMPH! Are you begging? Or are you selling something out of *that . . . thing*?" She pointed to the battered luggage.

Josie's face grew hot. "No. I'm not selling or begging."

A few seconds passed before the woman asked, "Is yours an urgent matter?"

"No . . . but it's . . . a personal matter."

The woman sighed. "Wait until Monday. I'm sure he'll meet with you at his office." She took a step back.

"No, I must see him today." Josie breathed in a long breath, blew it out.

"Is that so?"

"Yes, ma'am."

"Determined, aren't you?"

"Yes, I am. I won't leave until I've seen him. I'm willing to wait. So, where can I sit? How about . . . here would be fine . . . on the steps?" She plopped down, pulling her coat to her legs.

The woman bolted from the doorway. "Land sakes! You can't stay there. Why, what would the neighbors think?"

Josie tipped her head toward the woman towering over her. "I've been awake since three o'clock. I rode on a train for hours, and I lost track of the number of blocks I had to walk from the Union Station. I'm exhausted and hungry, but I'm not going to let anyone or anything get in the way of seeing my . . . of seeing and talking with Landon Matthews."

"Is that so?"

"Yes, ma'am. I'm sure Mr. Matthews would want you to ask me in."

"Oh? Why is that?"

"Because I'm a . . . a relative of his."

"Really? A relative, you say? Why didn't you say so sooner? What's your name?"

"Joselene Grace Matthews."

The woman put her fists on her hips. "Huh! He's never mentioned your name before."

"Please, I *am* a relative. He doesn't know . . . about me." Josie stood, stiffening her spine.

The woman pursed her lips. "I think there're some shenanigans going on here. Just go to his office on Monday."

"Oh, no!" Josie pressed the air with both palms. "That won't do. I'm quite sure he would want to meet me."

"Maybe. I'll find out, though. You wait here." She backed up and closed the door. Josie chewed at the corner of her mouth and shifted her weight from one foot to the other.

She walked to the edge of the porch, stopped short, and fixed her gaze on a 1930 Model A Ford—just like the one at Aunt Phoebe's home—trundling south on the brick street. Her mouth went dry, and she coughed.

The door opened again, and the housekeeper motioned for Josie to enter. "Sorry to have kept you waiting for so long. Mr. Matthews says for you to come in out of the wind." She stepped aside.

Josie heaved a sigh and entered. "Thank you," she said and stooped to set her traveling bag on an Oriental runner that ran the length of the polished oak floor. Straightening and looking around, she gaped for a moment and absorbed the feeling of grandeur. To her immediate right stood a tall coat rack. Slightly beyond was a pocket door pulled halfway through its wide opening. On the opposite wall, a grand multi-spindled oak staircase rose to the upper floor. A red-velvet-cushioned telephone bench sat near the stairs under a mirror in a gilt frame. Another door, this one closed, filled the wall space.

"You may leave your valise here. Follow me." The woman, walking like a Hessian soldier, led the way to the closed door. "Mr. Matthews'll join you in the library."

"Thank you." Josie's heart pounded. She took in three long breaths, forcing herself to calm down.

The woman opened the door and ushered Josie in. "He'll be with you directly. Now, just don't take up too much of his time."

"Oh, I won't. I promise." Josie glanced about. The entire room was oak-paneled except for the wall to her right that had floor-to-ceiling shelves crammed with books. To her left, an immense round window caught her attention. Inside the circle was a large, square, oak-framed inset of clear glass with four segments made of frosted leaded glass, each arc fashioned in the same fan design. The inset was curtained with oatmeal-colored linen. It had a padded window seat covered in the same linen as the curtain.

Josie's stomach growled loudly. She grimaced and pressed her palm to her midsection. How embarrassing.

The woman went to an impressive pillared fireplace, stooped down, and stirred up the small fire flickering in the grate. She straightened, brushed off her hands, and pointed to an oversized leather chair nearby. "Sit here."

"Yes, ma'am."

The woman nodded, turned, and left the room, closing the door behind her.

Josie's gaze fell upon a pleasing vignette nestled in a corner. Hung above a mahogany drop-leaf table with ornately carved legs was a beautiful oil portrait of a soldier dressed in a dark blue American Civil War uniform, handsome and regal in his attire trimmed with gold braid and brass buttons. His large hand rested on a sheathed saber. She rose from the chair, gravitated toward the portrait, and studied the soldier: red-gold wavy hair, green-colored eyes.

Sounds echoed in the hallway. The doorknob rattled. Josie scampered back to her seat.

The housekeeper edged around the door carrying a silver tray. With her foot, she snagged a side chair from its position at the drop-leaf table, dragged it to Josie, and set the tray down, clanking the contents.

"Mr. Matthews'll come directly. He's not here at the moment but has been called and is on his way. My name's Vertie."

"Vertie," Josie repeated.

"Short for LaVerta," she added, never looking at Josie while she attended to the items on the tray.

Josie pointed. "I appreciate your hospitality, but I've not asked for something to eat. I just want to meet Mr. Matthews."

Vertie raised her eyebrows. "I don't turn nobody away who's hungry."

"Oh . . . I . . ." Josie's attention went to the china cup in its saucer, a slender teapot with steam drifting out its spout, a plate holding a sandwich, and three frosted sugar cookies. "Thank you for your kindness, Vertie." She tilted her head. "Um, who's the portrait of?"

"Mr. Matthews's grandfather. Distinguished looking fellow, wasn't he?" She walked out of the room. The door clicked shut behind her.

"Yes, quite." Josie's words floated in the air. She dropped the tea ball holding tea leaves into the water to steep while she ate the sliced beef sandwich and the cookies. She then poured the dark, hot drink into her cup and stirred in cream and sugar.

Josie blew over the tea before taking a sip. She tried to envision Mr. Matthews. Would he still resemble the smiling young man in the sepia-toned photograph encased in the silver frame?

Ridiculous. Everybody grew older—unless they were dead. Which, until a month ago, he had been as far as she knew. She sighed over the impossibility of imagining what he'd look like now.

Her repast finished, she stacked the dishes together. Had he ever married? If so, would his wife want *her* there in the house? Where would she go if she weren't invited to stay with him?

She couldn't return to Bradford. She knew that much. Her aunts made it clear when she left. "What if you find him and he doesn't want to have anything to do with you? You can't come crying back to us. You made your choice to go with him. You'll just have to suffer the consequences." What if Aunt Phoebe's words prove true? The "what-ifs" worried her. The worst thing was not knowing. Uncertainty was such a curse.

She heard a heavy thud and footsteps. Josie's breath checked. Her stomach clenched. Any moment now, she would face the man she'd dreamed for weeks of meeting—imagined him and his greeting. Landon Joseph Matthews. She'd rehearsed dozens of things to say. That was then. Now it was for real, and at the moment, not one word came to her mind.

When the library door opened, she jumped to her feet. Her body tensed. Her sweaty hands trembled. Her heart thundered. Was *this* man the one she'd waited so long to meet?

Chapter 2

Josie gaped at the man entering the room. Was *he* Landon Matthews? He was not at all as she had pictured him. He vaguely resembled the smiling young man in the sepia-toned photograph of her mother's. This man's hair was faded reddish-gold, still thick and wavy, but touched becomingly on the temples with gray. He wore brown woolen trousers and a white shirt with the sleeves rolled up several inches, and brown-and-white saddle shoes—not the classy black suit and shoes, and no big, silly grin.

He came toward her. "Good morning. I'm Landon Matthews." His voice was deep and commanding.

She held out her sweaty hand. "Hello." The single word sounded awkward . . . much as she felt.

His large hand, firmly gripping hers, was cold and like stone. "Vertie tells me you're a relative." He did not smile. "What is your name?"

Shivers raced down Josie's spine. "I'm Joselene Grace Matthews." She envisioned herself as a country bumpkin in this stately room, standing before a man she really didn't know.

"Your coloring is certainly that of the Matthews's. How are we related?"

Josie touched her lips with the tip of her tongue and closed her eyes momentarily. "I'm . . . I'm your daughter."

Landon's head jerked. He gawked at her. "My *what*?"

She straightened her shoulders. "Your daughter. Mother was Sarah Charlene."

He squinted his eyes and cleared his throat. "Sarah's child? . . . And mine?" He ran one hand over his hair, turned away, and went to stand at the screened fireplace.

"Yes, she . . . named me after you and herself. She took the first four letters of your middle name, Joseph, and the last four of Charlene, to make Joselene. But everyone calls me Josie."

He said nothing as he came to her and took hold of her jaw, his thumb and fingers pressing into her cheeks. He yanked her face to one side, then the other.

"How old are you?" He released his grip and stepped back from her.

"Twenty. I was born on May 20, 1914." Josie could see his mind figuring the time.

"You think because you resemble me I'm going to accept you as my daughter?" He snapped his fingers. "Just like that?"

Her stomach flip-flopped. Her chest heaved in convulsive breaths.

He rubbed his chin. "Why should I believe you?"

She suppressed a sob. "I have the jewelry you gave Mother."

He huffed, "Those could've been bought . . . or stolen."

"No! No, they weren't! Mother gave them to me. I . . . I also have a photo of you two on what I was told was your wedding day." She twisted the snap-top on her pocketbook, bypassing a double strand of pearls and a ruby ring, grasped the silver frame, and handed it to him. "I'm not aware of anyone in Bradford suspecting you . . . uh . . . never married. I only recently found out from a letter Mother wrote and left for me that you were quite alive. She passed away a little over a month ago."

For a brief moment he focused on the picture, and then gave it back to her. "What brings you here to me?" He traced the arch of his upper lip with his forefinger.

"I wanted to find you. Mother had talked about you ever since I can remember. Course, I thought you were dead. Now, she is."

"What do you want from me?"

Josie's face burned. Her heart beat hard. "What do I wa—I'm here to meet my father. Don't you care that Mother's dead . . . or that you have a daughter? Why didn't you come after her and make her an honest woman?"

He glowered at Josie. "Mind your manners, young lady. You're being impertinent."

"I don't think so. I'm appalled—angry, actually, even troubled—but I am *not* disrespectful. Mother reared me better than that. I'll show you her letter." She removed it from her purse. "She said I should come to you." Josie had promised herself that she would search for her father after her mother's death.

"How did you know where to find me?"

"I didn't . . . not for sure. I remembered Mother describing the devastation of the tornado and flood in the spring of 1913 here in Terre Haute—the number of deaths, the thousands left homeless—and how she felt compelled to come and volunteer with the recovery. And that's when you two met."

The fire made a popping noise and poured a little shower of red embers through the grate. He turned his attention to it.

Josie continued. "It just made sense to begin here. After I got off the train, I located a telephone directory, checked for your name . . . and there you were. Mother had told everyone you died before I was born from a disease called sugar diabetes. Untreatable at that time, she said. But, of course, it is treatable now with the discovery of insulin. Mother chose to live the role of a widow raising a daughter."

Landon took the much-fingered envelope and withdrew the rumpled letter, limp from Josie's frequent handling. He rested one crooked elbow on the mantel and began to read her mother's final written words. Finished, he sighed. "She never married?"

"No."

A muscle flicked in his cheek. "I'm asking again. What do you want from me—money?"

She looked straight at him. "No, I don't want anything." Would he believe her? Of course she wanted something—an answer to her question of why he hadn't come after her mother. "I have money." She held up her bulging pocketbook and patted the mound made by the seventy dollars enfolded inside—everything she had left after paying her mother's medical and funeral expenses. "I came to you only because of her. Honest," she said, uncomfortably.

"Sounds to me like you thought you could waltz in here and allege to be my daughter . . . and I'd believe you. Is that right?"

Josie drew back and grimaced. "I thought—" She flattened her lips and shrugged. "I . . . guess so." She paused. "Oh, there's one other thing." She reached into the recesses of her purse, dug around, and pulled out a yellowed, crinkled, still-sealed envelope—her trump card. She held it up. "This is the last letter you sent Mother. She never ever received it because Aunt Phoebe hid it from her. Would you like to see it?"

"I don't need to."

"Why didn't you come for her? Didn't you love her enough to go to the trouble?"

He turned away and coughed. "She should have told me she was in the family way."

"When she thought you didn't love her? She didn't want you to marry her simply out of a sense of obligation to her."

"Marriages occur for less of a reason."

Vertie appeared in the doorway, and without the formality of a knock or even waiting for permission to enter, barged into the room. She glared at Josie. "Excuse me, Mr. Matthews, is everything all right?"

Landon beckoned her to come closer. He turned to Josie. "Vertie is not only my housekeeper, she's also a good friend. She's looked after me and run this house for many, many years."

He wheeled about to face Vertie. "This young woman"—he cleared his throat—"claims to be my . . . daughter."

Vertie's mouth dropped open. "Land sakes! Why, Mr. Matthews . . . how could the possibility even exist? You've never been married. I'm . . . I'm speechless at such a claim."

He glanced in Josie's direction and said, "She *says* she's my daughter and her mother has died."

Josie flinched. What kind of response could she give to such a display of condescension? She said in a tiny voice, "It was cancer."

"I'll grant that she looks like you, but . . . does she possess any proof?"

"*She* thinks she does."

Vertie raised her eyebrows. "But . . . I mean . . . does she have an honest-to-goodness birth certificate?"

"I do." Josie waved a folded paper in the air. "Here it is."

Putting her hand to her head, Vertie said, "Mr. Matthews, I don't know what to think or what to say."

"I'll admit she's got a modicum of evidence. But, right now, I question the authenticity of it."

"So, in the meantime, while you investigate who she is, where will she stay?"

"Not with me. I can't allow her to come in and make her assertion and let her take up residence here."

Josie shuddered. She swallowed hard and looked away, too bewildered to face him.

"Excuse me, Mr. Matthews, but even if she's not your daughter, you can't send her out to some Hooverville. She needs a warm, safe place to sleep, not any ole shantytown."

"What did I just say? She's not staying in this house. She can go to the YWCA until I get all this sorted out. She has money." He directed a cold stare at his daughter. "I'm sure you understand."

Josie's heart pounded. She breathed in shallow, quick gasps. She *was* bone of his bone and flesh of his flesh. The very reason she came to Terre Haute was to locate her long-lost father. *She* wanted a place to belong—with him. That dream had now vanished, but perhaps one day it would happen. Her lips trembled.

Vertie clasped her hands across her midsection. "Mr. Matthews . . ."

"Now what?" he barked.

"How is she going to get there?"

"I'll call a taxi," he said, shoving his hands into his pockets and walking out of the room.

Josie looked at Vertie. "He doesn't believe me, does he? I've done everything I know to show who I am and who my mother was."

Vertie reached out and touched her fingertips to Josie's arm. "Don't you worry none, miss. Mr. Matthews is an honorable person. He'll figure this out and do the right thing." Then she scuttled out of the room, and Josie was left on her own.

She wanted to believe Vertie. She bowed her head. "Lord, my father seems so detached and uninterested in who I am that I'm praying for Your Divine intervention. I want to live here—with him."

Landon stopped at the threshold. "A taxi's on the way," he announced in a curt tone. He pivoted and disappeared into the front hallway.

Josie sat still, her hands clutched tightly together in her lap. What would she do if he never came for her? She'd found her father only to have him reject her. No mother, no father—truly an orphan. A hollowness ached beneath her heart, and she shivered.

The taxi's horn sounded. Josie stood and yanked on her coat, her fingers fumbling with the buttons. She positioned her pocketbook on her wrist, straightened her shoulders, walked out of the room, picked up her suitcase where she'd left it, and marched out of the house to the waiting cab. Though her vision was blurred by tears, she managed to climb into the black-and-white vehicle.

The cabbie shut the door behind her with a soft clunk. "Where to, miss?"

"The YWCA," she mumbled.

He jumped behind the steering wheel, slammed his door shut, glanced into the rear-view mirror, and gave her a yellow-toothed grin.

She slumped in the rear seat. The fantasy of meeting her father— imagining how he would look, what they would say to each other— shattered in a matter of minutes. She could not have said or done anything more to prove who she was. Fear churned in her gut. What would she do now? How long could she pay her way? Bile rose in her throat.

"You all right? You don't look too good, miss," the cabbie said.

She plastered a fake smile on her face and barely nodded. Of course, she wasn't all right. Nothing was. Landon Matthews was her father. But would he ever claim her as his and Sarah's daughter, come for her, and take her into his home?

* * *

Ring-ring. Ring-ring. Ring-ring.

Elliott Jacobson answered the jangling telephone. "*Terre Haute Star.* Jacobson here. . . . Who's this again? Landon? What's up? . . . Young woman? . . . Yep, sure did. She was right at the door—in my way. Almost knocked her off her feet. . . . What's that? Did I get a good look at her? Uh, yeah, I'd say so. . . . Sure, I'd be able to recognize her anywhere. . . . You want me to do *what*? . . . Well, I suppose I could take the time to investigate her. What's this all about? . . . You know her? . . . Wait. What? She claimed *what*? . . . Uh, Landon, is that even a possibility? . . . Okay, then, where do I start my snooping? . . . Bradford in Harrison County. Gotcha. . . . I'll start on this right away. By the way, has it occurred to you she just might be paid by the labor union to make her declaration? . . . To infiltrate the management at the Stamping Mill? . . . Listen, I'll be as thorough as I can be. . . . I'll get back with you in a couple of days. . . . Yeah, bye."

Chapter 3

Josie stood at the window of her room. In the shadows of the mid-afternoon sun, she stared at a flock of noisy and messy pigeons fluttering about before finally settling to strut and preen. The birds reminded her of those in the barn at the orchard—home. She swallowed back the lump forming in her throat.

It took courage to find her father this morning. How brave was she this afternoon, though? Her fearlessness—gone. "God, I want to do what is right. Stop me before I make a mess of things. Is this the life I am to live—to belong nowhere . . . with nobody—facing the world alone? Surely there's a place for me. I want to be faithful to Your plans for me, to understand what they are, but no matter what I do, it's wrong. Your Word warns to wait for Your timing, and blessings will come. Have I simply not waited long enough?" She sucked in a deep breath and blew it out. "Would You please plainly tell me?"

She pressed her forehead against the coolness of the window's glass. The introduction to her father was not the welcome she'd hoped for or expected to find. *I'm not giving up. I won't go crawling to Aunt Phoebe and Aunt Ruth. They didn't want me to search for my father in the first place.* "You made your choice. Remember, you'll have to live with the consequences. If anything should go wrong, you better not think you can come back here," Phoebe had said.

"Well, don't worry. I won't. Nope. No way. Not if I can help it." Josie heard herself speak the words out loud. Her stomach tightened. What if her father never came for her? How long could she support herself? A week? A month? She paced back and forth, her heart storming within her. Goosebumps rose on her arms as she pulled in a quavering breath. She sat on the edge of the bed and covered her mouth and nose with both hands. *What can I do? I can live on less than a dollar a day. If I need to, I can make beds or wash dishes. I'll find a way to stay here somehow. But if worse comes to worse, I will swallow my pride and return home.*

Though it was only midafternoon, and certainly not the time for bed, she put on her nightgown. Her head ached dreadfully, and shivering, she crawled between the sheets. Drawing up the bedclothes, the sharp pain of loneliness stabbed Josie. Her hopes, her dreams for a future with Landon Matthews—dashed. "Awesome and Loving God, I believe in miracles. Please soften my father's heart so he'll want me in his life. I need him to come for me."

Hour after hour went by. The sun sank, twilight set in, and then came the darkness of night.

Josie, lying curled up in bed, stared at the streetlights reflected in odd little angles and squares on the walls of the room, thinking about the day. She resolved to stay put where he knew to come for her. How long would it be before she saw him again? She turned on her side, shifted the pillow under her cheek, and drifted off to sleep.

Night gave way to morning. Josie awoke to face the challenges of her uncertain future in Terre Haute. She located the Gillis and Hook's drug stores where she'd promised herself she could eat the one meal a day. On Monday, she found the Emeline Fairbanks Memorial Library, where she whiled away hours thumbing through the magazines and various newspapers and examined the stereograph pictures of the city.

Tuesday and Wednesday repeated the same routine as Monday. But on Thursday morning, something strange happened.

The front door of the library opened and a handsome man took some time perusing the place before ambling directly to where Josie sat alone at her usual place in the Reading Room. He backed up a step and studied her silently for several seconds. She put the stereoscope on the table for a moment to switch the picture, raised her head, and glared at him. He stooped, supporting himself on the back of a chair nearby. "Mind if I sit here?"

"No," she answered in a whisper.

The chair scraped against the wooden floor as he pulled it out. He glanced around and then let his gaze return to her. "You like those old photographs about Terre Haute?"

She nodded, not looking at him. "I want to learn all I can about this city. I hope to make it my new home."

"It does have an interesting history, that's for sure."

"Are you from here?"

"Nope, but I've lived in the city three years now."

"Well, that's probably long enough to know the place. I don't think we've had the pleasure—" Her voice trailed away.

"No, no. Not yet." He smiled a lopsided smile.

"Oh," she said. "You're the man who bumped into me at Landon Matthews's house last Saturday."

"Yep, I'm the guilty culprit. So, if you count that, this is actually the second time we've met."

"I still don't know who you are, but it was obvious to me you were in a hurry."

"I was."

"How did you know where to find me?"

"Just a coincidence, I assure you. I saw you come in and thought this was a perfect opportunity to show some manners. Now I've got to get back to work. See you, Joselene Grace Matthews." He scooted his chair back and headed for the door, then stopped and turned, and flashed a smile at her.

When he was gone, Josie pinched her lower lip as she considered the encounter. The man called her by name. She fidgeted because she still didn't know who he was.

The week came to an end, but no word came from Landon. Though she prayed every day for a miracle, none appeared. Maybe she didn't belong here—or with him. By Friday, with six days behind her, Josie decided if she heard nothing from her father over the weekend, then she must consider purchasing a train ticket and going back to Bradford the next Monday.

Saturday dawned. She lay wide awake, warm and cozy in the blankets drawn up over her shoulders, and thought forward to the day ahead. Would he come for her? She lounged in bed, pondering the possibility. "I wish this would've been so different."

The memory of the day she'd confronted her aunts about the years of deception was rekindled. "It was your mother's business to tell you the truth," they told her. And, "No, your father doesn't know about you." Josie had cupped both hands over her ears. She didn't want to hear any more of their lies and secrets. "I can't stay. I don't belong here anymore."

"Why not?" they'd demanded.

"Everything's changed. I'm going to find my father. And don't either of you think of interfering."

Now look at her. If she went back to Bradford, she'd have to listen as Phoebe and Ruth harped and carped about how they were right. Josie was tired of thinking about them and her father.

The day proved sunshiny and mild. She wore layers of clothes with no coat, and in the late morning, she left the Y to walk uptown on Wabash Avenue, the main street. She went west as far as Fourth Street, crossed over in the jam of Saturday traffic, and turned to the east. She strolled along the sidewalk, missing nothing in the stores' display windows.

The noise of the business district was almost deafening with the electric streetcars clicking and clanging, newsboys hawking the latest edition of the newspaper, and numerous motorcars with drivers screeching their tires and honking their horns.

Beyond her, a crowd had gathered, their attention focused on something or someone. What were they watching? She squeezed into the group and found a blind street musician playing the harmonica and strumming a guitar at the same time. The man appeared to be tired, and his clothes were dirty and tattered. She dropped a few coins in a tin can sitting on the sidewalk in front of him. "God's blessings be upon you," she said to the man.

In the next block, she came across a man with no legs who sat on a wheeled apparatus. The man sold pencils. She had no money to buy anything from him and walked away.

"Lord," Josie prayed, "people are in a world of hurt. They sell whatever they can and work at whatever they're able to do to make a few dollars to get by each day. I can sympathize with what they're going through. May You bless us all."

When Josie had seen enough of Main Street, she made her way back to the Y. She stopped short inside the entrance, her heart pounding. Her father sat on the edge of a chair in the reception area.

He hoisted himself up and came toward her. For several moments, Josie met his gaze. Why such a dour and solemn expression? Did he ever smile? She doubted it. Flustered, she held out her hand to shake his.

He looked surprised at the gesture but nodded at her and briefly took her small palm in his own cold, hard, large one. "Hello, Joselene Grace."

"Mr. Matthews. It's . . . um . . . a pleasure to see you. Why are you here?"

"I did some checking and came to the conclusion it's highly probable you are my child. I'm offering you a home . . . with me. We'll try an arrangement for a while. At the end of a couple of months, if either of us is not satisfied, we'll call it quits. What do you say?"

She stared at him a moment and nodded. "That seems fair."

"There'll be conditions, of course. I don't want any regrets about doing this. You may be my daughter, but if you try to put anything over on me, you're out and on your own."

Josie flinched and clapped a hand to her chest. His proposal seemed more like a trial basis for an employee than for a daughter. But it was more palatable than the one with her old-fashioned aunts. Better to be with her father in Terre Haute where she wanted to be than in Bradford where she didn't want to be.

Could she live up to the terms of their agreement? *Could she?* Josie vowed to herself to be agreeable with—or was it beholden to—him, however long she lived in his house. She may not prove herself to be the *consummate* daughter, but she would be the best she could be.

She heaved a great sigh of relief. "I guess a person has to be unlucky first to feel as blessed as I do now. Thank You, Heavenly Father, for answering my prayer. I promise I won't be any trouble to my father, and I'll trust You to help me keep that vow."

Landon opened the back door and stepped aside to let Josie enter the kitchen. He waited while she gave a cursory wipe of her shoes on the doormat and then closed the door behind her.

She gave the room a quick look over. It was orderly and bright but small and boxy, with many doors and windows.

"Oh, my," she breathed, mesmerized by the stove with coil burners, the refrigerator with its encased motor on top, and glass-fronted dish cabinets painted white.

Landon said, "Vertie?"

The housekeeper, hunched over at the sink with her hands in sudsy water, raised her head to glance over her shoulder. She broke into a big smile.

"Joselene Grace will be living here, now. Will you show her to her room, please?"

"Certainly, Mr. Matthews." She shook the water from her reddened hands and dried them on her apron. "Welcome home, Miss Joselene. I'll help you settle in." She shuffled over to Landon, took the suitcase from him, and led the way upstairs.

At the landing was a long hallway with doors on either side, all closed. On her immediate right, Vertie pushed open a door. "Here we go." She led the way.

Josie turned slowly and looked about the expansive room. It was full of light and smelled vaguely of furniture polish. A fancy light fixture in the ceiling's center caught her attention. She thought of the light in the long, narrow room at the orchard—actually the sloped-ceilinged attic, renovated for her and her mother—a naked sixty-watt bulb dangling by a green cord on which she or her mother had to grope in the dark for the thumb crank.

Vertie flung the old, battered bag on the bed—a majestic mahogany four-poster with an arched headboard carved with a scroll-and-acanthus-leaf pattern—released the catch, and lifted the lid.

"Make yourself comfortable, Miss Josie." She moved back and forth putting items in the chest of drawers and hanging the few faded dresses in the massive mahogany wardrobe. She pointed to the slightly ajar door next to the dresser. "Your bathroom's there. You'll always have plenty of hot water, too."

Josie slipped out of her woolen coat and slung it over the end of the bed. She ran her hands along the carving of the bedpost, her fingers making a soft squeak on the polished wood. "You mean I'm allowed this huge bedroom *and* a bathroom . . . *all to myself*?"

Vertie nodded. "Yes. All for you. Go ahead and look around."

Josie moved first to the wide bay window where two upholstered side chairs flanked a small table. She peered out into the upper branches of an oak tree and down upon the backyard, where an empty clothesline stretched almost the entire length of the lot. She roamed around the space, touching the furniture, fingering a blue-embroidered linen runner spread across the top of the bureau. She made her way to the bathroom and, nudging the door open wider, peeked in. She glimpsed a gleaming white porcelain bathtub, a pedestal washbasin, and a black-and-white hexagonal-tiled floor. She'd heard of bathrooms like this. At Bradford, there was only an outhouse. At the Y, there had been only showers. Finally, she sat on a padded stool at a dressing table with a swing mirror and little drawers.

"Unpacking's all done." Vertie shut the lid on the empty suitcase and stashed it at the back of the spacious armoire. She brushed her palms together and turned to face Josie. "Are you pleased—"

"The room's absolutely . . ." Josie interrupted, "beautiful. I can watch the sun come up each morning. Everything is"—she took in a deep breath and let it out—"perfect."

Vertie smiled and planted her hands on her hips. "Now, you've got a good amount of time to rest. Would you like a bath?"

"Oh, that sounds wonderful. I've never had a bathtub."

"You haven't!?"

Josie shook her head. "At home we just had . . . pitchers and basins . . . and a galvanized washtub."

Vertie folded her hands together at her chest and tilted her head. "Well, then, let me draw you some hot water so you can take a good, leisurely soak." She went to turn on the faucets and came back.

Josie swung an arm about the bedpost. "How long've you worked for my father?"

"Right smart while. Both me and my husband."

"You're married?"

Vertie nodded. "Forty-six years. Abner's his name. But everyone calls him Nub."

"Do you have any children?"

"We had two. Our son, George Henry, died years ago. We have a daughter, Elizabeth Delphine."

"Elizabeth Delphine," Josie repeated the name softly. "That's pretty. Does she live here?"

"No. She moved from Terre Haute years ago." Vertie left to turn off the booming water and came back. "Will the rest of your things be coming later?"

Josie's cheeks grew warm. "These are all of my clothes. We lived . . . um . . . in a very simple way."

Vertie wagged a finger. "You've got to ask Mr. Matthews to purchase you some."

"I couldn't."

Vertie frowned. "Why not? He's your daddy, isn't he?"

"Yes, but I think he may need some time to get used to that idea."

"Probably. Give him a chance to get used to it, then ask him. Remember the Good Book says if you won't ask, you won't receive. Plums don't drop without shaking the tree." She walked out of the room and came back with a green chenille bathrobe, a washcloth, a thick towel, and a cake of lavender soap. She handed them to Josie. "Here you go. The bathrobe belongs to Miss Mae, your daddy's sister . . . just in case you're wondering." She left again, this time closing the door behind her.

Josie entered the steamy bathroom. She slipped out of her clothes and climbed into the tub. Once in the hot water, she leaned back, stretched out, and gave a great sigh. "Mmm. The balm of Gilead." She soaped every bit of herself, squeezing the fluffy washcloth, trickling the suds over her.

A light tap on the door roused her. Josie sat up. "Yes?"

It opened almost instantly and Vertie poked her head around its edge. "I just want you to know you'll dine next door this evening. They expect you around seven o'clock."

"A dinner party?"

"No, no party to it. Just friends getting together to share supper. They want to meet you. I'll lay something out for you."

"I can do that myself. You don't need to attend to me." She pulled the plug to let the soapy water gurgle away, clambered out of the tub, and dried herself. Wrapped in the plush robe, she came into the room brushing her damp hair from her neck.

"Miss Josie, tending to you is part of my job. You want to impress the Van Allens this evening, don't you?"

Josie sank onto the soft bed and rested against the piled pillows. "Vertie, I've never slept on anything so big and comfortable."

Vertie, sorting through the garments hanging in the clothespress, said, "Don't you worry none. You'll become familiar with everything soon enough." She pulled out one dress, twisted the hanger, and then put it back. She took out another and held it up.

"Yes," Josie said, "that's the one. It's my funeral dress. I don't want to wear colors yet. How long's a person to stay in mourning, anyway? Do you know?"

The housekeeper hung the black serge on the door of the wardrobe. She turned to face Josie. "Now, I want you to always give attention to your appearance. Your father's an important attorney. He serves as General Counsel for the Columbian Enameling and Stamping Company and is much respected. I'm sure you don't want to do anything that jeopardizes his reputation in the community. Mark Schaumberg is his young, new associate. He'll be there, too. The Van Allens have lived next door for a long time. Mrs. Clarinda Van Allen is a widow, and her daughter, Priscilla, is about your age. You understand what I'm saying?" She raised her eyebrows and gave Josie a piercing stare. Then she left the room.

Josie remained silent. Were her social graces in question? Coming from Bradford she was no socialite, but she never thought of herself as being uncouth, either. She shrugged and turned back the heavy bedcover, wriggled between the smooth, ironed bed linens, snuggled down into the blankets, and positioned the puffy pillows. Maybe she could snatch a nap.

"Lord, You and Mother instilled in me a pride about who and what I am. You love me, just the way I am. I want my father to love me, too, just the way I am." She expected to lie awake for a while, but the bed was soft and her body was weary. Exhaustion winning out, she fell asleep.

It was dark when Josie awakened in exactly the same position she had taken when she slid between the sheets. She sat bolt upright, her pulse hammering. Where was she? What time was it? She pushed her tumbled hair back from her face and squinted at the bedside clock. Six ten. "Oh my," she mumbled. "I better hustle. Don't want to upset my father the first night with him." She threw off the covers and pulled herself to the edge of the bed. She dragged herself vertical and dressed.

The dress draped her slender build in a flattering way. Her hands shook with excitement as she fastened the white pearls about her neck. "Fabulous." Josie combed her hair, pinned back her bangs, and checked the results in the mirror. She smiled at her reflection, turning her head this way and that to see the effect. Her breath caught. "Oh my."

Josie descended the stairs. At the bottom, she stopped. The clink and clatter of knives, forks, and glassware came distinctly from the back of the house. The murmur of voices emanated from the front of the house. She followed their steady rumble and found her father in the library talking with a stranger—a man with blond hair. The two men stood by the fireplace, absorbed in a discussion, their heads bent over papers the man held. She inched into the room, then paused, not sure if she should continue. Her glance shifted from her father to the other man.

"Ahem." The blond cleared his throat and, with short jabbing motions at the air, pointed to Josie.

"I just wondered . . ." she began, flattening her lips.

Landon scrutinized his daughter a moment and nodded. "Very presentable, I must say." He gestured for her to come closer. "Mark Schaumberg, I'd like to introduce Joselene Grace Matthews."

"Hello," she said.

He extended his hand and she shook it. "How do you do?" His handshake was firm, his voice pleasant. He stood tall and lean, his blue eyes the color of a robin's egg. He wasn't bad looking, even though his face had been scarred by acne. The man looked quite debonair in his herringbone suit.

"Joselene is my daughter."

Mark's head jerked like that of a marionette. He gaped at Landon while he rubbed his temple and quirked an eyebrow. "Your *what*?"

"My daughter."

"Son of a gun! I didn't know you had a daughter." He peered at Josie while he held the papers out to Landon.

Landon took them and stacked them on the table. "I didn't either. But here she is."

Mark scowled. "Landon, I never knew you'd ever married."

"I hadn't." He turned away from his associate and toward Josie. "Ready?"

She nodded.

"We'll find your coat," he said.

The three walked out the front door into the twilight of a crisp, autumn evening and made their way to the neighbors' house. Dry, fallen leaves scrunched and crackled under their feet.

Josie looked at the velvet-black sky pricked with sharp, tiny white lights twinkling down.

"Isn't it a beautiful night? . . . 'When I look at the sky which You have made, Lord, at the moon and the stars, which You set in their places— what am I that You think of me; who am I that You care for me?'"

"Poetic," Mark said. "Is it Shakespeare?"

"No, um . . . King David . . . from the Bible . . . a part of Psalm 8."

"Oh-h-h. The Bible."

Josie nodded.

"Sure sounded like Shakespeare to me." They smiled at each other, and that ended the conversation.

They mounted the steps and sauntered onto the porch of the Van Allens's home. Would these long-time neighbors of her father accept her, or would she be a fifth wheel? Would they consider her a country bumpkin? Her stomach clenched. She straightened her shoulders. How much did the woman standing in the glare of the porch light know about her?

Chapter 4

"Clarinda, let me present my daughter, Joselene Grace."

She smiled at Josie. "Hello, there." She reached forward and latched hold of Josie's hands. "You're exactly as I pictured you. Come in."

What information was this neighbor privy to? She must have heard *something* because she didn't appear startled by the surprise arrival of Josie into her father's household. Well, after all, they had been neighbors for years. Were they more than *that*, though?

Clarinda led them into the spacious living room where she approached a young woman perched like an exotic bird on the edge of the sofa. "This is my daughter, Priscilla. You two are about the same age. I hope you'll become good friends."

Priscilla made a face, rolled her eyes to the ceiling, and mumbled, "I can't believe this."

"Now, my dear, let me take your coat." Clarinda stepped closer, ready to receive the garment.

Josie slipped out of the worn woolen wrap and handed it to her hostess, who promptly passed it to Mark. He left the room.

Clarinda tilted her head. "Landon, her resemblance to you is striking. How could you have even questioned if she were your daughter?" She peered at him. Not waiting for a response, she said, "Everything's ready. Come along."

They accompanied her into the dining room, where she flipped on the switch of a sparkling chandelier. Its light revealed a beautifully appointed table with glistening crystal, glimmering china plates, and gleaming silverware on an intricately patterned lace cloth, and a centerpiece of white candles in silver candlesticks with yellow chrysanthemums.

"Oh my . . . so magnificent . . . like it's arranged for royalty." Josie breathed the words more than she said them.

"We're celebrating your arrival, my dear. Mark, please seat Joselene. You men take care of yourselves while Priscilla and I bring the food from the kitchen."

Though the table setting was elegant, the fare proved to be simple: no meat, fried potatoes, green beans, and cream gravy over biscuits.

Clarinda sat. "Now then, I want to get acquainted with our guest of honor. Tell us about yourself, Joselene." She snapped out her napkin and laid it across her lap. "What do you like to do for fun?"

"Um . . . I . . . um . . . play the piano."

Clarinda passed the biscuits. "Lovely. Priscilla sings. Perhaps you could accompany her some time. Are you accomplished?"

Josie shrugged and quirked her mouth. "I took lessons for eight years."

"What popular songs do you know?" Priscilla asked.

Josie dipped cream gravy from the bowl and spooned it over her biscuit. "It's not that I don't know any show tunes, Priscilla, I just haven't played any."

Clarinda placed both arms against the table's edge. "What is a favorite of yours?"

"I don't have only one. I love all the hymns, but a favorite classical piece is Beethoven's *Adagio Cantabile.*"

Mark smiled at Josie. "Well, I'm impressed. That's a difficult composition."

Clarinda pierced the green beans with her fork. "Any other talents or skills?"

"I can cook . . . sew and knit . . . and I have a driver's license."

Priscilla's eyes grew wide. "How come you can drive?"

"It wasn't a choice. It was a necessity. Someone had to take Mother to the doctor's office or the hospital. It usually turned out to be me. Aunt Ruth wasn't interested in learning, and Aunt Phoebe was often too busy in the orchard. So, I was the logical one."

"Mother, can I learn? *Pl-ea-se*?"

"Priscilla, we sold our car, and at this point and time cannot afford to get another one. We must watch our pennies."

The discussion ended. Clarinda, shifting her attention to the men, obviously had no further questions for Josie—and neither did Priscilla.

Josie half-listened to the chatter while they ate. Much of it made no sense to her, anyway. For the most part, she observed the dynamics of the four. Had her father fallen in love with Clarinda? Wait! Was he capable of loving anyone? Did he love her mother years ago? Clarinda seemed fond of Landon. That came across quite clear. Was Mark in love with Priscilla? He ought to be. Priscilla, stunning with skin the shade of a perfect brown egg, thick hair the color of walnut and cut in a stylish, simple bob. They made a striking couple. Priscilla, animated. Mark, reserved. Priscilla, tall, brunette, and blue-eyed. Mark, tall, blond, and blue-eyed.

"Joselene, you need to eat more," Clarinda suggested, shoving the serving bowls her way.

"Your gravy is delicious. Thank you." Josie spooned it out, salted it lightly, but peppered it generously, and took a bite. Before she could swallow, an enormous sneeze erupted from her. The mouthful sprayed over her cheeks, down the front of her dress, and around her place. Mortified, she glanced from face to face. They were staring at her in horrified silence.

"Mercy," Clarinda muttered at last.

Josie sat speechless. Even if she'd thought of something to say, she couldn't have said a thing.

Priscilla slapped her palm to her forehead. She rolled her eyes and let out a huff. "Why didn't you cover your mouth?"

Josie glared at her. "It surprised me. I . . . I had no warning—"

"Well, no wonder, with all that pepper you shook out," Priscilla chided.

"I'll serve our coffee in the living room," Clarinda said. "We'll be more comfortable there." She flung her crumpled napkin onto the table. "Mark, please help Joselene."

A knot formed in Josie's chest. Too self-conscious to get up, she remained seated while the others left the room.

Mark returned from the kitchen with a dampened dishtowel. "Are you all right?"

"Just humiliated to death. I don't want to face anybody and wish I could just disappear."

He smiled, a kind gentle smile. "This could happen to any of us."

"Yes . . . but it didn't. It happened to me. On my first night with Father—and in front of his friends. I wanted to impress him . . . make him proud of me." She splayed her fingers over her chest. "Look at me. What a mess."

He handed the cloth to her. "White gravy on black dresses isn't in style this season, is it?"

"Father will despise me."

"Nonsense. I think you're making too much of this, Joselene. Don't be so hard on yourself. We forgive you."

Maybe he didn't think ill of her, but would her father? Her worries about doing something foolish proved true. Josie wiped and scraped and brushed. When she removed the obvious traces of food from her dress, she and Mark abandoned the dishes, switched off the light, and joined the others.

Josie, holding her coffee cup and saucer with both hands, sat in a chair under the soft arc of a lamp's light. She focused on the snapping and crackling logs in the grate and the changes in the fire as yellow flames spread over the wood, turned to blue, sank and flared, and sank again.

Priscilla, sitting with her feet curled beside her in the corner of the couch, thumped its arm with a balled fist and jumped up. "I've got the most marvelous idea."

"What is it?" Clarinda asked.

"Let's all go to the Trianon."

Josie leaned forward to place her empty cup and saucer upon the end table. "What's that?"

"A ballroom . . . on the east side of town. It's the cat's whiskers."

Josie's mind worked in a panic. "I . . . uh . . . this is . . . uh . . . too soon . . . for me to do something like . . . um . . . go to a dancehall."

"Be a sport, Josie. It'll give us something to do." Priscilla shuffled, swayed, and flitted around the room, pirouetting to imaginary music with an invisible partner. "There's a time for mourning and a time for dancing. You won't break any rules if you go." She reached to clutch Josie's hand. "Ple-e-ease. The Trianon is one of Terre Haute's premier recreation centers."

Josie shook her head and resisted Priscilla's tugs. "No, I can't!" For an instant, her breath stopped. "I . . . I don't dance."

Priscilla shot her a penetrating look, and frowning, freed Josie's hand. "*What?* You don't?" She flapped a hand. "Oh, well. If you don't mind what you do, you'll have a swell time. I promise. Trust me. Just come."

"I better not. I'll ruin the evening for you."

"You won't either. My friends will be there and I can introduce you to them. Surely you can do that much. We're all going. Don't be a wet blanket. You won't say no, will you?"

"I . . . uh . . ." Josie looked over at her father. "I won't say no."

Landon kneaded the back of his neck. "No real reason why I shouldn't go." He ran the same hand over the top of his head. "Got a stack of new contracts, though, needing to be reviewed."

"Then I won't go, either," Clarinda said.

"Mother!" Priscilla flung herself onto the davenport with theatrical flair. "Oh-h-h." She frowned and shook her head.

Mark turned to Josie. "You'll soon find out Priscilla's a party person. I call her 'the queen bee.' She likes it when men buzz around her like bees around a honey pot. She can't stand it if she doesn't have a swarm of admirers. I'm just trying to keep from getting stuck in the honey pot."

"If I were you, I'd be in love with her." Josie thought it, but of course, she didn't say it. Or did she? She must have, because everyone had exploded in laughter. Her stare met her father's. Had she embarrassed him again?

"Why would you?" Priscilla pressed. "Is it because of my hair or my eyes?"

"You're beautiful, that's true, and I can understand why others would want to be with you, do what you do, look like you, and act like you. You're sophisticated and sweet, and you must know everybody if you're the queen bee."

"Josie, you're the cat's pajamas." Priscilla came to her again, grasped her hands, and squeezed them. "What an utterly charming thing to say. See?" She looked at Mark and batted her eyelashes. "I'm glad someone appreciates me."

He gave no response.

At a quarter to nine, Josie, Priscilla, and Mark climbed into his blue Buick and headed to the Trianon. By the time they arrived, the expansive gravel parking lot was almost full. They left the car and went in through the well-lit main door of the eight-sided building.

The smell of hot buttered popcorn permeated the air, and the room jangled with live band music, voices, and laughter. Priscilla stood on tiptoe and craned her neck, surveying the crowd.

"There they are." She raised her arm and waved. With reluctance,

Josie trailed Mark and Priscilla as they wended their way through the well-filled tables and across the congested oak dance floor.

Lord, what am I doing? I don't belong here. Trying to fit into my father's world is one thing, but Priscilla's is way out of my league.

A couple half stood. Priscilla did a hand flick in the direction of Josie. "This is Joselene Matthews, Landon's daughter. Course you know Mark. This is Winnie Jenkins and Alex Heywood."

"Our pleasure," they said. They rearranged their chairs and sat.

Alex regarded Josie with an unnerving intensity. "I wasn't aware that Landon had a daughter."

"How do you know my father?"

"I work for the same company he does—Columbian Enameling and Stamping. I'm one of the union stewards."

"Oh?" Her glances wandered from Winnie, the most obvious of the new acquaintances with her rouged cheeks, painted eyelids, Chinese red lips and fingernails, and green enameled pendulous earrings, back to Alex, whose deep-set gray eyes were flecked with gold and who kept all of them involved in the lively conversation.

Alex, glib and engaging with a baritone voice, propped his forearms on the table and took control of the chitchat. Every phrase he said must have been a flash of wit, since the others laughed heartily. His hair, parted in the center and slicked with Brilliantine hair pomade, flowed in waves on either side of his head and bobbed when he spoke.

Josie studied the handsome, fun-loving man sitting across from her while sipping her Coca-Cola. An uneasiness struck deep within her gut about his sociable manner. Charming though he was, something didn't ring true about him—something secretive, mysterious.

She half-listened to the idle chatter and hoped she nodded or shook her head at the appropriate moments, but found it hard to concentrate on the boring small talk. She feared the possibility of offending the clique, but needn't have worried, for they gave her not so much as a second glance. She stifled several yawns until she noticed the man at a table a few yards away was watching her.

They stared at each other a moment. Then he smiled at her.

"Oh," she mumbled. "I've seen him before—twice, in fact."

He sat alone, angled about in his chair so he could watch the dancers gyrating and spinning their partners around while the music played. One elbow rested on the table, and with his other hand, he lifted his coffee cup.

"Priscilla, who is that man over there?" Josie hardly moved her lips. "Don't let him catch you looking. Just turn your eyes, not your head."

Priscilla's eyelashes never flickered. "Which one?"

Josie pointed with her chin toward the dark-haired man.

"Ooh, he's a Joe Brooks type. No, I don't recognize him. Mark, who's that man sitting by himself?"

"Son of a gun! He's Elliott Jacobson. I didn't see him when we came in. I'll invite him to come over here and say hello to everybody."

Mark went to Elliott's table and chatted with him. They looked back at the group and soon joined them.

"Hello there. So we meet again," he said to Josie.

Josie, flustered, unable to speak, simply nodded and extended her hand.

"Let me introduce you two," Mark said.

Elliott clasped Josie's extended hand, his gaze remaining on her face. "You don't need to. Joselene and I have already met. Twice, as a matter of fact. At her father's door on the day she arrived in Terre Haute. And this past Thursday I ran into her at the public library." He held her hand a second too long. "May I join you?" His smile showed even, white teeth, and his eyes crinkled at the corners.

Not waiting for an answer, Elliott pulled a chair away from a nearby table and wedged it in beside Josie. The others scooted to make room, introduced themselves, and shook hands with him.

"Elliott's a reporter for the *Star*," Mark said.

"Okay, I'm curious now," Priscilla said. "Why not give us the details of those meetings between you two? Bet you've got an interesting story in there somewhere. Come on. Tell us."

"The first meeting was all quite unexpected, wasn't it?" Elliott turned to Josie. She nodded. "I'd been to Landon's house. Time got away, and when I realized how late it was, I left in a hurry. Opened the front door and bam!" He smacked his hands together. "Plowed right into Joselene and almost knocked her down." He looked at the others around the table, from face to face. "Second time, saw her in the library studying the old stereograph photos of Terre Haute. Right?" He flashed a grin at her. "Now, here I am. Here she is. The end. Or maybe, it's just the beginning."

"Son of a gun," Mark said.

Alex faced Elliott. "So, you're a reporter for the *Star*, huh?"

"Yep. Morning newspaper."

"You know, of course, it reflects the Republican perceptions?"

"Yep. Love what I do."

"You're kidding," Winnie said. "You mean you actually love your job?"

"Yep. I don't joke about my work. I distinctly heard myself say I love what I do." Elliott placed three fingers in the air. "Scout's honor."

"Sounds like a ton of stress to me."

"Well, I suppose so, in a way. The job's certainly challenging . . . at times demanding with on-the-spot decisions and never-ending deadlines."

"You're not from here, or I'd have known you before now," Priscilla said.

He rubbed behind his left ear and pursed his lips. "You're right. I'm from Bloomington. Been in Terre Haute about two and a half years." He suddenly smiled. "Enough about me." Elliott sat up straighter in his chair and gestured at Josie. "Tell us about you."

All heads turned toward her. She took a sip of her Coca-Cola and set her glass down. She placed her forearms on the table, folded her hands together, lacing her fingers, and gave them a sweet smile. "Um, uh, not much to say. What do you want to know?"

"Anything you want to tell us."

"My story's pretty uneventful." She hesitated, but seeing interest on their faces, she began. "I lived with my mother and her two older sisters. Then Mother got sick."

"Has she recovered?" Winnie asked.

Josie fixed her gaze on her hands. "She . . . passed away." Tears pricked her eyes. Her nose started to run. She sniffled and turned to Priscilla. "Did you bring a handkerchief with you?"

Priscilla rummaged around in her purse. "No, sorry."

"I have one," Elliott said, producing it from his pocket. "Wrinkled, but clean. I guarantee there're no cooties."

She took it gratefully and blew. Now what? Never having used a man's hanky before, she didn't know what the proper protocol was. She wadded it in her hand and resumed her story. "After my mother's funeral, I found out the truth—that my father was alive. I was stunned, of course. Mother had always told me he died shortly before my birth from an incurable disease."

Winnie covered her mouth with her hand. "Omigosh."

Priscilla frowned. "Didn't you ever try to find out more about your father while you were growing up?"

Josie shrugged. "Oh, sure, I asked a lot of questions. They were probably the usual ones. But, when you're a child, you just accept life for the way it is. I asked everything I wanted to know at the time. My aunts would pull me aside and tell me to stop upsetting Mother. Now, I understand why. She had to invent her answers."

"I'm sorry for you about your mother. How sad she succumbed so young. Losing someone you love must be the most horrible hurt," Winnie said.

"It is. It's hard to say goodbye. Grief is like a hole in your soul, and only time will heal the wound. But after watching Mother struggle with life in her last days, it was a little easier to bear her passing. I believe she's in heaven now and at peace. Mother was a wonderful Christian."

"Christian? Her life was nothing but a pack of lies . . . and you had to live with the consequences of her choice . . . when you could have known your father all along."

"Oh, I knew him—not personally, of course, but through the stories she told me . . . and from her pictures of him."

"Don't you feel betrayed or even robbed by your own mother?" Priscilla pushed.

"Yeah. I find it amazing you don't resent her. You don't seem the least bit angry," Winnie said.

Josie stared at her. Angry? Oh, she was livid. Who wouldn't be? No one wanted to be deceived. Her entire life had been based on deception and lies. She had wanted nothing more in life than to have her mother . . . *and* her father.

Her voice lowered to almost a whisper. "When I learned the truth, it was terribly confusing. I could remain resentful, or I could believe Mother's choices to be the best at the time she made them. I chose the latter." While she spoke, Josie twisted Elliott's handkerchief around her fingers into a tight ball. Finished talking, she released the tautness of the wad. It sprang free, dropped to the floor, and rolled under the table. Josie bent over to retrieve it, now-uncoiled, just as Elliott did the same. Their heads collided.

She straightened, rubbing her head. She and Elliott exchanged sheepish glances and grinned at each other before turning their attention back to the others.

Priscilla looked first at Josie and then at Elliott. "What's going on with you two?"

They answered in unison. "Nothing."

The hour grew late. Waiters stacked chairs upside-down on empty tables, and band members packed up their instruments. It was midnight—time for everyone to leave. What had they talked about that made the evening pass all too quickly?

Alex rose from the table and stretched. "I'll see you around, Joselene. Nice meeting you."

Then he and Winnie left together.

Josie waved a hand in farewell, pushed back her chair, and stood. "Goodnight, Elliott. I'm glad to see you again . . . for the first time."

She held out her hand and expected him to shake it, but he grasped her fingers, bowed low, and said, "Goodnight, Josie. Now that we've been properly introduced, when do I see you *again*?" He raised his eyebrows and covered his upper lip with his lower.

Josie's heart gave an excited jump. "Do you want to?"

"Yes, I do." He whispered and smiled.

She gawked at him, opened her mouth, then clamped her jaw shut.

Chapter 5

Mark stopped his Buick in front of the Matthews's home and switched the engine off. He got out and waved to Landon, who stood in the opened front door. "Evening," he called. He rounded the car and opened Josie's door for her to clamber out.

"How'd it go?" Landon asked when she reached the porch.

Josie quirked her mouth. "I suppose all right. I met a couple of Priscilla's friends. Alex Heywood says he works with you."

They stepped into the house and Landon closed the door. "Not exactly *with* me. He's a union steward in the same company. A decent sort of fellow. Has looks and charm. Articulate and witty, I understand. Intelligent and ambitious, I hear. Some think he demonstrates leadership qualities and regard him as a young man on the rise."

She shrugged out of her coat and hung it on the rack. "Oh, and I was finally introduced to Elliott Jacobson, too. I didn't know his name until tonight, but our paths had crossed twice before."

"Elliott's a smart man. Charismatic. I predict a promising future in the newspaper business for that young man." He held out an arm. "Come. I want to discuss something."

Josie put a hand over her thundering heart. What was this all about?

She trailed him to his library where a small fire wavered in the grate. "Go on and sit down," he said.

She went to the leather chair, slowly lowered herself, and spread her hands to the flames, grateful for its warmth.

Landon pulled a chair over, sat, and fell silent. Then he rose and went to stand before the fireplace. For a while, he gazed into the fire, eventually turning to her. "Tomorrow I'm taking you to Indianapolis, to my sister's, Mae Anise."

Josie opened her mouth to speak, but his raised hand stopped her.

"Hear me out. I'll leave you with her for a few days to purchase a new wardrobe—a real shopping spree lasting two or three days. Arrangements have already been made with her."

Josie drew a long breath. "We can't stay here?"

He shook his head. "I never buy clothes in Terre Haute."

"Oh."

Landon arranged his hands like a little tent, fingertip to fingertip, and tapped them back and forth. "You need dresses and . . . other necessities, and Mae possesses a certain flair for fashion." He cleared his throat. "Morning will come soon enough, and tomorrow'll be a long day. Time to go to bed."

* * *

Alex Heywood carefully backed his Packard Phantom Coupe into a space in the lot at the Edgewood Grove Apartments. He shut off the motor and the headlights and glanced at his wristwatch. It showed five minutes till one. He was early. That was his practice. It always left him with time to catch his breath and case a place. He loosened his tie and got comfortable for the wait. It would be a while before the goon would happen along.

Twenty minutes later, a dark sedan slowed down and turned off Wabash Avenue. From the dim light of the streetlamp, Alex could make out the silhouette of a bulky man sitting behind the steering wheel, smoking a cigarette.

The man pulled into the parking lot and flashed his lights. Alex flashed his in return, and the car drew up alongside him and rolled to a stop.

Alex waited a couple of minutes before sliding out from the driver's side. Immediately, the passenger door of the other car flew open and smoke billowed out.

"Get in," a gravelly voice barked.

He scrambled in and slammed the door.

"I'm a very busy man, Heywood. What's so important it couldn't wait? This better be worth getting out at this hour," the man growled.

"It is, believe me. I discovered something ve-ry interesting this evening."

The man took a long puff. "So? Come on. Level with me, now."

"Landon Matthews has a daughter."

The man stubbed his cigarette in the car's ashtray and glowered at Alex. "Do tell?"

"Came across her tonight at the Trianon. Thought she might come in handy . . . at some point."

"Maybe. You know we don't like to dirty our hands. What's she like?"

"She's . . . uh . . . definitely a rube. Not sophisticated at all. Terribly naïve. But, she's a cute little bit of fluff. Ignorant about her father's work."

The man lit another cigarette and blew a cloud of smoke at Alex. "You sure?"

He nodded. "She arrived at his house only today. Really doesn't even know *him*, let alone what he does and what he's working on."

The man inhaled slowly and faced the window as Alex relayed the conversations of the evening. "Remember this, assume at all times she's more knowledgeable about him and his business than she's letting on."

"I'll keep that in mind. What's the next step? What am I supposed to do?"

"Find out the secrets and plans of the management with regard to the solution to the dispute."

"You think I can do that?"

"Wouldn't tell you otherwise."

"How am I supposed to get the goods?"

"Simple. Romance the daughter."

"Now, wait a doggone minute. I agreed to go after the airheaded neighbor of Landon's. Priscilla Van Allen. Couldn't make it to first base with her."

"Hurt your self-esteem, eh?"

"Maybe. She has her sights on Mark Schaumberg. He's probably the first thing she ever wanted she hasn't been able to have. Pro'bly ready to drive her crazy. Had to be satisfied with her best friend, Winnie. Now I'm saddled with the painted lady."

"You're handy. You've already made inroads in that clique. Play it right, and little Miss Matthews just might grow to trust you enough to tell you what's up with her father's affairs at the plant."

"I'll try."

"Nope. You'll get it done. You're to give us a heads-up on what the executives are planning. Understand?"

Alex considered the directive for a second, nodded, and opened the door. He went back to his car, slid behind the wheel, and turned the key in the ignition. Before he shifted into gear to leave, the other car pulled away, turned onto Wabash Avenue, and raced away into the night.

* * *

Sunday opened bright in a wave of October sunshine. Josie and her father left the house at nine o'clock. They went east on Highway 40, past the Trianon, out of the city, and into the rural area. The black

Chrysler sped past fields with bucolic scenes of tipi-like corn shocks, orchards of apple-laden trees, and pastures where Holstein cows grazed and lazed.

Josie drank in the changing scenery of green-shingled farmhouses, groves of walnut trees, and white-painted churches surrounded by cemeteries filled with leaning tombstones. From the towering spires, bells tolled calling worshippers to morning services. People, attired in their Sunday finery, stood in clusters on wide steps or at automobiles.

She half-turned toward her father. "Do you go to church?"

He kept his eyes forward. "Only occasionally. On Easter and Christmas."

"You don't go every week?"

"No. I don't hold much with that practice."

She stared at him, studying his profile. "Why not?"

He glanced sideways at her, then back to the road. "Self-indulgence, I imagine. I happen to believe it isn't necessary to go *every week*. You think it makes a difference in a person's life?"

"Yes, I do. I've learned to lean on God for guidance, strength, and wisdom. There're too many things in life I don't understand. I go regularly to worship and thank Him for blessing me."

Landon locked his fingers around the steering wheel so tightly his knuckles faded to white. "Your mother died. Would God deserve to be thanked and worshipped for that?"

"I don't pretend to know His ways or His purposes, but I can trust Him and gain peace of mind and security. Everyone needs a moral compass . . . something to be guided by. Even better, because of God, we have honesty and integrity, and . . . uprightness."

He glowered at her. "Are you some kind of religious fanatic?"

"Hmm. I never thought of myself as such. I do strive to be a faithful follower of Christ's teachings. The fact is, I choose to believe in someone who's greater and better than myself."

"Drop the subject. No more discussion," Landon insisted.

An awkward silence followed. Josie sat with her hands clasped in her lap and turned her face to the side window. Did her father have any faith in God at all? It sure didn't sound like he did. Her stomach burned and roiled. She would pray for him. At the moment, she settled back in the padded leather seat and heaved a great, secret sigh.

Finally, she broke the tension by asking, "What's my aunt like?"

"Mae Anise? Well, let's see. She's my younger sister. Possesses a lively, outgoing personality. Enjoys the company of a multitude of friends and spends a good deal of time with them. She suffers from wanderlust, travels quite a bit . . . been abroad numerous times—to England and France. Loves Paris and the English countryside. Mae's never married. It wasn't for the lack of suitors, either. She's just a very independent woman. A couple helps her from time to time, but, by and large, she does her own cooking and cleaning. Entertains a lot. Reads everything she comes across. Listens to classical music. Mae's a modern thinker. Into sports and politics. She's always well-dressed with perfect clothes sense."

"She sounds a lot like Mother . . . except for all the traveling. Mother hardly ever left the county, let alone the country."

He pursed his lips. "As a matter of fact, she knew your mother."

"Oh? I wonder why Mother never ever talked about Aunt Mae? It'll be nice to meet her."

"You two will get on with each other just fine."

"I hope so. How does she support herself? I mean . . . since she travels and entertains so much?"

"She's a writer."

"Wow! Like Booth Tarkington and Ernest Hemmingway?"

"She's not famous like them, but she does well enough to sustain her lifestyle. Kept our family's old home place, which is, by the way, in the same neighborhood as Booth Tarkington's home."

It was late morning by the time they reached the outskirts of Indianapolis. The skyline emerged in the near distance. Soon they were in the city proper, the traffic coming at them from all sides. Landon steered through the jungle of factories and imposing buildings and hulks of old houses, guiding the car to the north edge of the city.

"We're almost to Mae's." He slowed down, checked the rearview mirror, and swung the car sharply between stone gateposts with propped-open, elaborate wrought-iron gates.

The driveway swept in a great curve from the entrance, the gravel scrunching and popping under the tires. A thick, neatly trimmed privet hedge screened the house for privacy. "The place is well-hidden. It's just around the next bend. You'll have a good view of it in a little more than a second."

Josie craned her neck looking for her father's old home place. And there it stood, sheltered by sprawling branches of a gigantic oak tree, a three-storied gray stone house with a mansard roof and white shutters and an impressive, pillared front portico. "Is this it?"

"Yes. It is."

"It's marvelous. Like a French *chateau*." She breathed the words. "I've seen pictures of them in magazines. She actually lives here?"

"She does." He stopped the car and shut off the ignition.

Mae Anise appeared, waving. An instant later, she was at Landon's car door, welcoming him with both arms outstretched. "Big brother, you made it. I've been anxiously awaiting your arrival."

He grasped her hands in his, and before he could introduce Josie, Mae said, "Welcome to Indianapolis, Joselene." She went around the car to where Josie stood at the passenger side and pulled her niece into a warm embrace, rocking her side to side. "Here you are." She held Josie back at arms' length. "Now let me look at you. You're a Matthews, all right. I suppose you already know how much you look like your father? Come on in. It'll be wonderful to have you here." She slipped her arm around Josie's shoulders. "What shall we do first? Why not show you around the house? Oh my, we've so much to talk about."

Josie liked her aunt right off. Mae resembled her father—and herself.

That night, Josie lounged on the big bed wearing Chinese pajamas of mauve and silver-embroidered batiste, a set Mae gave her. The bed, higher than normal, was canopied with knotted netting.

She surveyed the guest room. It was larger than the one at her father's—high-ceilinged, elaborately papered walls, long windows hung with lace curtains, and a brass chandelier with frosted glass globes. An old-style mahogany suite of furniture outfitted the space. The dresser, with candle brackets and handkerchief drawers at each side, supported a tilting mirror which reflected the useless and over-abundant but cherished collection of souvenirs, treasures, and memorabilia from Mae's extensive travels.

Mae stood in the doorway. "Ready to say 'good-night?'"

Josie stopped all action of brushing her hair. "Thank you for your kindness, Aunt Mae. You don't seem the least bit leery of me."

She perched on the foot of the bed, making the springs creak. "Do I need to be?"

"My father is."

"He and I are different people—like the day is from the night. You are so much your mother. She was such a delight. I was very fond of her. Your father made a colossal mistake by not going after her."

Josie sighed and met her aunt's gaze. "You think they might have married?"

"Maybe. The might-have-beens are hard to know about." She smoothed the heavy jacquard spread on the bed. "We can't beat a dead horse, now, can we?" She waved a hand. "We can't fret about things we can't change because we can never go back to what was, because it's not there. It no longer exists. You and I must begin right here, right now. Landon and I differ in our attitudes about most things. How shall I say this? Ummm . . . I look at life as an adventure. I want to see and do as much as I can. *A joie de vivre.* A joy for living. Having fun, you know? On the other hand, your father is oh-so-serious about life. I love my brother, but he's the most intense man I've ever known. That's one of the reasons we live seventy miles apart." She laughed, and tilted her head, and studied Josie. "Your hair is so much like your father's. We need to fashion it into an attractive new style. Most of the girls now are bobbing theirs."

Josie bolted off the bed. "No! I might as well cut off an arm or a leg."

Mae pressed a finger to her cheek and shrugged. "The current trend says to—"

"I don't care what it is or says to do." Josie pushed her lower lip out and formed a childish pout, sulking for a moment. "My hair is me . . . as much as my eyes or nose are."

"If you keep it the same, you won't be able to get any stylish hats to fit properly."

Josie adjusted a curl of hair with a hairpin and surveyed her reflection. "What if I twisted it into a knot and pinned it at the nape?" She did so, turned, and faced her aunt. "Like this."

"Adorable. All right. I'll outfit you to suit your type. In that mauve and silver, you are like a lilac in the spring."

Josie flinched. "Are you expecting me to wear colors in public?"

"Of course. You're too young for black all the time."

She stomped over to stand before her aunt. "I'm not either. Wearing anything other than black would be like forgetting Mother. I told Father this morning if he couldn't mourn for her, I'd have to do it for both of us."

Mae stared at her. "You did? What did he say?" She cocked her head to one side.

Josie sat on the edge of the bed, pivoted, and slid her legs under the covers. "He said, 'Move on and live your own life. Yes, your mother is dead. Colors don't mean you've forgotten her.'"

Mae hoisted herself up and came around to the side, placed her hands on Josie's shoulders, and kissed her forehead. "I'm so glad you're staying with me." Tucking in the blankets around Josie, she said, "This house is too much for little ole me to rattle around in. Tomorrow morning, I'll fix you an honest-to-goodness British breakfast before we leave. We've got a full day ahead of us, so you need oodles of rest.

Goodnight, my dear."

Dawn came, clear and pale. Josie heard Mae's alarm clock tingling away in her bedroom at seven. She got up, brushed her hair and freshened her face, pulled on a dressing gown, and greeted her aunt in the kitchen. "I slept so well last night. It's quiet here. Like Bradford. What time should I be ready to leave?"

"Hungry?"

"Not especially. I'm too excited . . . I don't know if I can eat anything." But she could, and she did. She ate the fried egg, Canadian bacon, sausage patty, baked beans, mushroom, tomato half, and toast.

After the dishes were washed and put away, and the kitchen tidied, they got dressed for their day.

Mae brought the car around and Josie came out the front door. "Our schedule for today is to shop at L.S. Ayres Department store. There's nothing I like better than spending money on lots of new clothes. Remember, no one's concerned about cost."

Josie climbed in and shut the car door, her heart pounding. "I'm ready for our expedition."

They entered the multi-storied building a few blocks off the city circle. Josie was in departments in which she was not accustomed to finding herself and marveled at the display of garments. "I've never worn dresses like these."

"Time you did, then," Mae said.

A saleslady approached. "Good morning. May I help you?" They told her what they wanted to see and try on. "Come with me," she said, and pointed to several racks and rattled the hangers.

Mae presided over the selection, pushing some aside, and then held one up—a white and green silk print with tucks on the bodice and white lace on the collar and cuffs. "Try this one on, Josie."

She obeyed her aunt's instructions, and the frock was lowered over her head. When the shoulders were straightened and the many-gored skirt smoothed, Josie stared at her reflection, her breath catching. "Oh, my," she whispered, a hand going to her lips. "Is this me?"

"It is. See what stylish clothes can do for you?"

"I don't recognize myself. I'm looking at a new person."

Mae stepped back and smiled. "You're gorgeous, honey. We'll take this one. What else do you have?" She turned to the saleslady, who sailed away.

Josie gave her aunt a puzzled look. "I can't buy this."

"What's wrong with it?"

"Didn't you see the amount on that price tag? It costs too much."

Mae flapped her hand. "Folderol. Worth every penny, believe me. That dress was you. We need about six more."

"Seven?" Josie gasped. "I've never . . . owned so many *ever* . . . in my whole life." She stared at her aunt. "I can't . . . spend so much money on clothes."

Mae's forehead wrinkled. "Uh, how shall I say this? Yes, you can. Your father's sent plenty, and we're going to splurge."

Josie shuddered. More garments arrived. "Aunt Mae, I think I'm growing dizzy trying all of these on. Does that sound silly to you? I'm struggling to remember how each one fit me." The morning wore on, and the packages added up.

"I'm starved. Let's eat," Mae said.

"Do you always buy like this?" Josie asked. But no answer came. Being with her aunt proved to be hard work. She was hungry, too; her own stomach grumbled fiercely.

They headed to the L.S. Ayres' tearoom, where they were led to a table. Once seated, they piled their bundles and boxes at their feet. Mae and Josie laid aside their pocketbooks and gloves. Josie studied the menu card and wondered what to order.

"How about the chicken velvet soup, honey? It's world-renowned."

The waitress hovered above them while she took their orders. She nodded politely and moved away, and the two women got comfortable at the small table.

Mae greeted several of the patrons who came to chatter away with her, but she never introduced Josie. "This isn't the time or place to surprise them with Landon's daughter," she said.

"When we get back to Terre Haute, I'll write announcements to everybody, and they'll come to check you out." She reached over and patted Josie's hand.

"Now, this afternoon we'll hunt for more dresses. With the right colors and styles on you, the young men will fall in love with you, like moths drawn to a candle's flame."

"Will the new clothes do that?"

"Not by themselves, of course. But with you in the right kind of attire. Yes, certainly." Mae stopped talking as the bowls and spoons were placed on the table. "Your green eyes with their long, black lashes are your most striking feature, and since you insist on keeping your hair long, we'll emphasize it, too. I'll make people take notice of you."

"I'm not sure I want others to pay attention to me." The image of tall, dark, and handsome Elliott Jacobson popped into her mind. Why had she thought of *him* just now?

"Come now. Every girl wants to be admired. The thing you don't want is an inferiority complex. If your mother had been more gutsy, she wouldn't have run away from your father."

Josie flinched and choked. "Huh? I always thought of Mother as having a strong backbone."

"Hmm." Mae held her elbow cupped in one hand, a finger on her lip. "Sarah did have a grace of spirit and body, but she greatly under-estimated herself. She was sensitive enough to realize she lacked certain . . . umm, social skills, and it's unfortunate she became her own harshest critic. She saw herself as a crude, back-woodsy girl, unable to adapt to polite society. Everything she did to change—manicures, penmanship, apparel, and hair—she did for Landon's sake, out of love for him. But Olivia was able to interfere, anyway."

"Who's Olivia?" Josie asked.

Mae dabbed her lips with the napkin. "The woman who, in my opinion, chased your mother away." She splayed her fingers over her breastbone. "You didn't know about her?"

"No. Mother never mentioned an Olivia."

"Of course, she wouldn't. How much do you know about your mother and father?

"What do you mean?"

"Oh, you know, as to why they never married."

"Well, as far as I was concerned, they had married."

"Of course."

"You might as well have me tell you the story than hear it from someone else. Landon and Olivia were quite the couple. He'd known her all his life . . . they'd been together . . . well, ever since childhood, I guess . . . and everyone expected them to marry. Then he went to Terre Haute to help with the tornado and flood cleanup, met Sarah, and got caught in the grips of passion. Olivia was *livid*. It killed her pride that he chose another woman. Someone said she vowed to break up their relationship. I always thought she staged the scene that caused the misunderstanding between your parents."

Josie caught her breath and raised her eyebrows. "What happened?"

"Your mother came upon them together. I can't remember the place she found them, or the circumstances of how she knew where to find them, but I suspect she was told." She leaned closer to Josie. "I guess Landon was holding Olivia's hand." Mae straightened. "When Olivia saw Sarah, she jumped up and said, 'We might as well tell her the truth now.' Landon claimed he tried to stop Olivia from exaggerating what that was, but she said, 'Landon has said he still cares for me.' Now, whether or not he said those exact words, I don't know, but I guess he had said something like that. And that was it. Sarah should have said to Olivia, 'No, you can't have him,' but she didn't. Your mother came to the wrong conclusion about what was going on. She never investigated. She never fought for him. She simply upped and left, and Olivia got her way again."

Josie digested this information for a short time. "Did she marry my father?"

"No."

Josie shook her head. "Mother never married, either. What a pitiful story . . . both of them lived lonely lives because of a conniving woman."

The ticket was slipped on the table. Mae Anise glimpsed the total and reached into her pocketbook for the correct bills and coins.

"Perhaps I shouldn't have said anything, Josie, but it's better to see things as they are. What can't be changed has to be endured. Love your father for who he is, and not for whom you want him to be. People seldom ever do as we wish they will. Sarah could have done anything with him if she'd had more moxie. But lacking quite enough, she relinquished any hold on Landon, gave up a fight for him, and ran away from him."

Maybe her mother had more grit in running away than staying. No, Mae was right. Her mother had acted cowardly, finding it easier to lie and make excuses—because that's precisely what she'd done. For her to have gone back to him once she knew she expected his baby would have required her to be courageous.

Josie swallowed. "All I ever heard from Mother were enchanting stories of my father. I loved him because of how much she did. Do you think he loved Olivia?"

"Um . . . hard to say. She was statuesque and attractive—the sort of woman who would turn heads—the epitome of sophistication. Slender, perfectly groomed. She always wanted to be correct. The right handbag and the right shoes. The right words at the right time. She never omitted doing the right thing—except when it came to your mother. I think he took great satisfaction in being seen with her. But love, hmm, your guess is as good as mine."

"Was he happy with her?"

Mae Anise stared off into space. "Happy? I don't think so. Well, in a strange way, perhaps. Frankly, though, she wasn't a woman who engendered happiness. She brought out the worst in Landon. Your father was quite dispirited after your mother left. He became more impatient, more withdrawn. I think it was depression—anger at himself for losing Sarah. Olivia played life as a game, and your father toyed with her. Anyway, they had a huge quarrel and she left.

"Whatever happened to her?"

"She went away, to Chicago we heard. Married, had children. We've lost track of her."

The conversation ended. Mae scooped up the check, tendered the requisite bills and coins, and gathered up several of the parcels stacked neatly on the floor. She led the way out of the tearoom, leaving Josie to collect the remaining bags and boxes.

"This is what we're going to do this afternoon," Mae said. "New dresses necessitate new accessories. We'll visit the shoe department, then look at hats, handbags, scarves, and jewelry."

Josie staggered with the thought. More clothes? During the morning, she got caught up in the excitement of trying on beautiful garments, permitted dress after dress to be slipped over her head, considered, and then removed as yet another was produced. She ended up purchasing a royal blue dress with a pleated skirt; a modest honey-colored wool crepe; a green crepe; a toffee tweed suit with a beige silk blouse; and the green-and-white print with the tucks. In the coat department, Josie found a dark brown wool coat with a soft beaver collar and a brown hat trimmed in beaver.

"Aunt Mae, do I really need so many new clothes?"

"Of course."

"Aren't you afraid Father'll hit the ceiling when he sees how much all these cost? After all, we've spent a lot of his money . . . for me!"

"What? You don't want the new wardrobe we've bought?"

"Oh . . . my . . . yes, of course. I couldn't be more pleased with everything. But with the Depression so great, shouldn't we be more careful with his money? I don't want to bankrupt him."

Mae raised her hand. "Folderol. Aren't you enjoying your day?"

"Well . . . yes, it's thrilling to own so many beautiful dresses. But the number seems extravagant. I've never been able to indulge myself like this . . . ever. My mother and aunts wouldn't have spent this much . . . for all of us put together."

"This is what your father wants for you. You'll need them. Trust me."

Chapter 6

Thursday morning, Mae Anise drove Josie back to Terre Haute. While they rode, she glanced over at her niece. "How about inviting Mark and the Van Allens for supper tonight?"

"Could be fun."

"Nothing elaborate, of course. Just a little casual supper. That'll give you an opportunity to wear one of your pretty dresses. I'm itching to show off your new clothes to everybody."

Josie regarded her aunt warily for a few seconds. "You want me to actually *parade around*?"

Mae laughed. "Well . . . yes."

Josie chose a green crepe with flounces around the shoulders and an uneven hem. She lifted the garment over her head, straightened it out, and turned to survey her appearance in the door's mirror, first on one side, then on the other. When she twisted to inspect the back view, the skirt fanned out in soft folds around her. The effect pleased her so much, she smiled at her own reflection. She made her way downstairs to the library and positioned herself before the flickering fire in the fireplace.

Mark sauntered in. He gave a low whistle. "Wow! Son of a gun! You look swell, Josie. What a perfect dress for you."

She could not resist holding her arms out at her sides and turning about before him. "Do you like it?"

He smiled broadly. "Green is quite your color. It accentuates your eyes." A few seconds passed before he cleared his throat and spoke again. "A wood fire is very companionable, don't you think? I love one."

Josie nodded. "Burning logs can carry on quite a conversation." The flames made a crackling and popping noise and poured a little shower of red embers through the grate. "See what I mean?"

A babble of voices sounded in the hall, and Priscilla pranced into the room. "Josie, you're delicious. That new frock has expensive written all over it. Very la-dee-da. Mae Anise certainly knows how to select stylish dresses."

At dinner, Mae guided her niece to the foot of the table—opposite her father. Josie objected to the arrangement, but her aunt insisted on it. "The place of honor belongs to you."

Josie winced and clenched her jaw. She didn't want a replay of the fiasco at the Van Allens's: no sneezing, no coughing, no choking.

After the meal, everybody moved to the living room. Mae arranged a black folding table. "Why not enjoy a rigorous test of our mental skill by putting together this complicated jigsaw puzzle? . . . There're a thousand pieces." She dumped the contents of the box.

"Can I just observe?" Josie asked.

"Of course." Mae touched her niece's chin with the tip of her finger. "We all think you are quite lovely."

"Thank you, you're so kind. I think it's the new clothes and your good taste."

"Folderol."

With the others hunched over the table and focused on the puzzle pieces, Josie slipped out of the room. Stopping for a moment at the doorway, she looked back at the four. No one had noticed her quiet exit. She ascended the stairs to her bedroom.

A short time later, a cursory tap sounded. Priscilla opened the door partway and peeped around it. "May I come in?"

"Of course." Josie, wrapped in a quilted robe, and situated in the middle of the bed, sat cross-legged, making it possible to cradle her writing tablet. "Is anything the matter?" She set the notebook aside, sat up straighter, and drew her knees to her chest.

"I could ask you the same thing." Priscilla glided across the room and positioned herself at the foot of the bed, leaning back on one hand, her perfume filling the room with the fragrance of gardenia.

She stared into Josie's green eyes. "You're the hostess of the house now. I just came up to say you made a terrible social blunder by sneaking off from your guests. The polite thing to do was to excuse yourself, or at least say goodnight."

Josie gasped. "I'm . . . sorry. I wasn't trying to be rude and disrespectful."

Priscilla reached over and patted Josie's shoulder. "Poor little scared bunny. You no doubt felt out of your depth tonight. I'd be delighted to teach you the rules of etiquette."

"You're very kind. I always seem to do the wrong thing and suspect my father is put out about it. I do so want to please him."

"Don't worry. I'll help you." Priscilla smiled and gracefully pulled herself to her feet. Before she left the room, she turned back toward Josie. "By the way, Mark thinks you're charming." Her footfalls echoed in the stairway as she descended.

Josie got up and shut the door. She plumped and stacked the pillows, climbed back on her bed, and relaxed against the headboard. With the notepad close by, she gave her fountain pen the shake it always required before it would write and began a letter. 'Dear Aunt Phoebe and Aunt Ruth.' She stopped and sighed before she continued. 'Here I am in Terre Haute. It's amazing what's happened to me, almost overwhelming.' Did they ever think of her? She supposed they did. She threaded some stray strands of hair off her face and tucked them behind her ears. She wrote and wrote. 'Father took me to Indianapolis to shop with my Aunt Mae Anise (his sister). I have an unbelievable wardrobe now. Father is most generous with me. He loves to give me new things.'

Finally, she concluded with 'I send you both love and kisses,' and signed her name. She capped her pen, laid it down, flexed her cramped fingers, read over what she'd written, folded the pages, stuffed them into an envelope, and licked the flap to seal it. She wrote the address, affixed the stamp, and got up to put the missive upon her bureau to mail the next day.

Josie went to the bathroom and brushed her teeth and her hair. She came back, turned off her light, and went to the bay window to peek at the night sky. The moon, almost full, softly illuminated the backyard. Wait. Was there movement in the shadows of the alley, or did she just imagine it? She leaned her forehead against the cool glass and focused on the garage.

Yes, she could see a big, burly man appear out of the darkness walking around, moving into the beam of the streetlight and then going back into the shadows. What was he doing there? Was he a prowler? A tramp? A hobo passing through? He stopped, glanced around furtively, rested a wide shoulder against the side of the garage, and lit a cigarette. A shiver ran through Josie. Her heart pounded against her rib cage. She stood rigid, unable to move. What was he doing there besides enjoying a smoke? Was he spying on the house? It was a chilling thought. The man threw the butt on the ground, crushed it with his shoe, and meandered away into the shadows. Josie watched him until he was gone. She let out a breath she didn't even realize she'd been holding. Relief.

Her hands icy and shaking, she took a step back from the window, went to bed, and slid under the top sheet and blanket. But she couldn't sleep for a long time, her thoughts twisting and turning, and the roller-coaster emotions of the evening events wheeling before her mind's eyes: the stranger loitering in the back yard; Mark complimenting her on the new dress; Mae directing her to an honored seat for the evening meal; Priscilla offering to instruct her on the trivia of manners and conventions. "Course, Priscilla supposes she can manage everything better than anyone else . . . even when it comes to other people's own concerns. Gracious, my life has taken a more exciting turn since coming to live with my father."

Josie awakened early the next morning to the sound of the horses' clip-clopping on the brick pavement as they pulled the Model Milk delivery wagon. Their steel shoes clanked as they slowly advanced to each stop on the street, and the glass bottles in the milkman's metal carrier jangled as he carried them door to door. These now-familiar street noises heralded the beginning of another day. Her eyes flew open. She saw the wallpaper, the bed, her personal items. She was back in Terre Haute at her father's house. It was good to be home again. She gathered the warm blankets closer about her neck, hunched herself deeper into bed, and waited for the night to fade into the pink light of dawn.

Once the sun edged its way above the horizon, Josie dangled her legs over the side of the bed and yanked on her dressing gown. She took a hairbrush from the kidney-shaped vanity table and pulled it through her tousled hair, brushing it off her face with great sweeps. She turned off the light and went down the stairs.

She could hear the soft murmur of voices, but no distinct words, coming from the kitchen. Josie pushed open the swing door, and the delicious aromas of cinnamon and nutmeg, as well as that of freshly brewed coffee, welcomed her. Vertie stood at the stove. A man sat at one end of the table, buttering a popover. The two stopped talking when she inched her way in.

"Morning, Miss Josie. I'm surprised you're up. Thought maybe you'd catch up with your rest. Half expected to see you later in the day."

Vertie shuffled over and gestured toward the man. "This here's my husband, Abner." She slid two fried eggs, over easy, onto his plate.

He held up his coffee cup to acknowledge her. "Howdy, young lady. Just call me Nub, though. Ever'body does."

Josie came forward, smiling, and extended her hand. "Hello." The man's hand felt dry and calloused to her, and he smelled of Aqua Velva. His skin was wrinkled and weather-beaten, his cheeks netted with red veins. Clear blue eyes glittered like stars beneath owl-like eyebrows—their thickness contrasting with the thinning gray hair. He wore faded bib overalls, a red flannel shirt frayed at the collar, and unpolished leather boots scuffed at the toes and so worn down at the heels that no sole was left on.

Nub took a noisy swig of coffee. "You're younger looking than I thought."

"Oh?" Josie went to the dish cabinet, grabbed a cup, and filled it. She gouged four spoonsful of sugar from the bowl and flung them into the dark liquid.

Vertie raised an eyebrow. "Land sakes! You like a little coffee with your sugar, don't you?"

Josie grinned, stirred, and sampled her coffee. Satisfied, she sat opposite Nub.

He wiped his mouth with the back of his hand, then pointed to the discolored muffin tin. "Hot popover?"

"Sure." She took a knife and lifted out the quick bread.

Vertie held the cast iron skillet in one hand and a pancake turner in the other. "Eggs?"

"Please. Only one egg, though, and two sausage patties." She slathered butter over the popover, allowing it to soak in before she bit into it.

Vertie flattened the ground sausage into two patties and put them in the skillet to fry.

While they sizzled, she came to the table and topped off Nub's coffee.

After finishing his breakfast, he rinsed off his dirty dishes and put them in the sink.

"Reckon I better get started on my day."

"What'd yuh decide to get done today?" Vertie asked. She poured some orange juice into a swanky swig and handed it to Josie.

"Clean up the yard."

Josie gulped down her mouthful, still holding the glass in midair. "May I help?"

Nub stopped in the doorway and ran his tongue over his lips. "Uh, well, uh . . ." He looked at Vertie, who now stood with her backside against the kitchen sink, quirking her mouth and shrugging.

Josie lowered her empty glass. "Please?" she pleaded. Her glance shifted from one to the other.

Nub's lower lip covered his upper one. He stroked the back of his neck and passed his hand over his chin. "Don't rightly know what your father'd say about that."

"Please? I'd really, *really* like to help you."

"Well, uh. . . . all right, come on out when you're ready."

"I won't be long." After breakfast, she went to her room, pulled on a plain white shirt, knelt in front of her chest of drawers with the bottom drawer opened, and removed a thick, persimmon-colored wool sweater and a pair of brown flannel trousers. She tied back her hair with a colorful ribbon and appeared outdoors a short time later.

"Got another rake?"

"Yep, I'll get it." Nub went into the garage's interior and came back with one. He and Josie were at the south of the house, working on opposite sides of the lot. The two spent the next three hours raking.

Nub, closest to the alley, built a brush fire. Josie took in deep breaths when she toted armfuls of leaves and dropped them on the flames, the pungent, vaporous cloud curling and fuming upward. "I love to be out in the fresh air and have the warm sunshine soak into my bones. Fall is my favorite season. It has its own sweet scent."

Nub methodically swung his rake first right-handed and then left against the grass, making the piles higher and higher. "Aw, you're just smelling the burning of dried leaves."

The sun grew warmer and Josie's face became wet with little beads of perspiration. Wisps of her red-gold hair escaped from the confines of the ribbon and stuck to her damp forehead. She pulled off the work gloves, shed her sweater by stripping it off over her head, and slung it over her shoulders, where she knotted the arms around her neck like a muffler. She stared at the burning pile as the smoke rose like a waving blue-gray banner, swiped her brow with the back of her wrist, and leaned against a maple tree, lingering long enough for her heart to stop pounding.

A voice called from behind her. "Hey, you two!"

Startled, Josie peered over her shoulder, but the sun picked a path between the trees and blinded her. She squinted, lifted a hand to shade her eyes from the dazzle, and saw Elliott Jacobson approach. The sight of him whipped her up inside like beaten egg whites.

What did he want? She stood frozen in place, tongue-tied.

He stepped over to create a shadow for her. "Whatcha doing?"

"Raking." Josie bent down to pick up a brittle leaf skittering across the lawn and started shredding it between her fingers. "Why are you here?"

"You. Came to see you."

"Me?" She put her hands to her disheveled hair and made an attempt to bring control to it. But with only her fingertips, and without a brush and comb and hairpins, she did little good. "You want to see me?"

"Yep, hey, such a nice fall morning. Thought with a bit of luck, you'd be home. Sure enough, here you are. Maybe you'll let me show you Terre Haute and buy you some lunch."

She ceased in her half-hearted efforts to arrange her hair. "What? Go with you . . . right now?"

"Why not?"

"I'm not cleaned up."

Elliott gave a short laugh. "You look all right to me. Come on."

She never moved. "But I stink . . ."

Nub pulled out a large, red paisley handkerchief from his back pocket, mopped his forehead, and blew his nose with an aggressive toot. "Well, don't you want to go with him?" he asked, with a sidelong look at her.

Josie swirled around to face him and glared at him. She shook her head in small, jerky movements. "Nu-u-b," she growled through clenched teeth, her eyes squinted, her brows furrowed.

The man wiggled his eyebrows several times and waved his hand, shooing her away. "Go on, Miss Josie, I'll finish up. You can't turn down an offer like that. Go ahead." He jammed his handkerchief back into his back pocket and drew a long, satisfied breath.

For a moment, she fell silent. "I'm not used to people ganging up on me." But she was. How about her aunts in Bradford?

Elliott smiled in triumph and clasped his hands over his head in the gesture of a champion as they walked across the lawn together. He held the car door open for her to climb into the passenger seat and closed her door with a thump.

Josie turned to wave at Nub. "I can't believe I'm doing this," she said. She knew very little about this man. He was from Bloomington and had been in Terre Haute a few years working as a newspaper reporter. But Nub must have known him—and he seemed okay with them leaving together. She looked back over her shoulder. Nub was leaning on his rake, smiling at her.

Elliott drove north and turned east onto Wabash Avenue. He imitated the voice of a master of ceremonies. "You'll find the best smells in town on this street, Josie. Roll down your window and take a whiff. Planters Peanut Store." He pointed. "Breathe in."

"Mmm, popcorn and caramel corn," she said. "It does make one's mouth water."

"Coffee's coming up."

"I'm just learning to be a coffee drinker. I do love its fragrance, though. Where's it coming from?"

Elliott motioned toward a magnificent multi-storied brick building.

"Over there. Hulman and Company. They're probably most famous for the Clabber Girl baking powder."

Josie twisted about in the seat to get a longer look out the car's back window. "I've used that, but had no idea it was made here in Terre Haute."

"The odors at this end of town make one hungry, don't they? Hey . . . it's almost noon. Let's stop here." He pulled his gray Studebaker to the curb and turned off the ignition.

"Hm . . . The King Lem Inn. What kind of restaurant is that?"

"Chinese."

"I've never eaten that before."

"We're not eating there. Sorry to disappoint you. We're going over *there*. Next door to it. The Coney Island." He indicated by the slight direction of his left hand. "A great little eatery. The menu is limited, but they've got the best hot dogs in all the world. They're smothered with onions, relish . . . and Clay Ginapolis's special sauce."

"Sounds mysterious," Josie razzed.

"You won't be able to stop at one, I assure you."

She shrugged. "We'll see."

He came around to open her door and help her out. "Naw, you'll want more, I guarantee it." He cupped Josie's elbow to guide her across the busy street, and they made their way to the small and unpretentious hot dog place. The two seated themselves on stools at the counter and placed their orders. Already many diners were busy with their own meals.

"Wait 'til you taste them. They're fantastic."

When the sandwiches came, Josie and Elliott looked at each other, but neither of them said a word. Elliott draped his tie over one shoulder and bit deeply into the hot dog. He chewed and swallowed his mouthful. "Your father's working on a certain development at the plant."

"You asking or telling?"

"Do you know anything about it?" He wiped his mouth with the edge of his hand. "Your father's run into a spot of trouble there."

Josie glared at him. "Oh . . . so this morning really has to do with my father."

"Now, wait a minute."

"I know he's a lawyer. He never discusses his work with me." She nibbled away on her hot dog and reached for her napkin.

"*Never*? He doesn't ever talk about the Stamping Mill?"

"No." Josie bit a small crescent out of her sandwich. "Why should he mention anything about it to me?"

He scratched his head. "Thought maybe he might have, that's all." He arched his eyebrows. "Something's brewing. I don't like the smell of what's happening there."

She swiveled to face him. "What is it? You tell me."

"The labor union's trying to get a foothold in the plant."

"Hmm. Better for me to know nothing about the goings-on there than open my mouth and say the wrong thing at the wrong time to the wrong person. Wouldn't you say that'd be a good policy for me?"

He tilted his head. "Yep, I do. I tell you what, for your sake, let me enlighten you about the situation. The unrest has been going on for several months."

She fingered the remains of her hot dog bun. "Alex Heywood is a union steward there. He seems a capable man. Can't he manage things?"

Elliott puckered his brow. "Apparently not. Last month, four hundred fifty of the five hundred production workers joined the Federal Labor Union. I've been snooping around, trying to ascertain the source of the dispute. A good reporter does that, you know." He winked at her. "Listen, something's going on underhanded. I can sense it. Someone's causing controversy—stirring up the folk." He took a breath. "And your dad never mentions anything about the company?"

Josie fiddled with her napkin a while and smoothed it against the counter. "I've already said my father does *not* share *anything* about his work with me."

"Okay, okay." Elliott pressed open palms against the air. He remained silent a long moment and let his gaze return to Josie, and then rubbed the underside of his nose with a knuckle. "Say, how did you like your hot dog? They're the best, aren't they?" He grinned. "Want another one?"

"Sure. I musta worked up an appetite raking."

Elliott ordered three hot dogs with the works—one for her and two for him. "Told yuh you couldn't get away with eating only one, didn't I? Hey, I hope I'm not prying too much, but did you ever wonder what your life would've been like if your father'd known you all along?"

Josie had just taken a big bite of her sandwich. She flashed a fast glance at Elliott while her cheekful of hot dog nearly dropped out of her mouth. She swallowed and cleared her throat. "Always . . . in my imagination . . . even in my dreams. When I found out he was alive, I became obsessed with him." She stared straight into Elliott's eyes and smiled wryly at him.

He put his index finger to his lips. "You can trust me. I'll keep your secret. I'm as safe as a sealed tomb."

She looked away, staring off into space, and said, "I vowed no one and nothing could stop me from seeing him . . . from meeting him. I wanted my wish to come true."

They finished their sandwiches without further conversation and left the little restaurant.

On the way back to the Matthews's home in Farrington's Grove, Josie said, "Thank you for showing me Terre Haute . . . and everything else."

Elliott pulled to the curb and meant to turn off the engine, but . . .

"You don't need to get out," Josie said. "About earlier . . . I shouldn't have said what I did."

"It's all right. I didn't mind. Actually, I'm flattered you did. Part of my job is asking the questions, then listening for the answers." He smiled at her.

She meant to yank on the door handle when he reached over and covered her hand with his own. Why couldn't she make her hand move away from his? She glanced at him, her heart fluttering, to find him watching her. It had been the lightest touch, but definitely a deliberate gesture, one that sent a strange prickling sensation—like a current of electricity—zinging up the length of her arm and out her fingers. She was hot and then cold. She didn't know what just happened, except that nothing like it had ever happened to her before. And all because of the touch of his hand upon hers.

Elliott gave her a mock salute. "I'm going to be gone a few days, but when I return to town, I'd like to call on you."

Josie nodded, opened the door, and maneuvered herself out. She took a few steps from the curbing and stood on the sidewalk until Elliott put the car in gear and pulled away. The Studebaker was completely out of sight and the hum of the engine could no longer be heard before she turned toward the house.

He was so handsome and fascinating. She blew out a sigh, strolled to the back door, and entered the kitchen.

Vertie never looked up. She dunked the mop head into the hot, soapy water, wrung it out, and slapped it against the floor.

Josie halted in mid-stride and rested a hand on her breast. "I'm sorry. Have I tracked on your clean floor?"

"Nope. Ain't been that far over." She stopped and waved her hand. "Go on through." She braced herself against the mop handle. "How's your young man?" Her eyebrows went up whimsically.

"He's *not* my young man," Josie countered. "He's *not*! I don't even really know Elliott Jacobson." She spun on the ball of her foot and stomped out of the kitchen. However, she moved in a dream of him for the rest of the day. That night, when she lay in bed, she thought about him, going over everything he'd said and every nuance of his voice. Was he thinking of her? She hoped he was. She settled into a more comfortable position to sleep and checked herself. Why should she even care about whom Elliott Jacobson thought?

Chapter 7

Elliott opened the front door of the Jacobson's house on East First Street in Bloomington, Indiana. His mother, Lillian, a slim woman of average height, sat erect on the edge of the green-and-cream brocade-covered sofa. She wore a gray tweed skirt, a white silk blouse with a scatter pin at the collar, and a red cardigan.

"It's about time you got here. I was worried about you. You're much later than usual. I've imagined all sorts of mishaps." She glanced at the clock and laid aside her gold-rimmed glasses. "What happened?"

"Nothing." He sank to a low leather hassock by the fireplace, folded his legs like jackknives, loosened his tie, and undid the top two shirt buttons.

"There must've been something wrong. It's half past six."

"No, no. Not a thing." He planted his elbows on his knees, bowed his head, and locked his fingers across his eyes. Couldn't she, for once, greet him without complaining about something? What could he say or do now to pacify her? Probably nothing. "Just took longer to wrap up loose ends at the newspaper, that's all . . . and time got away. Started later from Terre Haute than I thought I would." He popped to his feet.

"Any mail for me?"

She pointed. "Over there."

He picked up a stack of letters and shuffled through them.

Lillian arched forward and glared at him. "Elliott Randolph Jacobson, don't you dare take the time to read them now! Supper's ready."

He stared at her. "It is?" He chucked the envelopes onto a small table in the corner and moseyed down the hallway to the bathroom.

Twenty minutes later, they sat at the kitchen table and ate supper—Elliott heartily, but Lillian had lost her appetite she said.

They returned to the living room, where she fluffed and rearranged the pillows on the couch. Elliott stirred the embers in the grate to new blaze, added a log, and watched it catch fire, the flames brightening the room. He tossed the just-plumped pillows onto the floor and stretched out on the couch, crossing his ankles.

Lillian lowered herself into the wingback chair under a silk-shaded porcelain lamp. She prattled about things of no consequence and finally asked, "What are you up to nowadays? Anything new or exciting going on in your life?"

He rested a wrist on his forehead. "Umm, could be."

She breathed in, held it a moment, then expelled the air. "Well, don't keep me in suspense. What is it? Something with your job? . . . A promotion maybe? A move to a bigger city?"

He chortled. "No, no. Nothing of that sort. I met someone . . . a girl. Nobody's quite like her—no one I've ever come across, at least. I'm tossing around the idea of settling down."

Lillian clamped down on the arms of the chair. "You can't mean that."

"Yep, sure do. Why not? There comes a time when a man needs a wife." He scratched behind his left ear.

"Stop! . . . Stop it. You're considering marriage!? How did this happen? I wasn't aware you were seeing anyone socially. Why didn't you let me know something about this before?"

His head came up. He braced himself on his elbows, and with the merest hint of a smile, said, "I guess I thought you wouldn't be so interested in my love life."

"Why Elliott, that's absolutely ridiculous. Of course I am. You're my only child. Whoever she is, she's a lucky girl. What do you know about her?"

He leaned back, clasped his hands behind his head, and stared at the ceiling. "She's a peach. You'll be impressed with her."

"What's her name?"

"She's called Joselene Grace Matthews."

"Were you properly introduced?"

He sat up and planted his feet on the floor. "Good grief, Mom, this is the twentieth century."

"We still adhere to certain standards. Things must be proper."

"Oh, yes. Everything according to the rules. Whose are those, though? Yours?"

"Don't insult me, Elliott." Lillian released a snort. "When will you bring her here for me to see her with my own eyes?"

"In time. I've known her only a few weeks, but found she's pleasant company."

"Charmed you, obviously," Lillian said in an ugly tone. "Where's she from?"

"Bradford."

She waggled her head. "How in the world did you come across a girl from there . . . wherever that is?"

"Here in Indiana, in Harrison County—along the Ohio River. She came to live with her father."

"Huh! A split family. Divorce. Doesn't sound too—"

"Actually, her parents never divorced because they never married."

Lillian's hands went to her cheeks. "Elliott! What are you saying? I'm not sure I want to hear any more about this girl. What are my friends going to think? You . . . sparking a . . . a girl of no account. How will I ever be able to hold my head up and face them? The disgrace of it all. How could you do this to me?"

Elliott blew out his cheeks and expelled his breath through his lips. Here she goes again. Off on one of her tirades. He closed his eyes and wobbled his head from side to side. She was forty-four years old, but her mouth, molded over the years because of stubbornness and discontent, made her appear older. "Mom, I'm trying hard not to laugh at the conventions of the society in which you choose to live. Josie can't help the circumstances of her birth."

She screwed up her face into the expression of one who just bit into a lemon. "Josie? Is that what you called her?"

"You'll find she's a beautiful person. Smart and sweet . . . and honest, and hey . . . she's completely unpretentious."

Lillian fidgeted in her chair. "Well, I should think so. A girl like that." She laid one hand on the other. "You can't be serious about . . . someone of that . . . uh, you're not in love with her, are you?"

Elliott said nothing. He spent some moments enmeshed in the illusion he and Josie were a couple, earnest about their relationship.

"Did you hear me, Elliott? You're not in love with her, are you?"

"What? . . . Oh, I'm quite attracted to her."

"How'd you ever attach yourself to someone with no status symbol?"

"Josie's a fine girl and I'm extremely fond of her. We met when I ran into her at her father's house—literally."

"What on earth were you doing in Bradford?" She plucked a horsehair poking through the chair's arm.

"No, you misunderstood. I'm talking about Terre Haute."

Lillian drew a quick breath and pressed four fingers over her mouth. "*Terre Haute.*" She almost hissed the city's name.

"You make it sound like Timbuktu or . . . outer space."

"I just want you to be happy."

"I want that, too, and I will be."

"Not with her you won't. Come now. I cringed when you got that job in Terre Haute, but I held my tongue because I figured it wouldn't last long owing to the Depression. Terre Haute is the hotbed for . . . for all kinds of sins—gambling, political corruption, and labor problems . . . not a desirable city by any means. I don't understand what has got into you to fancy a girl from there and with that kind of ancestry? You can do better, Elliott. There're so many lovely girls from good families here in Bloomington. Any of them would be more suitable."

He rubbed the hollow of his temple with two fingers. "Not any I've come across. Mom, I like Josie for the way she is and . . . well, the way she looks. I'm twenty-five and I know what I want."

"Oh, piffle, son. You've not lived long enough to figure out what's crucial in life and love. Think of your future. Be sensible. Marry money and social standing, not . . . some poor country girl. I'm afraid when you find the right girl, it's going to be difficult for her. Are you listening to me, Elliott? . . . *Elliott*?"

"What? Sorry." He'd been picturing him and Josie as a couple and came out of his reverie with a start. "What were you saying? What is it my wife isn't going to like?"

"Nothing she won't like. That wasn't what I said. Pay attention." Lillian huffed. "I don't know what to do with you anymore. I *said*, it will be difficult for your wife because we're so close. And, what about your career? You're just starting out and much too busy to be tied down with a wife and babies."

"Mom, I'm not even engaged, yet. I have no wife, nor do I have any babies coming along. I can't see that any of those would adversely affect my work."

"You better believe I want to meet this girl."

"You're going to be crazy about Josie. You two are fine women."

"Be careful, Elliott. Don't risk your happiness. Promise me one thing—"

He got up, headed for the door, then stopped and swung back to look at her. "What is it?"

"Promise me that nobody, not even your wife—whoever she might be—can ever come between you and me."

He clasped his hand over his forehead and left the room.

* * *

Josie fiddled with her pocketbook. "I can't wait to see Fred Astaire and Ginger Rogers on the silver screen."

"*The Gay Divorcee* is advertised as the hit of the decade," Alex Heywood said. He parked his Packard Coupe on Wabash Avenue, and he and Josie crossed the street to the Orpheum Theater.

Alex bought the tickets and the two entered the auditorium. They found it almost filled to capacity and seated themselves as the lights dimmed.

"Right on time," he whispered.

After the trailers for the coming attractions, the Universal Newsreel showed Germany's Chancellor, Adolf Hitler, meeting with Sir Robert Anthony Eden of Britain, the appointed Lord Privy Seal, where Hitler hinted that Germany possessed an Air Force—in direct violation of the Versailles Treaty. Josie shuddered at the implications.

The movie began. She settled back in her seat and got caught up in the fantasy of the story being shown. Fred Astaire, bigger than life, sang and danced his way through the "Night and Day" song with Ginger Rogers. Together they twirled and tapped the "Continental," and fell in love. When the picture show ended, everyone filed out.

"How about a strawberry ice cream soda?" he asked.

Josie smiled and nodded. "Mmm, delicious."

They walked to Gillis's Drug Store and slid into a booth. Promptly, a young waitress wearing a stiffly starched white apron appeared.

Alex placed the order with her and turned his attention on Josie. "How'd you like the show?"

"It was cute . . . and funny. Kinda screwball, I guess. "Let's Knock Knees" was a catchy tune. I love to watch Fred Astaire and Ginger Rogers dance together. I'm amazed how she can maneuver around in those long gowns and high-heeled shoes. She did every step perfectly."

The two broke off their chitchat when their sodas came. Josie plunged her straw into the tall soda glass and savored the taste.

"Say, how about you and me go together to see a stage musical at the Hippodrome next Monday?"

She stirred her drink with the straw. "What's that?"

He twitched his eyebrows. "Which one? A stage musical or the Hippodrome?"

She slapped his arm playfully. "Oh, you . . ."

"The Hippodrome is Terre Haute's premiere Vaudeville Theater with unbelievable acoustics. The musical is about old Kentucky, titled *Sunny Skies*, billed as a comedy."

Josie looked away, turned back to face him. "Uh . . . I . . . I'm not sure, Alex."

"Why not? Everyone who's anyone important in the city will be there. Believe me, you'll be sorry if you miss that production." He flashed a charming smile. "Now, don't be a stuck-up snob. Who else would even ask you? So, come on, go with me."

Josie flinched and stared at him. Had she heard him right? Who did he think he was, anyway? God's gift to women? It took great effort on her part to keep from revealing what really was on her mind. No, she didn't want to see the play, especially with him. She forced her attention back to Alex, who'd kept rattling on.

"Besides," he was saying, "the musical's a charity affair . . . an annual event . . . a benefit to raise money for the Rose Orphan Home. The monies defray the cost of their Christmas party. Just say you'll go."

Josie gripped the stubby base of the soda glass with the fingers of both hands. "So-o-o, if my answer is 'no,' are you thinking I don't care about orphaned children? Not fair."

"Then don't argue with me."

"I'm not arguing, Alex." She sighed long and deeply. "If the show is going to be as fine as that, then . . . all right." Immediately, she wished she hadn't agreed to go. On the surface, Alex was charismatic, but deep down . . . well. She glanced at him and gave him a feeble smile, an uneasiness filling her heart.

"What? Something you want to ask?"

"Only—" Josie began. "How can you go to the movies and shows as often as you do when the economy is so poor? Don't you want to be more thrifty? What if you lose your job?"

He sat back and folded his arms across his chest. "A little Miss Worry Wart here? Answer's simple. I'm a union man—one of their faithful servants. The bigwigs have me pegged for something. At least, they've made definite overtures in the form of giving me assignments to complete for them. They'll make sure my job's secure . . . one of the purposes of unions. I see things differently than you do. The worse things get, the more we need a way to escape the misery. Entertainment does that. Besides, when I go out, I'm helping several people hold on to their jobs. If everyone decided to stay home and stuff their hands in their pockets, all these other people would be out of work. I consider it my responsibility to help them as much as I can."

"Very admirable of you."

"Yes, it is. But after all, I am a wonderful, kind, and considerate person."

What did he say? Had she heard him right? "I thought one's virtues were discovered by others, not by oneself. So . . . I'm guessing . . . you are . . . some sort of . . . a prize?"

"Sure! Yes, I am. The man who is ambitious for power usually thinks rather highly of himself. If he doesn't like himself, how can anyone else like him? Gosh, I'm surprised you haven't perceived that about me. Come to think of it, though, it probably does take more than one or two dates for a woman to find out how awesome I am."

* * *

Josie pushed open the swing door into the kitchen. "What smells so scrumptious it called me from the library?" She took a glass out of the dish cabinet.

Vertie swirled white icing in snowy heaps over a four-layer chocolate cake. "I wondered where you got off to."

She turned on the faucet to get a drink of water. "Who's that for?"

"Thought you could take it to the Van Allens's tonight. Want to finish frosting it for me?" Vertie held out the spatula and spoon.

Josie set down her glass and took the utensils. "Sure. Now I can say I helped make it." She spread the remaining creamy confection over the outside of the layers and stood back to admire the fluffy peaks while she licked off her fingers.

The five sat down to dinner. Josie sat to the left of her father, across the table from Mark, and Clarinda, sitting at the head of the table, handed a plateful of cornbread to her. "Did you find *Sunny Skies* as spectacular as everyone's been saying?"

Josie took a wedge. "I loved every minute of it. The songs and the costumes were wonderful. Alex was right when he said I'd enjoy it."

Priscilla smoothed a napkin on her lap. "Didn't you go with Elliott?"

"No." Josie never looked up as she lavishly buttered the cornbread. She took a bite and swallowed before she said, "I went with Alex."

Priscilla stopped dipping the sweet-and-sour chopped cabbage from a china bowl. "Alex Heywood? I thought he was stuck on Winnie. At least, he seemed gaga over her. I thought they were getting pretty thick. You don't suppose he's throwing her over?" She glowered at Josie. "By the way, practically everyone in the city who's got any talent took part in that . . . singing or dancing or playing in the orchestra."

"How come you weren't in it?" Josie asked. Priscilla remained silent, but Mark snickered.

It was the first Tuesday after the first Monday, November sixth—election day—and the conversation buzzed about at the table finally came around to the topic of politics. Landon laid his knife on the edge of his plate. "Are you saying you voted the other way? Different from your own mother?"

Priscilla began nodding before he finished his questions. "Yes."

A small muscle at the side of his mouth twitched. "I can't understand why women even want to get involved in the voting process," Landon grumbled. "Can anyone explain the reason?" He raised his water glass to his lips.

"Why shouldn't we? I love the excitement of the political scene. What's the matter with that? Somebody has to run things. Someday, whether you men like it or not, there will be plenty of women elected to government offices."

Landon set down his glass with such force that the water splashed out and splattered onto the table. "I hardly think so. Elections are dirty business. If I had my way, they wouldn't even get involved. It's not any of their affair." He shifted in his chair and studied his daughter. "You're awfully quiet. Where do you stand in this? Do you agree with Priscilla's point of view?"

Josie tipped forward, a forkful of food halfway to her mouth when he addressed her. Her glance flicked over to him. "At the moment, I take little if no interest in what is going on, and I don't know enough about the local candidates to express an opinion about them."

"I, for one, am glad to leave the voting to men," Clarinda said.

"Good for you," Landon said.

Josie's eyes narrowed. She admired Clarinda, but she didn't like her father's praise of such a nonsensical statement. Women worked long and hard to get the right to vote. It was a milestone in American history, and she secretly vowed that when *she* was eligible, she definitely would exercise that right.

Landon switched his focus to his associate. "What do you think of Priscilla's liberal stance?"

She hurriedly answered before he had a chance. "Mark's never asked me what my political beliefs are. But Mother knows my viewpoints. She's always told me to form my own opinions, and I have. In fact, I believe the President's New Deal is the only way we'll come out of this appalling malaise. After all, he had to do *something*."

Landon glowered at her. "Bah! FDR's philosophy for recovery rubs me and many others the wrong way. It's thinking like his that'll propel our country into trouble down the road. His alphabet soup of new programs will ensnare us all into a dependency forever. He's a radical . . . a socialist."

"He simply wants to redistribute the wealth of the people," Priscilla argued.

"Exactly. Why should anyone work hard? Our very own President is luring the general public to trust in Uncle Sam to provide for them. With what he plans to do, a person's self-reliance is depleted. Welfare goes against our country's founding Constitution. And, by the way, have you noticed there's still double-digit unemployment?"

"Give him time."

"Harrumph! Time? The very thought of granting handouts says to me government bureaucrats have become far too powerful and meddlesome, and I strongly object to that."

She rolled her eyes. "Oh? Do you have a better idea?"

"No, a better solution. The wealthy need to stimulate the economy with large expenditures."

"The *wealthy*? Who are they anymore?" She dropped her fork. It clattered onto the table. "I can't believe you!"

"Priscilla," Clarinda rebuked. "Landon is our guest. Mind your manners."

"Mother, he is the only man who'll discuss this issue with me." She looked over at Mark.

He smiled wryly. "I've got to admit you have an idea on everything and are always up for an argument."

Clarinda shook her head, stood abruptly, and pushed her chair into place. "I think we're finished here. I, for one, look forward to eating a slice of delicious-looking cake. Let's eat our dessert in the living room while those inclined to do so may listen for the radio broadcast of the election returns."

"You go ahead," Josie said. "Priscilla and I will clear the table, make coffee, and bring everything in." Priscilla gaped at Josie.

"How nice, girls, for you to do that." Clarinda laid her napkin on the table and led the way out of the room.

Josie stacked the dirty dishes and carted them to the kitchen, where she jumbled them in the sink, crumbs and fragments of food still scattered on them. "How can your mother be so agreeable with my father?"

"Mother agrees with everybody. She's as comfortable as a feather pillow." Priscilla went to and fro between the cupboard and table, gathering the necessary china items.

Josie slashed through the four iced layers and then paused with the knife in mid-stroke. "But doesn't she have any convictions of her own?"

Priscilla put her index finger above her lips. *"Convictions?* Ha! She's from another time and place. Her generation was trained to be captivating to men. A woman wouldn't be considered appealing if she had too many of her own ideas."

"You're attractive to men, and you have definite persuasions."

"Things're different now from what they were in Mother's time. Today's men are more enlightened. More tolerant." She put the coffee pot, cups, and saucers on a tray. "Hurry up," she said, and left the kitchen.

Josie followed with her tray laden with the slices of cake. Clarinda stood at the Zenith console adjusting the volume. Her hostess struck Josie as graceful and poised, an unusually handsome woman in her red polka dot dress, her hair in Marcel waves. Maybe her father was enamored by this woman.

Shortly after eight o'clock, the group sat silent as the sprinkling of comments were broadcasted. By ten, the reports came in fast, and Josie grew uncomfortable when the numbers indicated that Landon's choice of candidate would, in all probability, be defeated.

She didn't want to get trapped in the crossfire between her father and Priscilla again. "I'm going home. Thank you, Clarinda, for an interesting evening." With that said, she moved toward the door.

Landon stood up. "Wait. I'll go along with you. Ladies. Mark." He nodded his goodbye to them.

Walking home, he said, "Don't know what your political persuasion is, but you'll learn two things soon enough. Number one, Priscilla supports the progressive movement, so be cautious she doesn't trip you up with her arguments. She tends to get on a soapbox to push her position. And number two, this city is a strong union town . . . a hotbed for liberalism. Eugene V. Debs was from here. Unions and progressive ideas are foremost in the fabric of Terre Haute."

Chapter 8

"I can't believe Thanksgiving's only two days away. Can you?" Josie leaned against the kitchen sink peeling the skin and pith off an orange, the juice dripping from her fingers.

"This fall's gone by in a hurry. That's for sure," Vertie said, sorting through a pile of clean clothes to be ironed. She plucked a crumpled white shirt of Landon's, shook it out, and flattened it on the table. "Happens it's my favorite holiday."

"How so?" Josie pulled apart a segment and stuffed it into her mouth.

"'Cause we're quite festive here." Vertie sprinkled water over the garment, rolled it up, and placed the bundle in a wicker basket on a nearby chair. "Everyone who works for your father comes to celebrate the holiday." She straightened and faced Josie. "We extend the dining room table to its full length and use the Spode china and the long-stemmed crystal goblets. I polish the silverware, and we use the best linen tablecloth and napkins."

"Who all comes?" Josie ran her tongue across her sticky fingers, turned on the faucet, lathered a bar of Ivory soap, and washed her hands under the warm water.

"Let's see." Vertie rattled off those who usually came. "Me and Nub. Florence Bedwell. Mr. Mark. Course your father, and the Van Allens—even though they don't work for him. We've always invited them, though. Kinda hard to celebrate Thanksgiving with a feast when only two people are there—so they join us. This year, there'll be you."

Josie grabbed a dishtowel from a bottom drawer in the cabinets, braced her backside against the counter, and dried her hands. "Who's Florence Bedwell?"

Vertie dampened and rolled a second shirt, and stuck it next to the other. "She's your father's secretary. She's called Flossie."

Josie cocked her head and looked off into space. "I haven't met her yet."

"Reckon not. No reason to."

"Why doesn't Aunt Mae come?" Josie hung the towel on the inside of a cabinet door.

Vertie lifted a white damask tablecloth from the heap and gave it a snap. "She always volunteers at one of the city's soup kitchens."

"Wow. I'd like to do that sometime . . . I think." She sat at the table, planted her elbows, and lowered her chin to her upturned palms. She glanced at the housekeeper. "Tell me about Florence Bedwell."

"What do you want to know about Miss Flossie?" Vertie busied herself with the linen table covering.

"Oh, the usual stuff. What's she like?"

"You'll meet her on Thursday."

"I know. Just give me a little preview. Short, tall? Older, younger? Is she married?"

"No."

"Is she nice?"

"Well, yes. Very competent. Always professional. Dresses appropriately. Gracious."

"Is she a special friend of my father?"

Vertie put her fists on her hips and looked at Josie with a long, steady gaze. "I don't know what you're meaning . . . but she's very loyal to your father. Dependable and trusted. She's proficient. Loves details and regulations and rules."

"Anything juicy about her?"

"What kind of question is that?"

Josie shrugged and quirked her mouth. "Just curious."

"Miss Flossie is an ordinary person. Probably the most shocking thing I could say is that she has a habit of sucking on a troublesome tooth."

"Oh, yuck!" Josie made a sour face and shivered.

Vertie continued to sprinkle down the articles to be ironed. "Come on, now, let's not harp on the poor woman. We've work to do."

"I'll make a list." Josie stood and glanced around. "Where might I find a pencil and paper?"

Vertie pointed. "Look in that top drawer there. Maybe something with all the flotsam and jetsam."

Josie pulled it out and rummaged around until she found a leaded stub and an old, rumpled envelope. "Mother was a great planner. She decided the jobs to be done and wrote them down . . . always wanted everything organized. She marked each one off as the task was completed." Josie stopped, allowing several seconds to slip by. "I miss her so much my heart hurts." Her lip quivered and tears formed in her eyes. "It's hard to think of life without her," she said, her voice breaking. "In my mind, I can still see her so clearly. She was always somewhere, and I'm miserable with the thought of her not being anywhere. I'm twenty years old and want my mommy . . . I want to touch her and hold her."

Vertie went over to Josie. "You need more time to grieve. No one is ever prepared to see a loved one go. It's painful, I know." She reached into the front pocket of her blue gingham housedress, produced a flimsy handkerchief, and handed it to Josie. It smelled of Fels Naptha soap.

Josie gratefully took it, wiped her eyes, and blew her nose. "I'm sorry," she croaked. "The one person who'd been most important to me is now gone . . . forever. The pain is almost more than I can bear."

"It's the people left behind who suffer the most. Remember this, Miss Josie, time gradually pushes down the bitterness of the grief and allows the happy memories to come to the surface. When you keep looking back at what might have been, you spoil things not only for yourself, but also for others. Your mother wouldn't want you to do that. She will always be in your heart, but you must move on with your life. Trust me, it gets more bearable as the days go by. Time is a blessed thing. Let go of the old so you can receive the wonder of the new. Life is meant to be lived."

"You think there's something wrong with me?"

"Land sakes, no." Vertie looped an arm around Josie's shoulders and pulled her close. "Mourning's different for everybody. Acceptance doesn't come all at once . . . but in stages . . . a little at a time. I think you're being hard on yourself. Be patient. Give time time."

Josie blew her nose again and waved the hanky in the air. "I'm afraid I'll never feel normal again."

"Then create a new one. Only one person died, Miss Josie, not two. It's better not to dwell on the past. Hold on to the recollections of your mother, treasure them, but don't let them keep you looking backward. Nothing's gained by that." Vertie paused. "The best way to honor her memory is by living a good life."

Later in the afternoon, Josie retreated to the library. She relaxed, sitting crossways in the leather chair, her legs slung over a wide arm, wriggling her stockinged feet near the flickering fire.

"Here you are." Vertie, poking her head into the room, pressed a hand on either side of the doorway. "I'm leaving for the grocery store . . . be gone about an hour. Your father'll bring me home. Do you need anything before I go?" She waited only a moment for Josie's response, then pushed off and disappeared. Soon the back door banged shut signaling her exit.

Josie got the basket from the back porch, located the ironing board in the kitchen pantry, unfolded it in the dining room, and plugged in the iron. While it heated, she flicked on the Philco Baby Grand radio, fiddled with the dials, and tuned to station WBOW. She jerked up the damask, which she could do without difficulty since it was a flat piece. The starched linen crisped beneath the heat and emitted a pleasant fragrance. Finished, she smoothed the fabric after each fold.

She unrolled a white shirt of her father's and shook it out. "Hmm, this can't be that much different from ironing a woman's blouse." Pressing the long sleeves last, she held up the garment, wrested a metal clothes hanger free from the stack on the table, slid it in place, and fastened the collar button.

She turned around to hang it on the door handle . . . and found herself face to face with Elliott Jacobson. His shoulder leaned against the doorjamb, his hands held behind his back, with one foot crossed in front of the other, toe to the floor.

"Oh!" She flinched, her heart fluttering.

He raised his eyebrows whimsically and smiled broadly at her. "Hello."

She stared, mouth open, hand clutched to her chest. "You scared me. Where'd you come from?"

He casually pulled away from the doorframe. "Hello, again."

She switched off the Philco. "I never heard you come in."

"Got here as your father and Vertie were carting in groceries and offered to help."

"Oh . . . well, thank you." She unplugged the iron and set it on the table with a thump.

Elliott folded the ironing board and placed it out of the way. "Just trying to be friendly."

Landon entered the room, wiping his hands on a towel which he promptly dropped onto the table. "I see you've been busy this afternoon, Joselene."

She looked back at the tablecloth and the one shirt and shrugged.

Landon turned to Elliott, pushing a fallen lock of hair back in place. "All right, young man, let's go take care of business." The two men left the room.

Josie watched them go. "Elliott has movie-star looks," she said, aloud to no one but herself.

After dinner and the evening news, father and daughter settled themselves companionably in the library. Josie curled up in the armchair by the fireplace with the latest edition of *Harper's Magazine* on her lap, alternating between flipping through its glossy pages and watching the flames lick the logs in the grate. She looked over at her father to find him staring off into space. "Can I ask you something?"

He started from his reverie. "What?"

"You're daydreaming."

"Hardly," he said, and hunched over the papers spread out on the drop-leaf table. "Did you want something?"

"Would you answer a question?"

He hesitated, reached for a file folder, uncapped his fountain pen, and scribbled something on the flap. "Maybe. If I can."

"Why did Elliott show up this afternoon? Did something happen at the Stamping Mill?"

He sighed. "Yes."

"What's going on there . . . or can you tell me?"

He pursed his lips and shifted in his chair. "Well, in a nutshell, we're headed toward a walkout. Doesn't sound too good, does it? The unrest started in September, when many of the employees joined the labor union."

Josie squinted and tilted her head. "I thought to unionize went against the company's founding policies."

"It does. But the Department of Labor informed us the union's request for a closed shop was not unreasonable."

"Why are they pushing so hard?"

"Mainly money." He rubbed his eyes with his fingertips. "They want a twenty percent increase in salaries. The plant manager told them the market made it impossible to grant such a huge rise in wages."

"Would it be beneficial if you went to the federation's president and laid it all before him?"

"Not a chance."

"What're you going to do, then?"

"We're trying mediation. Yesterday, management met with union officials. I'm not sure where the negotiations will go. Someone's stirring up discontent with the company's open-shop policy, and I don't like it one bit."

Josie waited a minute. "What if . . . well . . . maybe it's not some*one*."

He put down his pen, leaned back in his chair, and looked at her. "I have my suspicions as to who he is. Even if I'm wrong, he sure is pushing for organized labor to be recognized." Landon shook his head. "Heaven help us."

"I wish you would have told me about the disagreement."

"Why? This is none of your concern."

"You may think so. But it still doesn't explain why Elliott comes *here* from time to time."

"He's been able to keep the controversy off the front pages of the newspapers and stave off some mighty bad publicity. I'm grateful for that. However, the press's silence can't continue indefinitely."

Josie stood and tossed the magazine aside. "I'm going to bed. Now that I know about the problems, I'll be praying even more earnestly for you . . . and about the situation."

"You put too much stock in your prayers. God isn't concerned about a company whose union wants to go out on strike."

"God's interested in everything that affects us. *And* He's bigger than any problems we'll ever face. With His help, we can overcome the hard times that discourage us. If we don't go to Him in prayer, to whom shall we go?"

"Bah! The union people have their heels dug in . . . making ridiculous demands. They're not going to budge. You're expecting some sort of miracle with those petitions to the Almighty."

"Of course," she said.

Chapter 9

Josie sat at one end of the kitchen table, reading articles aloud from the most recent *Vogue*. Vertie rubbed flour and lard through her fingers, making pastry for pies. Nearby were peeled and sliced apples sprinkled with sugar, cinnamon, and nutmeg.

Landon strolled into the room. Vertie half turned toward him, resting her floury hands on the edge of the earthenware bowl. "Happy Thanksgiving, Mr. Matthews. Coffee?" She made her way to the sink. "Let me wash this here dough off my fingers."

"I'll get it, Vertie. You go ahead with what you're doing. Morning, Josie."

She lowered the magazine to peer at him over its top. "Morning."

Landon stopped in the act of pouring coffee into his cup. "What's so engrossing?"

"The November issue." She held up the publication for him to see its name. "Debutantes and Winter Season edition. There're features on Amelia Earhart and Princess Marina of Greece. She's marrying the Duke of Kent today at eleven o'clock. Sounds oooh so romantic."

He took a long pull of coffee. "Is that so?" He flung the question over his shoulder as he left the room, leaving the door swinging behind him. In no time, he came back and stopped at the threshold. "Remember, Joselene, be ready by one. We don't want to be late and keep the others waiting for us."

She closed the magazine and laid it aside. "You mean, we're still going?"

"Of course. Why not?"

"Today's so dark and dreary . . . not actually raining, but looks like the sky could open up at any minute and pour down."

"Typical November weather." He raised his index finger in the air. "Neither rain nor gloom of day will keep us from the Turkey Day game."

Josie turned to Vertie. "Just like the postman's motto."

Some seconds slipped by in which there was silence, and then Landon burst into a deep-chested guffaw with nothing held back. He spun on his heel and left the kitchen again.

"That's the first time I've heard my father laugh," Josie said. "He's always been so grim. I've never even seen him smile before."

Vertie stopped working. Her whole countenance changed in an instant. She beamed. "Land sakes, it's been forever and a day since I've heard him . . . It was nice, wasn't it? Heartwarming. Hmm. I think you've been good for him, you know it? . . . Looky here, Miss Josie, the best way to learn anything is by doing, so come stand beside me, and I'll show you how to make pies. We'll each make one." Vertie dabbled water into the bowl and mixed it in until what had resembled cornmeal was moistened sufficiently to gather into a ball. "Now comes the tricky part—rolling it out. You've got to have a nice, floury space."

Josie dusted flour on the table surface. "Like this?"

"Not too much, now, 'cause it'll make your dough tough. It takes a light hand to make a good, flaky crust, and you want yours to be a marvel of flakiness."

Josie took the rolling pin and pushed first one way and then the other, flattening the mound into a circle. She fitted it into a pie dish.

Vertie dumped the prepared apple slices into it, dotted the fruit with butter, and rolled a second round for the top. "Now, watch to see how I crimp the edges." She brought the two layers of dough together, trimmed the overhang, curled the top edge under the bottom edge, and pressed until a fluted border ran around the pan. "You can put the pies in the oven to bake now," she said to Josie, and then she went to the pantry, returning with the blue enamel roaster.

Josie then hauled the cold, limp turkey from the refrigerator. "A lot of work goes into this dinner, doesn't it?" She set a large saucepan of the already-mixed sage stuffing on the table.

"Fussy stuff, mostly. But it pays off. Makes the whole holiday a party, not a burden." Vertie opened a cabinet drawer and rummaged around in it until she plucked an upholstery needle and spool of coarse thread from its contents. She trussed the bird and took it to the stove. "When those pies come out, I'll put this in to bake."

"I better go upstairs and get ready," said Josie. "Don't want to hold anyone up." She'd bathed and washed her hair earlier that morning and now chose the toffee-colored tweed suit with its beige silk blouse and her brown wool coat with the beaver fur collar.

Right on time, Mark appeared at the door with Clarinda and Priscilla. The five climbed into his car for the ride to the stadium—men in the front seat, women in the back.

"I'm sure you'll not understand the football game, Josie, but you'll enjoy yourself, anyway. This is something we do every year. It's our Thanksgiving-y thing." Priscilla chattered away, jumping from one subject to the next with obvious disregard for context.

Arriving at their destination, Mark parked the car and killed the engine. They clambered out and got in line to purchase their tickets. The two men waved to someone Josie couldn't see because of the thicket of spectators.

The five, each with a ticket in hand, jostled their way through the throng to the stainless steel seats. Landon sat next to Clarinda, then Priscilla and Josie, with Mark on the end.

Josie said quietly below Mark's ear, "Don't you want to sit between Priscilla and me? She doesn't look too happy with this arrangement."

He whispered back, "If I didn't sit on the end, I wouldn't be much of a gentleman."

With their heads together, a hand clapped down on Mark's shoulder. He jerked his head. "Elliott! Son of a gun. Want to sit with us? Or do you have to stay in the press box?"

"I prefer being with the fans. Way more exciting. I can get the statistics later." He looked down the row to Landon and doffed his hat in greeting. "Hello, everybody," he called.

Mark cleared his throat and hoisted himself up. "Tell you what. Take this seat on the end, Elliott. I'll move over here between Josie and Priscilla."

"Works for me." Elliott turned his full attention to Josie, his gaze lingering, clasping her hand, holding it longer than necessary. "Do you mind if I sit here by you?" The breeze ruffled his dark, wavy hair.

She shook her head. It was too uncanny how she kept bumping into this man all the time. Somehow, he seemed able to mysteriously appear wherever she happened to be.

He sat. "Do you like football?"

Josie refrained from looking at him. "I don't know. My high school was too small to have a team. I'm afraid I don't know anything about it."

"Hey, no problem. I'll explain what's going on." He pointed to the field. "Those players down there in the purple are the Purple Eagles from Garfield High School." He indicated the opposite direction. "The ones down there in the red are the Red Streaks. They're from Wiley High School. Now, the gist is for each team to get the ball to their goal without being stopped. And the opposing team tries to stop them from scoring. Got it?" He grinned. "Things'll really move as soon as the Boy Scouts raise the American flag."

Everyone stood at attention, right hand over their heart, and sang the national anthem. When they finished, Josie said, "I get goosebumps when I hear it sung with such fervor. I love it."

* * *

It was almost dark when the five stormed the Matthews's front hall-way, chilled and ravenous. Josie yanked off her wraps, draped them on the coat tree, and hurried to the kitchen. She'd been anticipating meeting Florence Bedwell and wondering what the woman whom her father had hired as his secretary was like. The others lingered, chatting as they shrugged out of their coats and hats, and hung them up.

"We're back," Josie announced, bursting into the room. "The aroma is more than our stomachs can bear."

Vertie, crouched at the opened oven door, had pulled the roaster forward and was basting the turkey. "Did you have fun?"

"Uh-huh. But now we're *star-ving*. Everything smells scrumptious. How can I help?"

Vertie stood, shut the oven door, and braced her backside against it. "Don't know as there's much left to do. Miss Flossie's putting the cranberry relish on the table now. Turkey and stuffing are done. Sweet potatoes and green beans can be dished up, if you want to do that. Or you can fill the goblets with water. I'll put in the yeast rolls now that you all are back. By the time everyone gets washed up, the rolls'll be done."

Flossie sailed into the kitchen bearing an empty tray. "Miss Florence, come and let me introduce you to Mr. Matthews's daughter, Joselene," Vertie said.

"How do you do? I'm delighted to meet you," she said in a nasal voice, shoving her wire-rimmed spectacles up on the bridge of her prominent nose before extending her hand. "My pleasure."

Josie greeted a tall and big-boned woman with eyebrows that were drawn on like commas and a strong suggestion of a mustache covering her upper lip. The woman's hair was mousy brown, but cut and curled in the latest style. She wore a simple crepe print dress and sensible low-heeled shoes.

Vertie took the pan of rolls from the oven, brushed the tops with melted butter, and glanced at the clock. "Go tell the others to get a wiggle on, Miss Josie. Unless they hurry, these rolls'll be cold."

The eight gathered in the dining room, where the table was beautifully appointed with the best damask cloth, crystal glasses, and polished silver. Landon invited Josie to offer a blessing on the food before they sat down.

She stared at him until his voice bridged the awkward pause. "Josie?"

"Uh, yes." She nodded. "Heavenly Father, we give You thanks for Your love, for all Your goodness and kindness toward us, for good health, for warm clothes to wear, and for this food we are about to eat. We live in comfort, while many huddle in hunger and cold. Help us appreciate all that we have and be grateful. Free us from the selfishness and the self-centeredness that keep us from understanding and feeling more deeply the anguish of others. May we strive to be all that we can be through You and in You. In Christ's name we pray. Amen."

Nub put a hand on Josie's shoulder. "Mighty fine prayer, Miss Josie."

She smiled at him. "Thank you."

Landon disappeared into the kitchen while the others seated themselves. He came back carrying a huge platter with the steaming turkey, its basted skin a glistening russet color. He pierced the golden-brown crust, making its fragrant juices run down the sides, and sliced through the breast. He carved the meat with ease and stacked two or three slivers on each of the china plates along with a spoonful of the sage stuffing.

Conversations overlapped in an ebb and flow while the side dishes were passed, but once they began eating, little was said.

Josie gazed at the faces of those sitting around the table—people she hadn't known at this time last year, or even a few months ago, for that matter. Her life now was everything she wanted it to be—well, almost. She hoped and prayed her father would welcome her into his heart. But nothing had happened yet . . . at least the way she wanted it to happen. Oh, he treated her well. No doubt about it. He was polite, all right. But she saw herself more like a guest in his home than his daughter. All in all, though, she had much for which to be thankful. *I have entered His gates with thanksgiving in my heart. I have given thanks to Him and praised His name. For the Lord has been good to me.*

Vertie spoke up. "I want to hear about the game. What did you think about all the hoopla, Miss Josie?"

She snapped out of her reverie. "The opening ceremonies were impressive."

Landon lifted his water glass. "Did you understand the game?" He took a drink.

"No, not really, even though Elliott spent the entire time explaining it to me. It looked to me like the players simply ran on and off the field and at each other with the purpose of knocking them down. Football is confusing."

Vertie hesitated in slathering butter on a hot roll. "Elliott? Elliott Jacobson?"

Flossie turned toward Landon. "Isn't that the young newspaper reporter who comes to the office from time to time?"

He picked up his napkin and wiped his mouth. "He's the one."

"Mr. Jacobson was at the Turkey Day game . . . and sat with you?"

"Elliott Jacobson was there and sat beside Josie." Priscilla chided Vertie. "What's wrong with that?"

"Land sakes, nothing at all. Did you invite him to join us?"

"I . . . did. He was . . . that is . . . he was . . . going home."

"Home?" Vertie's fork clattered to her plate. "He was driving all the way to Bloomington after the game?"

Everyone around the table sat motionless—like statues. Forks stopped in the air, mouths stopped chewing. No one spoke. Everyone but Nub stared at Vertie.

"I guess so. That's . . . where . . . his home . . . is," Josie stammered.

Mark asked, "How'd you know Elliott's home is in Bloomington, Vertie?"

Her glance shifted from one face to the other all around the table. "I listen."

Chapter 10

Perched on her bed, hands clasped at her chest, Josie bubbled, "For me? It's too exciting."

"Mother and I always put on quite a good party during the holidays," Priscilla announced. "Everyone looks forward to them. This year, *you'll* be the guest of honor—no Cotillion, of course. That'd be too grandiose a name for our parties, but there'll be a dinner with a small number of my close friends and afterward a larger reception for your father's . . . uh . . . colleagues and associates. You'll be introduced to a lot of people. Christmas is the perfect time for a festivity like this. Mother's already sent out cards with the invitations worded something like . . . 'to welcome Joselene Grace, the daughter of Landon Joseph Matthews.' It'll be such fun. You'll have a whale of a time."

"Sounds like quite a crowd."

"About fifty, if they all come. And they almost always do."

Josie locked her hands on top of her head. "This is scary. You think I'm ready to come face to face with so many people . . . of polite society, at that? I don't want to appear gauche or commit some terrible blunder and embarrass you . . . or my father . . . or even myself."

Priscilla flapped a hand. "Don't be silly. With all my instructions, you're presentable now. So-o-o, the next step is to be seen." She used her fingers to make air quotes around "be seen."

Josie furrowed her brows. "What's 'be seen?'" She mimicked the gesture.

"It means getting invited to the best social gatherings. You've proved to be no rube. You'll do fine. Remember everything we've rehearsed. Besides, I'll be there. Just smile and be attentive to the people."

Josie's mind became a jumble of thoughts, the chief of which was what she should wear. She asked Priscilla about it.

"Something white."

"Maybe Aunt Mae can help me find a suitable dress. I'll call her tonight."

Priscilla pointed to Josie. "One other thing: be the last to arrive."

"Shouldn't I be the first in order to greet the guests?"

"No. I want you to make a grand entrance—on the arm of your father. He's presenting you."

The two chatted and giggled and missed hearing footfalls on the stairs. When Vertie tapped on the frame of the open door and came in, they stopped their conversation abruptly.

"Well, here you two are." She stood before them, a wicker basket jammed against her hip. "What're you up to, tittering away?"

"Priscilla's planned a celebration in my honor. Something like a Cotillion where I'll be introduced to lots of people. She'll have the whole shindig written up in the society column of the newspapers and—*everything*." She made a wide sweep of her arms. "Isn't that marvelous?"

"Could be," Vertie said, without much enthusiasm in her voice. "What's the date?"

"Saturday, the fifteenth."

She scowled at Priscilla. "Of December? Land sakes, you can't plan something like that to be held a few weeks away."

"I could put together any kind of event in a day if I had to," Priscilla boasted.

Vertie arched her head back, staring out of the bottom of her eyeglasses at Priscilla. "I don't think so. Not anything like a Cotillion." She shook her head as she crossed the bedroom and disappeared into the bathroom.

Priscilla turned to Josie. "Alex and Winnie always come. They've already got their invitations. What about Elliott Jacobson? Shall I send one to him?"

Josie gave a one-shoulder shrug. "If you want to."

"What do you mean if *I* want to? This party's for you, not me. Aren't you interested in him? I can tell he's fallen for you, no end." She patted Josie's knee.

Josie's eyebrows rose. "I'm not sure Elliott even knows I exist."

Priscilla rolled her eyes. "Come on, now. All you have to do is see how his face lights up when you walk into a room. It gives him away every time. Don't tell me you haven't noticed how he ogles you all google-eyed? He's madly in love with you."

"Pris-cil-la, stop it."

"Why? Don't you like him?"

"Yes, I do. How can I not? I'm bumping into him all the time and he turns out to be the most appealing guy I know. It's extraordinary how he puts me at ease, almost as though we've been friends all our lives. Listen, don't you dare tell a soul what I've said, Priscilla."

With theatrical flair, Priscilla used her index finger to sign an X on her chest. "Cross my heart," she promised. "He's quite a catch. A prize any woman would be happy to win. Your father appears to like him, too." She nudged Josie with her elbow. "He's a nice man."

Josie reflected on Priscilla's comment and admitted that *nice* was an inadequate word with which to describe Elliott Randolph Jacobson. "He's better than that. He's honest, a hard worker, and doesn't put on airs. He's confident to a fault . . . kind of pushy some times. Probably the way a newspaper reporter would be. I do appreciate the way he laughs and jokes around—"

"It doesn't hurt he's so good-looking," Priscilla added.

Vertie came out of the bathroom holding the now loaded-down basket with dirty laundry. She plunked it on the floor, stood in front of Josie and Priscilla, and planted her fists on her hips. She sniffled with an upward jerk of her nose. "Careful what you say about Mr. Jacobson. You don't realize some things about that fine young man."

The two exchanged glances. Vertie picked up the basket, hefted it higher on her hip, and huffed her way out of the room, mumbling under her breath.

* * *

Josie hesitated in the library's doorway. Her father sat bent over at the drop-leaf table, its top cluttered with sheets of papers and several piles of files.

He wrote something for a few seconds, and then glanced over at her. "Josie? Something wrong?"

She remained where she was. "I have a bit of a problem, but I hate to bother you with it."

He screwed the cap on his fountain pen and closed a file, shoving it aside. Two pieces of paper slipped easily off the table and fluttered to the floor. He retrieved them. "What is it?"

Josie came toward him. "I hate to interrupt, but there're only eight shopping days left till Christmas."

Landon twisted about on his chair to rest an arm upon its back and faced her. "Need some money?"

"No." She shook her head and frowned.

"What is it, then?"

"Could you drive me up town?"

He stroked his jaw. "I think I can manage that. Remember Priscilla's affair is this evening. You don't want to tire yourself out."

"I won't. But today is Jubilee Day at J.C. Penney's. Plenty of bargains."

He ran a hand across the back of his neck. "Give me another twenty minutes or so."

"You can let me out anywhere." Josie gestured. "Here's fine."

Landon swerved the car to the curb outside J.C. Penney's and stopped. "Call me when you're ready to come home. Got enough cash? Better take this." He reached into his pocket and handed over several large bills.

She looked at the amount of money and then at him. "That's not necessary."

"I know. But better to be prepared than to be sorry for not having enough."

"Thank you," she said, climbed out, and slammed the door shut. She stood on the sidewalk and waggled her fingers at him as he pulled away. She paused and then turned to examine the store's window display.

Josie entered Penney's, wandered in and out of the different departments, and sauntered up and down one aisle after another, examining the perfectly arranged jewelry, pocketbooks, and rows of thick socks. She found her way to the men's displays, where she spent a half hour looking at gloves for her father, and finally chose a pair of fleece-lined deerskin. She was waiting to pay for them when, from behind her, a voice said her name.

"Josie?"

She spun around. "Elliott!" Her heart danced.

"What a fantastic coincidence to see you here. What're you doing?"

"I'm browsing and buying." She positioned her pocketbook on her arm and lingered for her package and the receipt. "You?"

"The same."

Josie tilted her head and quirked an eyebrow. "I see no evidence of that."

"I'm just beginning. How far along are you?"

"One purchase so far."

"How about if you and I get some coffee? We can plan a course of action over our cups."

They rambled past the lengthy counter and the racks of merchandise. Elliott pushed the heavy plate glass door open for her. He put his black fedora on his head, giving the brim a tug, and yanked his fur-lined gloves from his coat pockets and pulled them on.

Out of doors, facing the cold, brisk air, their breaths flew back into their faces as they headed to the corner of Seventh and Wabash. Inside, Hook's Drugstore smelled of peppermint and cigars.

Elliott led Josie to the long lunch counter, where they sat on the red swivel stools. "Want a sandwich, too? Any pie?"

"Coffee's enough, thank you."

He ordered, and soon the waitress slid two saucers in front of them and set a cup in each. She poured the fragrant coffee.

"Who's left to buy for?"

"Let's see." She looked off into space and rattled off the names. "Vertie and Nub, Aunt Mae, Aunt Phoebe, Aunt Ruth, the Van Allens, Mark, Flossie, Alex and Winnie, and . . . you."

"Sounds like you're buying a present for everyone."

She shook sugar from a dispenser into the dark beverage and watched the spoon while she stirred it. "It's so satisfying to have people to shop for and not have to worry about the expense."

"Was there anyone in Bradford who was special to you?"

"Other than Mother and my aunts . . . no." She blew across the surface of the steaming liquid before she ventured a sip.

"No one . . . *in particular?*"

"Are you asking if I had a boyfriend?"

"Yes."

She shook her head. "Taking care of Mother didn't leave time for . . . for a friend."

"Really? Hmm, hard to believe."

She shrugged. "It's true."

He lifted his cup, but stopped midair. "What kinds of gifts are you looking for?"

She gave him a quick look and smiled. "Oh, no. I'm not going to say. You'll tell."

He lowered the cup to its saucer. "I won't, either." He put his left palm flat on the countertop and raised his right hand. "I solemnly swear I will not tell anyone what you're giving them for Christmas."

Josie rolled her eyes and shook her head. "Stop it. You act like a witness taking the oath in a court of law. You're not on trial here."

"Sure sounded like it to me. You accused me of something, and I want to verify I can keep a secret."

"All right, I'll tell since you've sworn an oath. You saw what I got for my father. I hope he'll wear them."

"Why wouldn't he?"

"He doesn't get his clothes in Terre Haute. He goes all the way to Indianapolis. I'd like to find a box of embroidered handkerchiefs for Vertie. Hers are pretty tacky looking. Bath salts for Aunt Mae. I haven't decided yet for the others. I'm sure something will call out to me."

Elliott finished his coffee. "You sound persnickety."

"I am. What can I get you?"

"Do you want me to make a list?"

"Oh, you—"

"Hmm. How long do you think it will take to finish?"

"Why?"

"Because we can shop together, and then I could drop you off at your house. No reason for you to ride the streetcar or have your father come pick you up if I'm already here."

"I'll see how much I can get done in a couple of hours."

"Good." He took her coat and held it up while she turned and plunged her arms into the sleeves. Josie fastened the collar snugly under her chin.

Elliott put on his black chesterfield and carried his fedora. "All set?"

She nodded. They went out of the drugstore and joined the crowd of shoppers.

Their breath issued forth like white smoke into the crisp winter air. "What d'yuh think, Josie? Does Terre Haute know how to decorate the town for the holidays, or what?"

"Have you ever seen so many colored lights? I can't even guess how many strands it must've taken to string them from light post to light post."

Elliott caught her hand in his and squeezed it.

* * *

Josie's long dress lay on the bed. It was white velveteen, simple in style, with a scooped neckline. After she bathed and dusted herself with scented powder, she lifted the soft fabric over her head and thrust her arms into the sleeves, and then did up the zipper at the waist.

She fastened a silver filigree chain with an intricate cross about her neck and screwed dangly cross earrings onto her earlobes. She slipped her feet into silver pumps and stepped to the mirror to study her appearance. She turned this way and that, fingering the necklace. She looked beautiful and gave a little wriggle. "You did very well, Aunt Mae."

She descended the stairs and came upon her father. "What do you think?"

Landon smiled at her. "You look like a fairy princess. This will be a notable evening for you, Joselene." He draped her brown coat with beaver collar over her shoulders, and they left the house. "You must be cold. You're shaking all over, and your hands are like ice."

Josie's mouth tightened. "I'm anxious."

"You don't need to be. Only friends will be there. They won't eat you."

The two were the last to get to the Van Allens's party—to make their grand entrance, as Priscilla had worded it. Tonight's gala was

Josie's "coming out" of sorts. She would be presented to her father's professional and social circles, to Priscilla's contingent of friends, and to a few of Terre Haute's "who's who" in general.

Talk and laughter flowed out of the living room's doorway. Josie checked her breath. She peeked in and stood amazed at the glimmering and shimmering dresses of scarlet and jade and sapphire. The mixture of fabrics made splashes of vivid colors and, as the women moved about, changed the combinations so that the scene had the effect of a kaleidoscope. She shivered, pulled away from the opening, and looked toward her father. "Aren't you nervous?"

"Me?" Landon narrowed his eyebrows and squinted. "No. Why should I be?"

She shrugged. "Well, I am . . . and excited . . . and nervous . . . and scared all at the same time. The room's so full."

"Joselene, relax. Try to enjoy the evening."

"But it's scary for me." She placed her arm in her father's, and together they proceeded into Clarinda's living room. Josie's stomach clenched into knots. *Lord, please give me courage and grace for this evening. I don't want to sneeze or fall on my face.*

Priscilla waved her hand. "Josie," she called. But when she started forward, someone asked her something, and she turned away to answer.

Alex stood with his back to the fireplace, talking with Elliott and another man Josie had not yet met. When he saw Josie, Alex strode away from them and stopped in front of her. "Hi."

She tipped her head, peered up into his face, and gave him a broad smile. "Hi."

"You look absolutely fabulous," he crooned. "What a perfect gown for you. In white and silver, you resemble the goddess Diana."

Priscilla came up to them right then and looped her hand through the crook of Josie's arm. "Come, I want you to meet everybody here. Please excuse us, Alex." The two young women worked their way around the room, greeting every one of Priscilla's friends—all except Elliott.

Josie spotted him, handsome in a gray pin-striped suit, speaking with Mark. She wanted to be beside him and hoped he would be her dinner companion. Surely Priscilla would seat them together.

However, it was Alex who tucked Josie's hand in the crook of his arm and escorted her to the table. Why would Priscilla pair her off with him? Baffled, she scanned the room to find who Elliott was with. It was Priscilla, who seemed in her best mood, babbling and giggling her worst. Josie stiffened.

Alex leaned forward and whispered into Josie's ear as he seated her. "Tonight, you're a beautiful enchantress."

Josie focused on spreading the linen napkin. "This evening seems magical. I feel like Cinderella. At midnight, a clock will strike, a fairy's wand will wave, and I'll be running down the steps in rags. I'll be transformed back into my old self and find this is only a dream."

He chuckled. "Having a good time?"

"Uh-huh. I'm breathless over all this and have to pinch myself to be sure it is really happening." She ate with gusto, taking small bites of the apricot-glazed chicken breast.

"What do you think of Terre Haute? Happy you're here instead of . . . where was it? . . . Your previous hometown?"

"Bradford. Oh, it's a million miles away right now. I'm happier than I ever thought imaginable. I doubt anything can spoil my enjoyment of this evening," she said, forking a bite of meat into her mouth while glancing around. Her gaze fixed on the two standing at the buffet table—Elliott and Priscilla—their backs toward her, their heads close together, chattering away like old friends.

Priscilla paused, an earring swinging against Elliott's cheek, and fanned the air with her hand. They drew away from each other and laughed.

Resentment prickled through Josie. Some nerve Priscilla had to flirt with Elliott. That was Priscilla, though. Beautiful and refined. The queen bee. What might be proper for others wouldn't faze Priscilla—the one who'd flirt with a snowman if that was the only man around. Maybe Priscilla was just trying to make her jealous—or Mark. Where was *he*, anyway? Josie surveyed the room and spied him sitting with Winnie—all painted up.

She looked back at the couple, gritting her teeth each time Priscilla's hand rested on Elliott's arm. She swallowed hard against the cottony feel in her throat. Her appetite now gone, she poked at the food on her plate.

What was going on with her? Was she in love with Elliott? Was *that* the reason for the fierce pangs of jealousy and the flip-flops in her stomach? Nobody had ever explained what it was like to fall in love with someone. But wasn't love supposed to be patient and kind? Without envy and not easily angered? She tried to understand the hateful feelings boiling up inside her and swirling around her.

Alex's voice broke into her muse. "Are you all right?"

Chapter 11

Josie stood in the middle of the living room, hands on her hips, surveying the space. She crossed from one side to the other, walked to the bay window, and back to the room's center.

Vertie, carrying a stack of clean, folded towels, stopped in the opened doorway. "What're you up to?"

"I'm trying to figure out the best place to put a Christmas tree."

The housekeeper shook her head. "Won't need to worry none. We haven't had one for . . . land sakes, I can't remember. Mr. Matthews doesn't like the clutter that comes with them."

"*What*? I can't picture the holiday without one. Where did you heap your presents?"

"Aren't any. It's quiet around here. I don't even cook dinner. Me and Nub have the entire day off."

Josie touched her fingertips to her cheek and looked off into space. "Surely Father will let us get one . . . or at least decorate the house. He has some ornaments, doesn't he?"

"Got a box of them in the attic . . . best I can recollect . . . no idea the shape they're in. Been stored away for years."

Josie clasped her hands at her chest. "Would Nub bring the box down for us?"

Vertie raised her eyebrows. "What d'ya mean . . . *us*?"

She said nothing to Vertie's question but rattled on with her own train of thought. "Just think, my first Christmas with Father. I'm so excited. I can't wait to deck the halls." She stretched out her arms and twirled around in the bay window. "This is the ideal place for a huge tree . . . one that'll fill this whole space. We can move the piano from here to . . . how about over there?" She pointed to a spot across the room. "We can mix some pine cones with orange peel and cinnamon sticks and put them here." She ran a hand along the mantel's edge. "What do you think?"

"I think you're dreaming big. I fear your father's not ready for what you've got in mind."

"No harm in trying, though, is there? Have faith, Vertie."

"For some reason, Miss Josie, I think you'll win the argument," she said, looking back over her shoulder as she clumped upstairs.

Josie followed her. "I intend to."

Later in the afternoon, Nub crawled into the attic, located, and carried down the box labeled "Christmas Decorations" to the living room. He lowered it to the floor, and Josie knelt to open it. She found two ropes of gold garland, and underneath them, glass balls carefully packed away in previous years. From the bottom of the box, she pulled out a tangled strand of multi-colored lights. Last of all, in its own box, she discovered a golden-clad angel with gossamer wings.

By the time Landon came home, the room was in disarray with the decorations scattered about. Josie was on her hands and knees, untangling the string that now extended across the room. "Just what do you think you're doing?"

She pulled her hair back from her face and let her gaze shift over him. "I'm checking out the lights you have . . . so we can decorate our tree."

"Bah!" he snorted. "We're not having one."

"Christmas will be ruined if we don't put one up," she wailed.

"I don't see how." He nudged the tangled cord out of his way with the toe of his shoe.

"We need a place to put our gifts," she said.

"Ahh . . . well, somehow we've managed to celebrate for years without a tree," he said. "I don't have the time to fool with one, and you have no way of getting one here."

Josie jerked her head up. "Nub and Vertie could help me."

He lifted both hands, pushing against the air. "I'm not paying them to put up any tree. And besides, who would clean up all those nasty needles after the holiday? I'm not paying them to do that, either."

Josie flinched at the sternness of his tone. How on earth would she be able to convince him this was important to her? *Lord, guide my words.* She took a deep breath, let it all out, and asked in a calm voice, "If I bought a tree, and got it here and put it up, decorated it myself, and promised to clean up all the mess, would you let me have one?" She was breathless as she finished speaking.

"HMPH. And who do you think you are? The little red hen?"

She gaped at her father. His question sounded so nonsensical that she couldn't keep from bursting into laughter. Her outburst was followed by a long silence.

Without a word, Landon stepped over the strand and left the room, and in a moment, Josie heard the door to the library close.

She still didn't know if she would have a Christmas tree.

The next afternoon, Landon took Josie to Haas Home Nursery, where they found a small forest of cut pines. The two wandered through the rows, stopped over and over again, examining each prospect from every angle to ask, "How about this one?"

Josie shivered against the cold. She buried her chin in her coat collar, cupped her gloved hands over her mouth, and blew to warm her stiff fingers. She was not about to complain, though. She wanted a tree.

Landon paused in his search and looked at her. "You frozen? Your teeth are chattering."

"I think my feet are becoming blocks of ice. I have to stomp around to keep them halfway thawed."

"We've taken long enough. Let's decide. You found one yet?"

She shook her head. They continued admiring or criticizing this one after that one until at last she spotted an eight-foot Scotch pine. "This is it."

Landon pulled the tree off the mound. "It certainly is a fat monster."

Josie backed up to get a better perspective. "Lots of character, too."

"No broken branches. Fresh, piney fragrance. That settles it, then. We'll take this one," he told the salesman and paid him.

"Merry Christmas," the man called as the two pulled away from Haas's, the tree tied onto the roof of the Chrysler.

They got it home, where Nub made a wooden stand for it. "Know it don't look like much, but that there contraption'll work, I guarantee it."

Nub and Landon set the tree upright, set the whole shebang inside a galvanized tub, and poured in water. Vertie pulled an old, Christmassy tablecloth out of the buffet drawer and spread it around the tub.

"Come on, let's trim it," Josie said, excitedly. "We can turn on the radio and listen while we work."

Nub puffed out his cheeks. "Yes sir-ree, bob. What better way to spend an evening than listening to the creepy and demented laugh of *The Shadow* asking us who knows what evil lurks in the hearts of men? *The Shadow* knows."

Josie made a small snorting noise. "I meant the news and *Amos 'n' Andy* . . . or music."

After the evening meal, Nub brought the stepladder from the garage and opened it in the living room.

Vertie gave mild suggestions about the decorating, but Josie had strong, definite preferences. Up and down the ladder, she and Nub went throughout the evening. The glass balls and the lights made the branches droop under their weight and caused them to span the width of the bay window. After a quantity of tinsel was added, Nub climbed the ladder for the last time at about ten o'clock and placed the gossamer-winged angel on the treetop.

Josie plugged in the lights, their illumination casting colors on the floor. She stood back to admire the effect of the shimmering tree. "It's simply beautiful," she whooped. "The most magnificent Christmas tree I've ever seen! The lights look like shining jewels on the branches, don't they? This will be the ideal place to heap our gifts."

The next morning, the wind howled and whistled with enormous snowflakes slipping and lisping against Josie's bedroom window glass. The upper boughs of the great oak in the backyard creaked and groaned. It was still dark when she awoke. She kicked off the covers, jumped out of bed, dashed across the room to put her face against the glass, and peered out at the sparkling white world. She pumped her arms in jubilation. "Hooray! A white Christmas. Thank You, Lord."

After breakfast, she sat huddled on the window seat in the library. Even with a fire in the grate, the room was chilly, but cheerful. She pulled her legs up against her chest and locked her arms about them.

Vertie shuffled around the room, dusting the ceiling with a towel pinned around the straw end of the broom. "We're in for a big one today, that's for sure. The radio says our weather's going to get worse as the day goes on. If people don't have to go out in this, they won't."

The thick, drifting snow swirled and twisted down in pale blue and cream and pink and lavender flakes that blended themselves into a mantle of white.

"Everything looks so smooth and soft, like a glistening blanket covering the world," Josie said. The window glass fogged over from her breath. She rubbed a small circle with her sleeve to clean it and peered through as a city snowplow whizzed past going south, clearing the street and disappearing. However, the wind whipped up the drifts and obliterated the plow's work.

"I'm thankful we got our tree yesterday evening. It was perfect timing, wasn't it? Will Aunt Mae come for Christmas?"

Vertie straightened the side chairs at the drop-leaf table. "Don't see why not."

"Well" . . . Josie pecked on the frosted window glass. "Because of this."

* * *

"I'm glad you're finally here, Aunt Mae," Josie called from the opened front door. She liked her aunt's infectious laugh and generous heart.

Mae came up the sidewalk toting a large pine wreath adorned with a bright red bow. Waving her niece forward, her free hand gyrated like a windmill blade. "Help me with this."

"And do what?"

"Hang it right here." She stopped at the door and waited while Josie ran inside to grab her coat.

The two worked together to fasten the circular form to the door so that its ribbon dangled straight. Josie stood back. "Our house resembles one of those pictured on an old-fashioned Currier and Ives card."

"Let's get the rest of the things," Mae said. They hurried to the car, loaded their arms with tissue-wrapped boxes, and mounted the steps together.

"Where shall we put them?" she asked as they entered the house.

Josie's voice rose. "Oh. I'll show you. We have a special place this year."

"Don't tell me you have a tree!" Her eyes grew wide. "Will wonders never cease?"

The two reached the living room. Mae gaped. "Stunning! How did you ever talk old Scrooge into having one?"

Josie dropped to her knees. "He resisted at first, but he came around." She took charge of arranging the decorated packages. "Actually, I think it was the little red hen."

"You'll need to explain that to me." Mae yanked off her coat.

Josie leaned back on her heels. "Ho, it's a funny story. Aren't these beautiful here?"

Mae took her niece's hand and pulled her to her feet. "Is the kettle on? I'm ready for some scalding coffee."

Settled at the kitchen table, her fingers encircling a cup, Mae said, "Now, tell me all about the little red hen and how you got the tree."

Vertie came into the room just then. "Hello, Miss Mae. Pleasant trip?" Not waiting for an answer, she said, "Uh, Miss Josie, there's a young man here to see you. He has something with him, too, all decorated up, and good-sized." She gestured descriptively.

Josie looked at her aunt, then back at Vertie. "Who is it?"

Vertie shook the teakettle and took it to the sink. "Mr. Jacobson." She lifted the lid and turned on the faucet.

"Elliott?" Josie's heart raced.

Over the rush of water, Vertie said, "He asked for you. I happened to notice he had a fancy wrapped parcel."

Mae motioned with her hand. "Go on. Find out what he's got."

Josie hustled out of the kitchen and felt the peculiar sensation that her feet were never on the floor.

* * *

Elliott smiled at Josie as she walked to him. "Hi. I wanted to stop by and give you this." He held out his present to her.

Her gaze remained on him. "Oh, Elliott. I . . . um . . . have someth—" She turned her back on him and made her way into the living room.

He let her lead the way. "Wow!" He tipped his head, following the tree to its top.

She crouched, put the package he gave her with the many others, retrieved the one she had for him, and stood. "Isn't it marvelous?"

"I'll say." Rubbing his palms together, he reached for the present she handed him. "Want me open this now?"

"No! Keep it for Christmas morning."

"Naw, I won't be in town then."

She wagged her head. "All right . . . go ahead." She sat on the sofa.

He tore away the green paper and removed the lid from a long box to find a luxurious, hydrangea-blue wool muffler. He took it out and wound it around his neck.

"I knitted the scarf myself . . . to keep you nice and cozy . . . when you're out in the cold on assignments."

"Your gift of love means more to me than I can express." He stooped to the pile of parcels, picked up his to her, and deposited it on her lap. "This is yours. Open it." Their hands met, and for a long second, neither moved. Elliott then stood and planted himself before her, his hands sunk in his jacket pockets.

Her fingers trembled as she broke the thin red ribbon and ripped away the layer of white embossed paper to reveal a simple walnut-stained box. It was varnished to a high gloss and had a small brass latch and a tiny porcelain knob on its door. She opened the door, and on its inside was an oval mirror, attached vertically, and surrounding it were minute gold-colored hooks for necklaces and bracelets or keys. In the body of the box were five little drawers, each with a miniature white knob. She touched everything before she shut the chest and looked up at him, catching a special gleam in his eyes.

"Elliott, it's the most beautiful gift for keeping my treasures. Thank you."

Wordlessly, he took the box from her and put it aside. He helped her to her feet and drew her close to him, cradling her face between his hands, his thumbs gently caressing her cheeks. He dipped his head and kissed her lightly on her cheek.

"What's that for?" She squinted, frowning at him.

"I have no idea. Oh, yeah. Merry Christmas, Joselene Grace Matthews."

She smiled. "I wish you the same, Elliott Randolph Jacobson."

He took her hand, and they walked slowly to the hallway. They lingered there, looking at each other, reluctant to part. When the time got long, Elliott shifted his feet. "I better go." He opened the front door, winked at her, and was gone.

She closed the door, one hand hesitating on the doorknob while the other brushed the cheek Elliott had just kissed. She hugged herself with the ecstasy of it and, for a few moments, let her imagination play pleasantly with the memory.

Josie dashed to the living room, clutched the chest to her heart, and waltzed into the kitchen, her hands shaking. "Look what Elliott gave me." She sang the words more than she said them.

Mae Anise and Vertie stood behind her as she showed them the box with pride.

"What a splendid place for your trinkets," Mae said, turning to face her niece. "Well, it's obvious to me . . . that young man adores you." She chafed Josie's upper arms and smiled at her.

Chapter 12

"Vertie has fixed a perfect meal for Christmas Eve dinner," Josie said, leading the way to the dining room. "It's herbed beef rib roast, mashed potatoes, and Brussels sprouts with chestnuts."

"Sounds delicious," Mae Anise said, as she seated herself. "Your table looks lovely, dear. Very Christmassy."

"Thank you." The table, covered with a red linen tablecloth and decorated with sprays of pine boughs and sprigs of holly as its centerpiece, was elegantly appointed with gleaming silver, crystal, and the Spode china.

"Would you pray a blessing, Josie?" Landon asked.

Josie took in a deep breath and let it out. "Of course. Thank You, God, for this holy season. We celebrate Jesus's birth believing He was born so we might find salvation from our sins. We give thanks for Your great gift, for this day and time, and for this food. Bless it, nourish our bodies with it. May we serve You obediently. Amen."

Mae Anise unfolded the napkin on her lap and looked at her niece. "What are the plans for this evening?"

Josie settled back in her seat and looked over at her father. "Umm

. . . after we eat, I think we ought to open our gifts."

"And after that, how about we partake of the family's traditional Christmas dessert?"

"Vertie never made anything for us."

"I know. I did. I brought it with me. It's not a secret recipe, but almost."

"What is it?"

"Woodford pudding," Mae said.

The muscles about Landon's mouth twitched. He turned to Mark. "Little bit bossy, aren't they? Got the whole evening all planned for us."

When the four rose from the table after the leisurely dinner, they gathered in the living room around the tree and the mass of packages piled there. Mark squatted before the fireplace and stirred the embers with the poker. He stacked on two logs, swiped his hands on the seat of his trousers, and stood back until the wood ignited and crackled. "A fire always makes a room more cheerful," he said, though no one responded. When he joined the others, Mae passed out the presents.

Josie was handed a small, slender box wrapped in glossy silver paper and tied with a matching ribbon. It was from her father. She removed the wrapping, lifted the lid, and stared at an emerald hung on a fragile platinum chain. For a moment, she was speechless. "Oh . . . it's . . . beautiful," she finally said in a low, breathless tone. Her eyes welled up with tears. "How . . . how can I ever thank you?"

"I'm pleased you like it. The gem belonged to your grandmother."

Her hands trembled as she took the necklace out of the box. "This is absolutely gorgeous." She gave him a long look. "Shouldn't it belong to Aunt Mae? I mean, since it's a family heirloom."

"No, my dear." Mae leaned her head against Josie's. "I want you to have it with my blessings as well as your father's."

"I can't believe this is mine. I'll treasure it always."

Josie got a basket with Harriet Hubbard Ayer perfume and bath powder from her aunt. From Mark, she received two books written by Laura Ingalls Wilder: *Little House in the Big Woods* and *Farmer Boy*.

"The author lives on an orchard in a small town of south-central Missouri," he said. "I thought you might appreciate her stories of when she and her husband grew up. They're for young readers, but any age will enjoy them."

Alex sent Josie a leather-bound Bible with her name stamped in gold on the cover—quite an unexpected gift from him. Had she misjudged him? All too soon, the packages were opened, and she sat in a sea of rumpled paper.

Mae left and came back with a tray arranged with four small bowls. "Dessert time."

Josie took a bite. "This is as delicious as you said it'd be." She licked her sticky spoon. "What did you call this?"

"Woodford pudding with butterscotch sauce."

"I do believe I'll have seconds, if that's okay."

"Help yourself," Mae chortled. "We've got plenty."

Later that evening, at the Congregational Church, a man greeted the three Matthews's in the vestibule and handed each a small white candle. By the time they made their entrance into the sanctuary, only a few open spaces remained in the pews.

Josie worked her way down the center aisle in front of her father and aunt. A hand touched her arm.

"Alex!" She caught her breath. "What a surprise. I never expected to see you here."

"Sit with me." He slid over to make room for them. "What? Did you think a heathen like me wouldn't come to a candlelight service? Is that it?"

She made no reply and managed only a feeble smile. "Thank you for the Bible. I've never had my very own before—and one engraved with my name. It was a lovely gift."

Just then, a great surge came from the pipe organ. The choir stood and sang *"Cantique de Noel."* The familiar strains thundered throughout the sanctuary, the melody rising and falling like the tide.

Fall on your knees! O hear the angels' voices!
O night divine, O night when Christ was born;
O night divine, O night, O night divine.

Josie scanned the chancel area where the minister, braced to stand, waited to address the congregation. She glanced sideways at Alex—dressed smartly in a tweed suit. She thought he was likable enough—though he was more than a bit pompous. She knew he could never be anything but a friend. He was handsome and athletic, the kind of man many women fantasized about, except for her—and, at the moment, she couldn't put exact words to the reason. To her, Alex tried too hard—to be funny, to be liked, to be noticed. It boiled down to the fact that he failed to make her hair and fingertips tingle with excitement.

She chastised herself for allowing her mind to wander and concentrated on the reading of the scripture—the story of the messenger angel's visit to the Virgin Mary. Do not be afraid, the angel said to her, for she would be the mother of the Savior, Jesus Christ. She never protested about the event, only questioned how it could happen, since she and Joseph hadn't married yet.

The clergyman began his homily. When his speaking moved on in dull cadences, Josie tuned him out. She gazed at the beautiful altar with its masses of red poinsettias and branches of pine emitting their sharp scent.

Three rows in front of her sat Clarinda and Mark with Priscilla sandwiched between. Where was Elliott? She shifted in her seat and looked around. Maybe he was behind her, but she couldn't very well turn around and look without being too obvious about it. Then she remembered he went to his mother's for the holiday.

The mention of his name made her fingertips tingle and her heartbeat accelerate. She admitted to herself that every time she was with him, she encountered a new facet of his personality, and what she found out she admired, more and more. He was an easy man to talk to, and she enjoyed his picturesque way of describing things and people—probably the reporter in him coming out—and his deadpan humor was never unkind.

She imagined herself and Elliott as a couple. What was *that* all about? Could she be in love with him? Josie had asked herself the same question over and over for several weeks now—ever since Priscilla's party.

Something she heard caused her to come out of her reverie—"life would be full of changes. We all will have our hopes, our dreams, our plans altered at some point. Mary's were. Though they are difficult to accept, we can face them with courage . . . just as Mary did, trusting God to work in our lives, for our benefit."

Was God working on her behalf? At the moment, Josie couldn't see much of anything happening.

The organ sounded again. People stood as they were able, held their candles up, and lit them from one to another while singing "Silent Night."

Josie's candle flame dipped and danced from her breath as she sang. "Silent night, holy night, wondrous star, lend thy light; with the angels let us sing, Alleluia to our King; Christ the Savior is born, Christ the Savior is born!"

She glimpsed her father—strong, honest, generous, but not demonstrative, his facial features as relaxed as she had ever seen them. She thought of her mother. Her parents must have been lonely without each other. They might have been a family all these years except for Phoebe's interference. She would pray harder and work at being intentional in forgiving her aunt.

The singing ceased. For a long moment, a hushed silence pervaded the place. Then candles were extinguished, feet shambled, and everyone spilled out of the pews, making their way inch by inch up the aisle. It had been a good service to attend.

Josie awoke midmorning, earlier than she had anticipated after having been up so late the night before. "My first Christmas with Father." She lay comfortable and toasty under the blankets in the gloomy winter light. But when she caught a whiff of the aroma of bacon, and mingled with it the tantalizing smell of freshly brewed coffee, they tickled her nose too much.

"Who's cooking? Aunt Mae?" She got out of bed, pulled on her dressing gown, and made her way to the kitchen.

Josie pushed on the swing door and stopped short in its opening, staring in amused disbelief at the sight of her father at the stove wearing one of Vertie's aprons. Beyond her father, her aunt was braced against the counter, clutching a bowl to her stomach, whanging away with a wooden spoon.

"What're you two up to?" Josie asked.

Landon spun around and grinned—a big, goofy grin. "We're fixing breakfast. See?" He held up a fork with a rasher of bacon stuck in its tines. "Merry Christmas!"

"Oh, my goodness. I'll say this much, you never fail to amaze me."

He raised his eyebrows. "What? That I can cook? . . . Hungry?"

"I am now. My taste buds are wide awake, and they won't let my body go back to sleep." She went to the dish cabinet, grabbed a cup, and filled it with coffee, lacing it with sugar.

"Pancakes are ready." Mae pointed toward the table. "Sit down." She flipped three of them onto a plate and placed it in front of Josie. She spooned more batter onto an iron griddle. "Don't wait for us. Go ahead and eat them while they're hot."

Josie smeared butter over each pancake and poured warm maple syrup over the steaming stack, drowning them. "Yum," she said. She ate every morsel with a hearty appetite. "No more. I'm stuffed."

"What? You're stopping at three?" Landon went to the sink and washed his hands. He sat at the table with a stack of four for himself, hot off the grill.

"What're we doing today, since we opened our gifts last night?" Josie asked.

"We could take down the tree," Landon said, as he slathered butter over the pancakes and drenched them in syrup.

"Isn't it unlucky to take down the decorations before the Twelfth Day? Why can't we leave everything up until then?"

Mae brought over her own plate and sat. "Twelfth day of what?"

"Christmas. January sixth. The day the church celebrates the coming of the wise men to see Jesus," Josie said.

Landon and Mae looked at each other and rolled their eyes. "Oh-h-h."

"I thought they went about the same time the shepherds did. That's the way the pageants always show it," Mae said.

"I know, but it's wrong." Josie got up to refill her cup with coffee, then returned to the table. "The magi didn't go to Bethlehem for two years after Jesus was born. And when you read the Bible, it says they entered the house to worship the young child with their gifts of gold, incense, and myrrh. They didn't go to the manger and worship a baby."

"How interesting. Well, maybe the tree will last 'til then, who knows?" Mae questioned.

"With all the water it drinks every day, it'll last until St. Patrick's Day," Landon said.

Josie chuckled. "Whenever we take it down, can we ask Nub to cut it into small pieces and save them in a box on the back porch? We can burn them little by little and make the house smell Christmassy for a long time. Besides, good luck is supposed to follow for the new year."

"Hmm, never've heard of that superstition before," Mae said. "Come on. Tell you what, Josie, let's join forces, do the dishes, and clean up this greasy kitchen."

"Sure, okay."

All three helped to clear the table.

Mae turned on the faucet, filled a dishpan with soapy water, and began washing the dishes. "You dry and put away, Josie." When she finished, she tipped the dishpan and the water gurgled down the drain. "All done."

Everything was in its place and neatly stowed away, and the table and stove had been wiped off. She squeezed out the dishcloth and ran it over the faucets, then turned to her niece. "Let's go to the library."

Landon knelt on one knee in front of the fireplace, snapped twigs, jumbled old newspapers, and scraped together the ashes in the grate. He struck a match and touched it to the paper and kindling, and when they burst into flames, the room became brighter and cozier immediately with the firelight.

Mae pulled a large, leather-bound portfolio out of the bookshelves, wedged in so tightly it was not easy to dislodge, posited it on the drop-leaf table, and opened the tome. "Old pictures tell such interesting stories," she said. A handful of unattached photographs fanned out, half exposed, from the scrapbook's cover. She brushed them aside and sat.

Josie situated herself beside her aunt at the table and slowly turned the pages, studying each folio's spread while Mae offered commentary. Landon stood behind them and looked over their shoulders.

Mae scooped the loose snapshots together into a pile. She gathered them up in her hand and shuffled through them like playing cards. "Here's one you ought to see, Josie." She gave it to her.

"Mother . . . and you." She glanced at her father.

It showed Sarah sitting in a chair by a window, and Landon resting his arm on the chair's back. They were gazing into each other's eyes. "You two seem very much in love."

Mae gave Josie another one depicting the couple posed alongside an automobile. Sarah wore a dark suit reaching to her ankles, her high-top shoes showing, and a white lace ascot gracing the front of her jacket. She was smiling and squinting as if the sun blinded her. Landon was leaning against the car, his arms folded, his teeth displayed in a big, goofy grin.

Josie had seen that same broad smile just that morning. "You seemed happy."

"We were. A pity we can't go back in time."

Why had he kept these old photos, and why were they right on top? Did her father open this book of memories often and grieve over what might have been?

Josie swallowed the lump in her throat. She pondered her mother's lost years of happiness with the only man she ever loved, and her own emptiness for not having the father she always dreamed of knowing. Why couldn't they have been a family? She could do nothing about it now. She took a quivering breath. "What's the car?"

"A Marmon. Known as the easiest riding car in the world. Model 48. A dandy. Cast aluminum body. Electric starter. Lights. Nickel trim. A real beaut. Made in Indianapolis, Indiana."

She put the picture down. "Never heard of it."

"Musing over old photographs is sad," Mae said. "What a shame we get so busy with life. Before we know it, time's slipped away. Gone. We never get it back—ever."

"We have pictures and recollections," Landon said. "Pictures are more reliable, though. What we remember tends to become distorted. We better gather up all these and stick them back into the album. We need to get dressed for dinner."

Mae closed the book and rammed it back in its slot on the shelf. "Josie, our traditional Christmas meal begins with a bowl of hot oyster soup."

Josie wrinkled her nose. "Ewww. Sounds disgusting to me."

The three arrived at the Terre Haute House and were seated; menus were brought, and orders were given. A waitress immaculately attired in a black dress with white apron set down the brimming cereal-sized bowls of soup on a charger, and the milky sea-smell curled through the air. Small, plump oval crackers swam half-submerged amid specks of black pepper on the surface of the liquid.

Could she eat this? She might be able to get down the creamy part, but the oysters would remain untouched. Landon saved his until the last, peppered them, and slowly chewed the rubbery mollusks, one after the other. Josie's stomach turned.

Back home, Mae went upstairs to pack for her trip home the next morning.

"There're some correspondence and other paperwork I need to deal with," Landon said.

Josie followed him to the library and flopped down in the armchair. She replayed the day in her mind. She opened her eyes and turned her head to study her father's profile. Was he content? He obviously had the kind of life he wanted—a successful law practice, a small circle of friends, and a cadre of colleagues. All in all, her father appeared to have a pleasant life. Then she showed up. Was he proud to have her with him?

She thought about how much he'd changed in these few months she'd been at his home. Or was *she* the one who'd been transformed the most? Maybe she was. What was she thinking? No, it hadn't been *her*, it'd definitely been her father.

She scooted out of the chair and heaved to her feet. She wanted to tell him the day had been good—better than good. "My first Christmas with you was a wonderful day, Father. Thank you for everything."

Landon looked up from his papers. "Why, you're welcome. I'll admit today was an enjoyable day for me, too, Joselene."

What? That was *all* he had to say? Nothing endearing and tender? How could he have no trouble spouting out facts readily in matters of the court, but be tight-lipped in expressing matters of the heart? Why was exhibiting any affection hard for him? Could she not arouse in him one spark of warmth? Not even an embrace? Evidently not.

She yawned, tapping her fingers to her mouth. "I'm going to bed. G'night." She left the room and mounted the stairs, getting slower and slower, until halfway to the top, she paused. She took in a huge breath, shut her eyes, and emptied her lungs in a long, slow stream, somehow hoping to stop the ache in her chest. Why did it feel like a cold hand clutching at her heart? Was it anger rearing its ugly head? Or was it disappointment—*deep* disappointment? She opened her eyes and continued making her way to her room.

She undressed, put on her nightgown, and climbed into bed. She lay in the dark, telling herself to be thankful that at least he considered her worthy enough to provide a beautiful, spacious room, and a new wardrobe of expensive dresses, a Christmas tree, and the emerald—the family heirloom.

However, the consummate Christmas for her would have been a hug and something like, "I'm delighted you're here and fortunate you are my daughter." Perhaps sometime in the near future, he might take her in his arms and give her the hug she craved. She went to sleep on the thought.

Chapter 13

Josie sat at the dressing table and touched the perfume stopper to the base of her neck. She pulled out hairpins and fluffed her hair as it fell onto her shoulders. The royal blue silk dress with the pleated skirt hung on the wardrobe's door, but when she went to put it on, she changed her mind. This time, she chose the honey-colored wool crepe because it was warmer. Josie checked the results in the mirror and, liking what she saw, leaned forward and carefully painted her mouth. She heard the knock on the front door and her father's scuff of footsteps in the hallway to open it. She put down her lipstick and went to the stair landing.

"Elliott!" she called.

He came to the foot of the stairs, held on to the newel post, and stared up at her. "You look like a princess in a tower. Come down before I get a crick in my neck."

"Give me another minute or two." She dashed back to her bedroom, checked her reflection again, and primped one last time. Satisfied, she went quickly out of the room. As she descended the stairs, he turned and stared at her.

He flashed a bright smile. "You're gorgeous."

"Thank you."

Landon accompanied the two of them to the front door. "Have fun," he called out as they moseyed down the sidewalk.

Elliott ushered her to the Studebaker and opened the passenger door for her. He went around to the driver's side, relaxed behind the steering wheel, and started the engine. He glanced over at Josie. "I hope the Orpheum's not crowded, but Katharine Hepburn's very popular." He eased the car away from the curb.

Josie sank back into the seat, fiddling with her gloves. "The last time I was there, the place was crowded."

He stopped at the corner of Sixth and Poplar. Turning east, he asked, "You've been to the Orpheum before?"

"Uh-huh."

"When?"

"Um, it was right after we were introduced at the Trianon. You went home. We saw Fred Astaire and Ginger Rogers in *The Gay Divorcee*."

"Who's the we? Your father or Priscilla?"

"Neither one. If you must know, it was Alex."

He jerked his head. "Alex! I'm more than a little surprised your father would approve of you going out with him."

"What do you mean?"

"Your father probably knows him better than I do, but the truth is, I think of him as nothing but a wolf in sheep's clothing."

"Alex Heywood?" She eyed him warily for a few seconds.

"Yes, Alex Heywood. And don't look at me like that. Be careful around him. In fact, stay away from him. Just for the record, for myself, the less our paths cross, the better."

"You don't like him?"

"No, not much."

"Why? Jealous of him?"

"Of Alex? By no means."

"What is it, then?"

"I wouldn't put anything past him. In fact, I'm afraid of him."

"What could he do to you?"

"Not to me. I've got my reasons to suspect he's a thoroughly unscrupulous man. Don't trust him, Josie. I sure don't. Don't talk about your father or the plant to him—any."

"Alex works for the same company as my father. He might ask me a question or two. Am I supposed to say, 'I can't talk about him. Elliott said so'? I don't understand."

"You don't have to. Just believe me when I say he's not the person you think he is."

"So, you're telling me to stay away from Alex Heywood?"

"No . . . I'm *demanding* you keep your distance."

"Elliott, listen to yourself. You're not giving him any benefit of the doubt."

"I'm not intending to, either."

"Why not?"

"Because he's Alex."

"Uh-uh. Not enough of a reason for me."

"Okay. How about this? What if Alex is a mole?"

"You mean like a spy? Sounds crazy to me. For whom would he be a double agent?"

"For the labor union, of course."

"You mean he'd betray confidential information to the union?"

"Yes, exactly."

"Stop it. You're being ridiculous. I don't want to hear any more." She cupped her hands over her ears. "I can't believe you."

"Is it you *can't* believe me, or you don't *want* to?" He parked the car across the street from the movie house and switched off the ignition. He turned to look at her in the evening's dimness and pointed. "Take this as a warning. I'm serious, Josie. Don't ignore my words. Don't!"

There was no line at the ticket booth outside the Orpheum, but several people were milling around, looking at the display of glossy black-and-white photographs advertising the film. Neither spoke as they sauntered into the theater. Inside, the couple followed an usher down the aisle of the semi-dark auditorium to their seats.

Elliott angled himself and took hold of Josie's hand, lacing his fingers with hers. "You're awfully quiet. Penny for your thoughts."

She smiled sheepishly. "Just thinking."

"I could see that."

"I'm . . . puzzled about something. I'm trying to sort it out in my mind."

"Maybe I can help you become unconfused and all sorted out. What's the something?"

"Alex Heywood."

"What? How so? . . . Why in the world are you even considering him?"

"Well, because he gave me a beautiful Bible for Christmas, imprinted with my name in gold on the front."

"So what if he gave you a Bible? He's probably never cracked the cover of one or read even a single page."

Josie continued, "Plus, I sat with him at the candlelight service. We went out a couple of times, and yes he's been cocky and arrogant, but at Priscilla's party, he was quite attentive and complimentary . . . which is more than I can say for you. And then you're thinking Alex is a weasel and imagining him of being a mole for the union. That's underhanded kind of stuff. All of those things don't go together. So who is the real Alex Heywood? I'm trying to figure him out."

Elliott scowled. "Listen, just be careful around him, okay? Look, I don't want to spend our evening talking about him. Let's talk about us—you and me." A faint smile crossed his lips. "Didja make any New Year's resolutions?"

She nodded. "Being a woman of leisure makes me too uncomfortable. I want to do something to help others."

"What will the *something* look like?"

"I'm going to check into volunteering at the Light House Mission and would like to start next week."

He squeezed her hand. "Commendable."

"I want my life to count for something or someone."

"Your life does. You are important, especially to me."

"Oh, you." She withdrew her hand from his. "This is serious. I just need to be doing *something*. I can't sit around all the time. Changing the subject, what did you do over Christmas?"

"Mother and I went to church . . . ate . . . slept. The usual stuff." He brushed stray wisps of her red-gold hair off her cheek.

Josie got goosebumps from the tickle of it. "Anything else?"

He pinched his lower lip. "Talked about you to Mother."

"Me?" She positioned a hand over her heart, feigning surprise, and whispered, "Like what?"

"Um, for starters, how much I enjoy being with you."

"Am I ever going to meet her? Or are you trying to put me off?"

Elliott gave no response because the lights dimmed, the silver screen lit up, and a hush came over the house. He positioned an index finger over his lips. "Sh-h-h."

* * *

A February Wednesday broke with the sound of noisy, wintry rain lashing against the bedroom window glass. Josie snuggled under the cozy blankets, listening to the wailing and shrieking of the wind. Shuddering, she got up, peered out at the branches of the oak tree now coated with sleet, and dawdled while getting dressed, eventually making her way to the warm kitchen, where Landon sat with the newspaper spread out on the table before him.

Josie poured herself a cup of steaming coffee, sweetened and tasted it, and set it at her place to cool. "This better wake me up," she said. She put two pieces of bread into the toaster, and while they browned, she stood at the dark window and leaned her forehead against the glass. "It sounds wicked out there. Listen to the water gurgling through the eaves."

The rain fell like straight steel rods, spattered, and streamed down the windowpane. "This month's only half over, and yet seems like it's lasted *for-ev-er.*" She flapped her arms at her side. "I'm sick and tired of the winter's dreariness."

Landon raised his coffee cup and took a sip. "Appears to me like somebody's mood this morning matches the gloom outdoors. Got the winter blues?" He folded the paper and shoved it aside.

She removed the toasted bread and smeared butter on the crisp slices. "Probably. Been thinking—"

"About?"

"Um, getting a job."

His eyebrows shot up. "This is new. What about your volunteer work?"

She took a hard-boiled egg from a bowl in the refrigerator, cracked the egg's shell, and peeled it away. "I want to be able to make my way . . . earn some money. Support myself. Volunteering doesn't give me the opportunity to do that."

Landon made a steeple of his fingers, pressed it to his lips, and looked at her intently. "What are you qualified to do?"

Josie came to the table and plopped in a chair. "Hmm. Well, nothing, to be honest. I could apply at Quaker Maid or Davis Gardens. I wouldn't need any special skills to work at either of them. They'd train me. Or, I guess I could hire out as a lady's companion. Maybe get a job in the five-and-dime."

Landon laid his knife and fork in his plate, and his napkin beside them. "Ever considered going to college?"

She salted and peppered the egg. "No, I haven't really given it much thought because it'd be dreadfully expensive and I could never afford it . . . not without a job."

He stared into the remains of his coffee and slid the cup into its saucer. "Let me rephrase the question. Would you *like* to go?"

"Sure, but I don't have the money."

"No, you don't. But I do. Did you know you could receive a teaching certificate in two years? Right here in Terre Haute at Indiana State Teachers College?"

"Really? . . . I was a good student . . . and I like children. I want to build a worthwhile life for myself—do something to help the world. What would I need to do?" she asked, looking at him as she munched on the toast.

"First thing is to have your high school marks sent to ISTC. Then register, and you're there."

Josie stopped chewing. "You mean that's all I have to do?"

"Yes, it is. Registration Day for the spring quarter is March twentieth."

She stuffed the last bite of crust in her mouth. "How do you know?"

He patted the newspaper. "I just read it." He looked at the clock. "Time for me to find my umbrella and briefcase and head to the office. Have a nice day, Joselene."

* * *

The torrent hammered down throughout the entire day. That evening, Josie, entering the dim hall, shivered as she shrugged out of her wet coat and shook off the water. A gush of light flowed into the entryway from the library's slightly ajar door. She recognized the men's voices issuing from there—her father's and Elliott's.

Landon's voice sounded stern. "We must refuse the union's demands. A closed shop simply goes against the company's principles."

"What about their complaint that the plant favors non-union employees?"

"Unsubstantiated. In fact, quite the opposite is true. Those more recently hired are sympathetic to the union."

Josie joined them, stepping cautiously into the room. "I'm home from the Van Allens's."

Landon turned his head. "Did you want something?" he snapped.

"Yes. I should think that a person who's been out in this weather might need something hot to drink."

Elliott glanced at Landon and back at Josie. "I sure would. Sounds good to me," he said. He trailed her to the kitchen. "What can I do to help?"

"The kettle's on the stove," she said, and indicated with her head, her hands getting down the teapot.

He took the kettle to the sink, filled it, and put it on the coil.

When Josie brought the cups and saucers over to the table, Elliott reached into his jacket's pocket and pulled out a small package wrapped in red paper and boasting a little white ribbon bow. He placed it in front of her. She looked at it and then at Elliott and pointed. "What's this?"

"Find out. Go on, open it," he said. "Happy Valentine's Day." He caught her hands in his own and held them. "Whoa! They're like ice!"

She laughed. "That's why I want something hot." She wrested her hands from his grip and struggled with the wrapping. With it torn away at last, she saw a blue velvet heart-shaped box. Inside was a golden locket on a gold chain.

"Oh, my, Elliott," she said.

"Take it out and open the heart."

She fumbled with it. "My hands are too cold."

"Here, I'll help." He took the necklace and pushed in a little catch on the side, and it unlatched. Inside was a tiny oval picture of him. "Let me put it on you."

Josie turned around and pulled her hair to one side, allowing him a clear view to fasten the clasp. She felt his fingers on her neck, and then, centering the locket over her heart, she whirled around to face him.

Elliott stepped back and looked down at her. "Now I will always be close to your heart, no matter how far away you are from me." He put his arms about her and held her tightly to his chest, his fingers tangling in the cascade of hair at the back of her neck. "I love you, Joselene Matthews," he whispered, his lips skimming her ear. "Always remember that."

She pulled away only far enough to see his face and the gleam in his eyes again.

"Did you hear me? I said, 'I love you.'"

She squinted at him. "Oh, I heard you. But . . . you don't even know me."

He raised a single eyebrow and smiled. "You're wrong. I know you, all right . . . been watching you for months." He dipped his head and lifted her chin to him and lightly pecked her on the cheek, like greeting a friend. "I'm waiting around for you to fall in love with me." He kissed her again—unhurried this time, soft and sweet. For Josie, it wasn't the first time she'd been kissed on the lips. But it *was* the first time she'd been kissed so thoroughly.

"Hey . . . I'd better say goodnight." He put on his raincoat, and at the back door, he paused. "I look forward to the time—maybe someday soon—when you realize you love me, too." Then he walked out into the darkness, and the house became silent.

Josie crossed the room and turned off the stove's burner, the teakettle's steam rising in a swirling pattern that twisted toward the ceiling. She hadn't had the hot tea, but felt warmed anyway. She put the unused dishes back in their places.

At half past nine, to the drowsy drizzle, Josie went to her room. She grasped the necklace and sashayed around and around in the center of the floor. Elliott loved her—his words now inscribed upon her heart for all time.

"I love you, too," she said. "I just couldn't say anything to you because it's plumb scary for me. Golly, what might it be like to be Mrs. Elliott Randolph Jacobson and have the responsibility for your meals, your clothes, your comfort, your honor, your children? You haven't yet proposed, but still—" Josie's heart danced and her fingers tingled. Was this for real?

She knelt at her bedside and buried her face in her hands. "Lord God, You've blessed me beyond anything I could have ever imagined. Thank You for Your graciousness, and for Elliott, who's given me a new sense of belonging. Amen."

She stood, put on her nightgown, and crawled into bed. She tried to sleep, but couldn't. She lay awake in the night a long time, going over Elliott's words, searching her mind, and finding no logical reason why the tall, dark, and handsome reporter with the quick smile should be seriously attracted to her—that out of a whole world of waiting girls, he had chosen her to love. What would the future bring for her? For him? For them?

Chapter 14

The first Saturday of spring, March twenty-third, dawned bright and sunny with a western breeze that propelled puffy white clouds across the azure sky. The sycamore trees were fuzzed in green, the maples in red, and the yellow trumpets of the daffodils bobbed on their stems.

Josie walked on her knees, grumbling under her breath. "What's wrong with the employees at the Stamping Mill that they'd just walk off their jobs?" She grubbed in the dirt at the south side of the yard using brusque, angry motions.

"Hey, those aren't your enemy."

She recognized Elliott's voice, excitement whipping through her. She flung clumps of weeds into a bushel basket and looked back over her shoulder at him.

"Might as well be." She slammed the trowel into the musty-smelling damp earth. "This little space has been sorely neglected, and I'm trying to make a beautiful garden spot. What're you doing here this time of day?"

He pushed back his fedora with an index finger and wrinkled his brow. "Thought you could use a little word of encouragement today."

"You mean because of the labor walkout at the plant?"

"Yep."

"I call it absolute foolishness."

"Yep. You're right." He crossed his arms at his chest.

"Would you like to help me here?"

"No reason I can't . . . at least for a little while." He squatted down on his haunches. "I can see you're more than a little upset."

Josie sighed dramatically and jabbed harder at the soil. "I keep telling myself this can't be happening. Thankfully it's not the general strike they've been threatening. I've been praying about the situation for quite some time."

"I know you have . . . here, give me the trowel . . . at least until you calm down. I'm afraid you're going to injure yourself."

She tossed the garden tool his way and sat back on her heels, clapped her hands together to pat the dirt from Nub's old work gloves, and yanked them off. "My heart aches for Father. I wish I could close my eyes and somehow it'd all just go away," she said, wiping beads of perspiration from her forehead with the back of her arm. "But it won't."

"Nope. The rumblings began when so many of the employees joined the labor union. That was before you ever came to Terre Haute." Elliott hoisted himself up, pulled a clean handkerchief from his pocket, and wiped his face and hands. He turned to Josie and hauled her to her feet.

She brushed off the back of her skirt, straightened, and knuckled an ache in the small of her back. "Wherever this strike leads, it isn't going to be beneficial to anyone, is it? Father said the Stamping Mill is closed for . . . well . . . goodness, who knows how long?"

"For sure, the controversy won't be resolved quickly."

"Father said negotiations have been going on since November . . . and still no change in the company's policy. I'd hoped the union'd come around. Why can't those in charge understand striking never accomplishes what they want?"

He shrugged. "It's an emotional issue. When emotion overrides logic, common sense goes out the window. By the way, Alex been around here much?"

"Alex?" She wagged her head from side to side. "Why are you so hung up on him?"

"I've been investigating the conflict and found something very interesting. What would you think if I said the discontent got stirred up after he became a union steward?"

"Are you implying he's been the driving force for the problems?"

Elliott nodded. "It appears so. I have strong suspicions he's involved."

"Father never told me who he thought it was. Do you really think it may be Alex?"

"I have no actual proof, but according to the evidence I've gathered, yes, I do."

Josie chewed on her lower lip. "Why would he have any reason to do that?"

"Want to hear my theory?"

Josie nodded.

"He wants to win favor with the union so he cooperates with them—which probably means a promotion for him within its ranks. Then there's a more obvious reason." He rubbed his first two fingers and thumb together. "Money."

"Do you think so? That would mean Alex has sold his soul to them."

"It's the only logical explanation. I suspect he's calculated every move he's ever made. He's proving to be determined to advance his career . . . whatever it takes."

"Elliott, if you're right about this, then Alex is a traitor to the company . . . betraying father's trust by acting like a friend and peacemaker. Do you honestly believe he's only *pretended* to want a settlement?"

"Yep."

"This makes me sick to my stomach. If your hunch proves true, he's a skunk."

"A snake in the grass."

"Yeah. He's pathetic," she said.

Elliott stood close to her and caught her hand in his. "I'm sorry about all this."

She nodded. "It's awfully upsetting, to say the least."

"No doubt. Say, didja get started with classes at State?"

"Uh-huh. I'm all set. I think I'll enjoy them, too."

"I'm proud of you." He stooped and kissed the tip of her nose, and said, "Listen, I gotta get back to the office. Now, don't forget."

She arched her eyebrows. "Forget what?"

"That I love you." He touched two fingers to his hat brim in a salute, thrust his hands in his pockets, and walked back to the car.

Was she nervous about the strike, worried about her father, or ruffled at Alex? Josie wasn't sure which it was—maybe all three—but her inner turmoil gave her boundless energy. After weeding the garden space, she now swept across the front porch's painted wood floor.

She'd made her way to the swing and back of it, jabbing at some trapped black dirt and dried leaves in a corner, when . . .

"Josie," a man's voice said behind her.

She stopped sweeping and looked over her shoulder. On the second step stood Alex, his muscular frame in a smart tweed jacket. Her mouth fell open and, for an instant, she released her grip on the broom, sending it clattering to the floor.

"Hello," he said.

"What are you doing here?" she snapped.

"I beg your pardon?" He stayed right where he was.

"What do you want?" She bent over to retrieve the broom while an awkward silence ensued.

He stepped onto the porch, removed his hat with a gallant gesture, and held it in one hand. He ran the fingers of his other hand through his thick, dark hair, glanced around, and said, "I had to see you and tell you how sorry I am for what has happened. I worked hard to keep the workers from walking out. Ask your father."

She bristled, rolled her eyes, took a long breath, and puffed out her cheeks as she let the air out in a long, slow stream. She looked at him warily. "Oh, stop it, Alex! How did you think I'd feel?"

"I knew you'd be riled up, but you can't blame me."

"Oh, yeah? Well, I think somebody's causing trouble, and I don't like it one bit." She clenched her jaw. What if he had instigated the whole mess as Elliott suspected? If Alex'd played any part in the events there, he was a weasel in her book.

"I figured as much," he said.

"Then why did you bother coming over, if you'd already surmised how I'd feel? It's downright sinful to fight against the company's founding principles."

Alex cleared his throat. "I wouldn't go so far as to use the word 'sinful.'"

"What *would* you call it, then, and what're you going to do about it?"

"Not much I can do."

"Wait a minute. Aren't you a union steward? Can't you steer the people to agree with the long-standing course of action?"

"Josie, think about it. I'm a union man, not a non-union man."

She moved away from the swing, strode across the porch gripping the broom handle like a man might carry a rifle, marched up to him, and smacked the straw end to the floor right in front of him.

Alex jerked and staggered backward. He lost his footing and teetered at the edge before tumbling down all five steps to the ground, his arms flailing. He lay in a heap at the bottom, his eyes tightly shut, his breathing labored.

Horrified, Josie clapped her trembling hand to her mouth, hurried down to Alex, and leaned over him. "Are you hurt? Any broken bones? Can you stand?"

He slowly opened his eyes, moaned, and sat up with an effort. "What do you care?" He scrambled to his feet, brushed off his suit with his hands, collected himself, and blew out a shaky breath.

"I think you better leave," she barked, shaking the broom at him.

"What's wrong with you? Have you gone daft?" Glancing around, he tucked his shirt inside the front of his pants. "I'll not forgive you this in a hurry," he sneered, and headed down the sidewalk. When he got to his car, he climbed in and drove off.

"Good riddance," she mumbled.

Josie told her father what had happened when he came home that evening. She waited for him to say something—anything. However, he was silent about the matter, and a deep quiet sank onto the room and settled onto the house. Josie didn't know what to do next.

* * *

The last Monday of April, Elliott Jacobson stopped at the Matthews's home. "Mr. Jacobson's here to see you, sir," Vertie said, standing in the open door to the library, knocking with her knuckles as she spoke.

Landon, sitting in the leather armchair behind *The Terre Haute Star*, lowered the newspaper. "Come on in, Elliott." He folded the paper carefully, laid it across his lap, and motioned for the young man to enter. "What brings you out on this nasty, rainy evening?"

"Forgive me for intruding."

"Nonsense." Landon pointed to the drop-leaf table. "Grab a chair."

Elliott dragged one from across the room to Landon and sat. "Is Josie here?"

Landon chuckled. "Ah . . . no, no, she's absorbed in the great adventure of college, the thrilling experience of spending her evenings doing research."

"Tonight!? In this weather?"

"I took her there and will pick her up when she's ready to come home."

Elliott nodded. He rested his hands on his thighs and squirmed in his chair. He let out a gust of breath, swallowed hard, stood, and walked to the fireplace. "Landon, I'll be brief."

"Sure. What is it?"

Elliott ran his fingers through his hair. "I'm seeking your permission to marry Josie."

The older man stared at the young man and then at the paper. Silence fell across the room.

Elliott walked to his chair and stopped. He remained standing behind it, his hands grasping its back. He coughed. "You know little about me personally, but I believe my salary, with frugal living, will amply provide for her. I'll be the best husband I can be."

Landon stretched out his legs. He tilted his head slightly, stroked his chin with the back of his hand, and met Elliott's gaze. "Have the two of you talked about this?"

"Actually, no. In fact, Josie hasn't given any indication she's even interested in marriage."

"Then why talk to me now? Maybe you're moving too fast for her. She's just started her first quarter at State and has another year and a half ahead of her."

"I realize that. But the truth is, I've never before known a woman like her. Her qualities of womanhood appeal very much to me. I love her with all my heart and want to spend the rest of my life with her. I'm asking for her hand."

Landon settled back in his chair meeting Elliott's stare. "You haven't known each other long."

"Long enough."

He grinned. "A man can never really know the woman in his life well enough. What are your plans?"

"I'm not sure." Elliott tinkered with his tie. "I knew if you didn't approve, there'd be no reason to make any."

"This is rather unexpected, but I have no objections to her marrying you."

Elliott shook his hand. "Thank you, sir. I assure you I'll take good care of her. I never want to disappoint her . . . or you." He let go of Landon's hand and gave a sheepish grin. "Now comes the hard part."

Landon dropped the paper to the floor, pushed himself up and out, and came to stand beside Elliott. "What's that?"

"Convincing Josie to marry me."

Landon's mouth curved in a smile, he crooked a hand over Elliott's shoulder, and gave a squeeze. "I can only wish you luck, there."

Chapter 15

Josie flumped into the porch swing and, with her foot, moved it slowly back and forth at a steady rock, the chain creaking and grinding above her.

In no time, Priscilla mounted the steps. "Golly, but I'm tired of all this rain, aren't you?"

Josie shrugged and said nothing.

The constant drizzle spattered from the eaves. Priscilla dropped her opened umbrella onto the painted floor, where it went wheeling along in the current of air, making a scraping sound, and dribbling little pools of water wherever it stopped.

She perched on the wide railing. With her back to the street, she flung one arm about a post and swung her legs, her heels bumping the porch's balustrade.

"Don't sit there," Josie cautioned. "You'll be sopping wet in no time."

"No, I won't," Priscilla argued. "The roof hangs over too much for me to get wet. Besides, I'm not made of sugar. I won't melt."

Josie chuckled, noiselessly. "I know." She scratched her head.

Priscilla put out a hand to examine her fingernails. "Your birthday's coming up, isn't it?"

Josie gave a slight nod. "Uh-huh, in a little over two weeks . . . the twentieth of May."

"If I remember right, that'll be a Monday: a good day for a party."

Josie held her breath. "Please don't plan anything grand, Priscilla."

For a few moments, they looked at each other without speaking. Then Priscilla asked, "Aren't you going to be twenty-one?"

"Yes, but don't—"

"Don't, schmon't. If I want to make a big deal of it, I will. We've got to celebrate the big one." She tapped a finger to her lips and stared off into the distance. "Now, what theme would be the right one for you?"

Neither spoke. The dripping rain, the grinding swing, and the hum of sparse traffic making its way on South Sixth Street were the only sounds.

"I got it!" Priscilla snapped her fingers and pointed at Josie. "A treasure hunt."

Josie stopped swinging. She quirked her mouth. "I don't know about that."

Priscilla flapped her hand. "Come on. It'll be fun. We can go around the neighborhood searching for clues, which will lead everyone back to your house with the presents at the end of the wild goose chase."

Josie raised her hands, palms up. "Priscilla! Do you always try to manage other people's lives?"

Priscilla drew her eyebrows together and glared at Josie. "Is anybody else planning something?"

Josie shook her head.

"Then it's up to little ole me. No more discussion. Have Vertie make a cake. I'll take care of everything else." Priscilla pushed off the railing and brushed her hands together. "That settles it. I'm going home. There's work to do, so I better get busy. Invitations to send out, for one thing."

"Don't invite Alex," Josie said. "Personal reasons."

Priscilla stooped to snatch up the unfurled umbrella. She glanced over her shoulder as she headed home. "I'll have to include Alex on Winnie's account."

Josie watched her go. "No, you don't!" she yelled back.

* * *

Elliott eased his car next to the curb in front of his mother's house. He switched off the ignition, peered at the mullioned living room window, and saw his mother. He waved to her. By the time he yanked the sheaf of spring flowers and greeting card off the seat beside him and climbed out of the car, Lillian stood at the open door.

"Is everything all right?" she called. "I was getting worried. Been looking out the window for you. Wondered if there'd been some kind of problem. You've always come on Saturday evening and stayed over so we could have breakfast together on Mother's Day and attend church. I had to endure all kinds of questions this morning. 'Where's Elliott, Lillian?' 'Why, he always worships with you on Mother's Day.' It was awful."

He made his way up the sidewalk. "I told you I wouldn't be here until later in the morning. I have responsibilities with my job. Things have been kinda hectic at the *Star* office."

"A mother can still worry, can't she?" She spun and disappeared inside the house.

Elliott hesitated, stepped over the threshold, and followed her into the living room. He held out the card. "Happy Mother's Day! I love you, Mom."

Lillian took it and traced each word of the elegant, embossed printing with her fingertip. "Lovely."

He presented the bouquet to her and gave her a peck on the cheek.

"Elliott, they're beautiful. But you didn't need to do that."

"You don't enjoy getting them?"

"I didn't say anything of the sort. Of course I do."

"Which restaurant am I taking you to this year?"

"Surprise! We're going to eat here—at home. Can't you smell it?"

He made little jerking motions with his head, noisily sniffing the air. "Amazing! You cooked your own Mother's Day dinner? I'm more than a little surprised. Uh . . . how about we put these blooms in some water? I'm sure they're thirsty."

"Yes, of course. I've not seen snapdragons since . . . last year."

"Where would I find a container for them?"

Lillian gestured vaguely. "In the pantry, probably. Oh, wait, look on the top shelf in the cupboard." She unwrapped the green-glazed tissue paper from around the long-stemmed blooms.

Elliott passed through the kitchen, opened the cabinet door, and snatched a glass jar. On his way back, he stopped and checked the oven, which was emitting mouth-watering smells. He found a roasted pork loin and candied yams.

"I'm waiting," Lillian called.

He banged the door shut, went to the sink, and half-filled the container with water. "Coming," he said, and carried it to his mother.

She slipped the snipped stems one by one into the vase and fanned them out. "Look at these. They always brighten up a place, don't they? I'll put them on our dining table." She fiddled with a stray carnation. "You're such a good son."

He patted her arm. "You're the best, Mom."

After the two o'clock meal, they retired to the living room. "Leave the dishes, Elliott. I'll wash them later," Lillian said. "I want to spend as much time as I can with you."

She sat rigid in the wingback chair, both her feet firmly planted on the floor and her hands gripping the chair's arms. "Why so quiet today? Maybe I kept the food warming too long waiting for you to appear."

"Huh? Oh, no. Dinner was swell." He sprawled out on the sofa and closed his eyes.

"What's wrong, then?"

He opened his eyes, half-raised himself, and looked at her. "Nothing.

Got a lot on my mind, that's all. Had quite a time keeping the story of the strike off the front pages of the newspapers." He sank back again.

"I dare say the paper isn't the only distraction. I knew something was bothering you when you got here. I can tell these things. Are you still consorting with *that* girl from there?"

"Sure am."

Lillian poised on the edge of her seat. "Have you still got a horrible crush on her?"

"Um, suppose so."

"I never heard of such nonsense. I don't understand what you find remarkable about . . . *her*. What's her name, again?"

He sat up. "Joselene Grace Matthews. She's adorable and sweet and has changed everything for me, Mom. That may sound silly to you. But, well . . . she's a fine girl, and I'm extremely fond of her."

Lillian plucked a wayward thread from her skirt and twisted it in her fingers. "Is she aware of how serious you are about her?"

"I haven't talked about marriage to her, yet. Listen, when you know her—"

"How can I, unless you bring her here? When *will* that be? Are you ashamed to introduce her to me?"

"No, not at all." He put up his hands to stop her. "Josie's kind and gentle and well . . . spiritual like."

Lillian puffed out her breath. "Don't be utterly ridiculous. She's not the caliber of woman that would—well, I just want you to be happy."

"I want that, too, but my happiness is determined by me, not you."

"You won't be happy with someone of her ilk."

"You're wrong about her."

She sat like a woman of stone, her head held high, her eyes flashing. "I am not, and someday you'll recall this conversation."

"I've prayed for someone to come into my life. Josie's the girl, and because her parents weren't married and she lives in Terre Haute, you don't want her and me to experience happiness and companionship. What rot. She's done nothing to earn your rejection of her . . . nothing."

Lillian bolted from her chair, her chest heaving. She paced back and forth in the room, wringing her hands. "So on Mother's Day, even, you come here and tell me that everything I ever did for you in these twenty-five years since you were born is thrown away?"

Elliott raked his fingers through his thick hair, making it stick up and out into two antlers. "No, I'm not saying that."

"This is supposed to be the day you honor *me*!" She jabbed her finger in his face and glowered at him, her breathing shallow and quick. "I don't understand what's happened to you."

When Elliott spoke, it was slow and deliberate. "You're right, Mom. This is your special day. Let's talk about this another time."

* * *

The birthday party guests traipsed into the Matthews's house, shrugged out of their rain gear, and toed off their soaked shoes.

"That was fun—in spite of the lousy weather," Josie said.

"Told you a treasure hunt would be a hit," Priscilla bragged.

Everyone went into the living room, where Vertie had positioned a table in the bay window. Arranged on it were dessert plates, cups, silverware, and the silver coffee pot along with a multi-layered banana cake smothered with caramel frosting and holding the necessary number of yellow candles.

Vertie struck a match and began lighting them, one by one. "Somebody better help me, or these first candles'll be down to nothing by the time I light the last ones."

Elliott and Priscilla quickly pulled one after another out of the thick icing, lit them from those already burning, and poked them back into their holes. Before long, all were afire.

"Make a wish," Priscilla said.

Josie rolled her eyes, but said nothing, and took in a deep breath. She bent over the flickering flames, and blew. A smattering of applause broke out when the last sputter faded to swirling smoke.

"What was it?" Elliott asked.

"Can't tell," she said.

"Why not?" he bantered back.

"Because, if I tell, it won't come true. The power of wishes is in the waiting, not the telling."

Elliott rambled over to the piano, sat down on the bench, opened the key cover, and, after lightly fingering a flight of chords, drifted into, "Dream a Little Dream of Me," and then, "Happy Birthday." They all sang to Josie. When they finished, he played various familiar bits of show tunes, sometimes looking down at the keys for a moment as he maneuvered one bit of melody from a popular musical into another.

Priscilla stood beside him and giggled as she thumbed through a stack of loose music sheets. She chose one, leaned toward Elliott, and said something to him.

He nodded and she placed it before him on the music rack. His accomplished fingers rippled an accompaniment on the keyboard. Priscilla's soprano voice lifted, clear and strong, and filled the room. One after another of the group stopped their chatter and listened.

"Say it's only a paper moon
Sailing over a cardboard sea
But, it wouldn't be make-believe
if you believed in me.

It's a Barnum and Bailey world
Just as phony as it can be
But, it wouldn't be make-believe
if you believed in me."

Josie, cutting and serving the cake and pouring the coffee, became distracted by Elliott's playing and Priscilla's singing. She paused at her task and looked across the room, her gaze meeting Elliott's. He winked in recognition of her glance, and they smiled at each other. He was the most talented man she knew.

* * *

Elliott remained seated. He removed the sheet of music, set it on the bench beside him, and continued to play songs from his memory.

Priscilla said over his shoulder. "We need to talk."

"Right now, or can it wait?"

"It pertains to Josie."

"What about her?"

"Mind if I sit?" she asked.

"Not much room here." But he slid over and she sat on the edge beside him.

"It took me awhile to decide whether to say this or not, but I think I'd better . . . though I can't see that it matters." She hesitated a moment.

"So?" He glanced her way and saw Priscilla watching him. "What is it? Go ahead and tell me."

"I overheard Josie and Landon talking the other night. She wants to go back to Bradford. Did you know that?"

"No," he said.

"She wants to decorate her mother's grave for Decoration Day."

He shook his head and quirked his mouth. "Not said a thing to me." Only one way to find out why she hadn't. He'd simply ask her.

Priscilla went on. "If I were you, I wouldn't let her go. She may not come back."

"I can't keep her from going."

"If I were a man who cared for a girl, I'd not let miles and miles come between us."

With an arpeggio, Elliott finished the song. "Is that right?" He barely looked her way.

Priscilla flattened her palms against the bench and hunched her shoulders. "I wish a man would pick me up and run away with me."

He gathered up the scattered pages of music, tamped them together into some semblance of order, and laid the pile aside.

"Heaven help him," he muttered under his breath.

He crossed the room, dropped into the empty chair beside Josie, drew up one knee, and clasped his hands around it.

* * *

She touched her fingers to Elliott's arm. "I had no idea you were such a fine pianist. You're very gifted."

Elliott looked down at her hand, then covered it with his own. "How can I get you away from here?"

"Why?"

"I want to ask you something."

"Oh? Does it need privacy? Just ask me here. I can't leave. I'm presiding over the table. I . . . guess I could meet you in the library when the party's over."

"All right, but don't forget me," he said, stood, and walked across the hallway.

Elliott whistled very softly between his teeth while he drew back the linen curtains. He looked out at the nasty weather, shook his head, and stretched enormously.

Josie entered. "Here I am. Now, what did you want to talk to me about?"

He came to her, took her hand, and led her to the window seat. "Sit," he ordered.

She did so with her back to the window and sighed. "What is it?"

He said, "You."

"Me?"

"Yes. Priscilla tells me you're going back to Bradford."

Josie leaped up, walked toward the drop-leaf table in the corner, and straightened a chair already in its place. She turned his way. "How did she find out?"

"I asked her the same thing. She said she heard you talking with your father."

"Eavesdropping? That would be like Priscilla. Well . . . I always planned to go back to visit. Decoration Day seemed like a perfect time. Plus, I . . . may be a little homesick . . . for the country . . . and maybe for my aunts, although I'm not so sure about that. I can't explain it. I don't intend on staying there very long."

He stuck out his lower lip. "The idea of not having you here in Terre Haute bothers me. If you don't come back, I'll have to go looking for you. I don't want to be forgotten."

She smiled at him. "Elliott, I would never be able to do that."

"Uh-huh. Is your father taking you?"

"Does it make a difference if he is or not?"

"Yes, it does . . . to me. Is he?"

"Gracious, no."

"How will you get there?"

"Same way I got here: train."

Elliott sighed. "Nope. Not a good idea."

"Why not?"

"Look, I fully understand your determination in going. The only thing I can do is drive you."

Josie caught her breath. Her heart beat fast. She shook her head and grabbed hold of the chair. "Why on earth would you want to do that? It would take too much of your time, and it wouldn't even be proper."

"I'll talk to your father. If he gives me permission, then I'm driving you to Bradford, regardless of what you say. We can leave early this coming Saturday and come back on Sunday. Your mother's grave would then be decorated for the holiday."

A silence ensued.

Josie stiffened. Her stomach clenched. "That . . . means . . . we'd stay overnight."

Elliott put his hands on her forearms. "Yes, it does."

No, we can't do that, she wanted to say, but his touch sent a shock of electricity through her. He mustn't be allowed to see the dissimilar lifestyles between her aunts and her father. She couldn't have him stay at the shabby old house and spend much time with those two old-fashioned, fuddy-duddy women. "You won't have anything to do there."

He dipped his head until his face was mere inches from her own. "So? I'm not going for me. I'm going for you."

"You'd give up a weekend to take me to Bradford?"

"Of course. I'd do anything for you."

"Why?"

"Because I love you." He took her in his arms and kissed her. She knew she'd lost the argument, but at the moment, it didn't matter to her.

Chapter 16

Early the next Saturday, the twenty-fifth of May, Elliott and Josie headed south out of Terre Haute on Highway 150. She stared out the window, and after a while, leaned her head back and shut her eyes. They rode some thirty miles in silence.

He glanced over at her. "You okay?"

She nodded, focused on her tightly clamped fingers instead of on him, and sighed.

"Have I done something wrong?"

She shook her head.

"What is it, then? I can tell you're angry, or at least irritated about something or someone."

She wouldn't look his way. "I can't believe Father allowed you to take me to Bradford," she snapped. "He never even discussed the matter with me."

"He didn't? Hey, what can I say? Take the issue up with him, not me. Landon trusted me to get you there and back, safe and sound. I'm going to do that since I don't want to be on the wrong side of your father."

She hung her head. "I prefer to keep on his right side, too." She took in a huge breath, then emptied her lungs in a long, slow stream. More relaxed now, she sank back in the seat, and peered at Elliott as he drove. He was a good man . . . a man who loved God . . . and he'd shown her nothing but kindness and respect.

Neither of them spoke further until Josie said, "Turn here." Elliott steered his Studebaker off the state road onto a rutted, packed-clay road. When they came to a T intersection, he slowed the car to a stop. "Which way?"

"To the left. You'll see the orchard just around the bend. The apple trees'll be all clouded over with white and pink blooms. There! Isn't it a magnificent sight?" She swallowed a lump in her throat.

"I agree . . . breathtaking."

Josie glanced Elliott's way to find he was staring at her. Her cheeks burning, she said, "Sweet fragrance, too, huh? The house'll be close to the road."

He pressed the accelerator, rolled forward following her instructions, and pulled up at the front of an old, weathered, wood-framed farmhouse with a high-gabled roof.

Josie gaped at the house. Her stomach dropped. Nestled under tall maples and oaks, it looked quite ramshackle—a picture of neglect with the white-painted trim cracked and peeling.

"Gracious, the place is going to rack and ruin. How could my aunts let it get so run-down in such a short amount of time?" She shook her head. The yard was a mess, too. The grass, yet to be mowed, displayed a plentiful powdering of dandelions. Untended, gigantic fuchsia peonies bordered the stone foundation.

"Who's at the porch swing?"

"Aunt Phoebe."

"What's she doing?"

"Looks to me like she's trimming her toe corns." Josie blew out a sigh and scrambled out of the car. She squared her blue hat with its wreath of gardenias about the low crown and smoothed the skirt of her blue suit.

Elliott slammed the doors, and they made their way to the house.

"Our girl's here, Ruthie!" Phoebe yelled in the direction of the screen door.

Ruth's voice came from inside the house. "I'll be right out." She appeared shortly, wiping her hands on a grease-stained apron, and stepped out, coaxing her niece forward.

"Josie, Josie, Josie, let me look at you. You're prettier than ever." She put her arms out and pulled her close. "We've missed you dreadfully."

Josie gave a guarded embrace in return. "What've you been doing?"

"Frying our supper. We killed the fatted hen—to celebrate!" Ruth announced. "Meant to be done afore you got here, though." She turned toward Elliott. "You must be Josie's new friend."

He snatched off his Panama hat, and with his hand thrust forward, advanced toward the women. "Hello, I'm Elliott Jacobson. Pleased to meet you."

Phoebe offered him a hearty handshake. "How nice of you to bring her all this way. Come on in and tell us . . . about everything . . . and everybody . . . and how you're doing." She looked from Josie to Elliott. "I wanta hear how you two came together."

Josie chortled. "Well, we bumped into each other at Father's house . . . my first day in Terre Haute."

"Go on in. I was just about to put the kettle on to boil. We can have a cup of tea while you tell us the story." She held the door open, but they all remained where they were.

"We'd like to go to the graveyard now," Josie said.

"Uh . . . sure, uh . . . yeah, go on. 'Fraid the site needs some tidying up," Ruth stammered. "I'll finish up getting everything ready. When you come back, we'll eat some supper. Then we can talk all evening."

The couple followed the tree-lined county road to the edge of town, where the cemetery occupied a small rise; a decrepit, sunken gate marked its entrance. They tramped among old, simple tomb-stones—sticking out of the ground like jagged teeth, now brown with age, and their inscriptions almost obliterated by time and weather—and more elaborate, tall monuments with family names carved in the heavy granite. Thick honeysuckle vines sprawled and crept along the hedgerow and weighed down the rusty wire fence encompassing the property, its heady scent sweetening the air.

"It smells good out here, doesn't it?" Josie said. "This way." She traipsed beside Elliott through the maze of stones to her mother's small marble slab.

Elliott relaxed with his back propped against the trunk of a great maple tree. He drew up one knee, tipped forward, and dangled a fore-arm loosely over it.

Josie knelt at the marker, brushed away the leaves matted around it, and yanked tufts of weeds invading the purple irises that were blooming *en masse*. She rubbed a palm over the inscription on the stone: Sarah Charlene Claycomb Matthews, born July 23, 1894, died September 8, 1934, at the age of 40 years, 1 month, 16 days.

Sinking back on her heels, she lifted her head to check on Elliott. He did not smile at her or move. He did nothing more than watch her and make her heart pound. She boosted herself up and walked toward him.

He pushed back the brim of his hat with his index finger and took a deep breath, letting it out in an exaggerated sigh. "It sure is quiet out here."

"Are you bored?"

He braced both elbows against his knees and clasped his hands together. "Believe me, I'm not."

"Sure sounded like it." She dropped next to him on the rough and long grass. "What was the sigh for?"

"It was a yawn."

She shook her head and made a little tut-tutting noise between her tongue and teeth. "I warned you it would be a wearisome day."

Elliott stretched out to his full length beside her, leaning on one elbow. "I was thinking about you and me."

She picked a handful of wild violets and formed a bouquet. "What about us? I haven't made any promises to you."

"I don't need any." He reached over, took the flowers from her, and, setting the bunch aside, grasped her hands and kissed them. "I'll make you love me."

She pulled her hands free. "You believe that?"

He grinned and winked at her. "I do. You just wait and see if I'm right."

The gleam in his eyes shone again. Her heart did somersaults as she hoisted herself up. "Very self-assured, aren't we?"

Quick to his feet, Elliott turned her around to face him. "Yep, I am."

She gazed into his eyes and exchanged smiles with him. After a lingering look back at her mother's gravesite, Josie locked her fingers in his, and together they wandered down the shaded road back toward the house.

The late afternoon of the balmy spring day was perfect for a leisurely walk. The only sounds were the scuffle of their shoes on the hard-packed dirt and the raspy cries of hawks flying overhead. The sun, descending, took on the shape and color of an orange pumpkin and touched everything with gold. For a time, it splashed an awesome array of vermillion streaks and swirls on the western horizon.

Elliott pointed to the heavens. "Tomorrow's going to be a beautiful day. The Good Book says, 'Red sky at night, sailor's delight.'"

"From Matthew's Gospel."

It was nearly five o'clock when the two ambled onto the home place. "What's the scoop on your family? Mother's been asking."

Josie chuckled. "Only natural. My grandmother was a member of a Shaker community in Kentucky. She left the religious sect and married an itinerant photographer. They made their way to Indiana and bought a farm at the edge of Corydon . . . our county seat. He kept his photography business and she helped with the farming. Had three girls, no boys. Aunt Phoebe's the oldest, owns this land, and runs the orchard. Aunt Ruth's the middle one and does the outside work like the chickens and bees and vegetable garden and home repairs. She hunts and traps in the winter. My mother was the youngest—by eleven years. She tended the flower and herb gardens and did the inside housework. She had a knack for making something out of nothing." She glanced at Elliott. "I wish you could have known her. Whenever I think of her, she's smiling. She lived quietly. She died quietly." Josie stared off into the distance and then back at Elliott to find his gaze fixed on her. "Their middle names rhymed. Phoebe Darlene, Ruth Arlene, and Sarah Charlene."

He smiled, his lower lip covering the upper. "Did any of them ever marry?"

"Uh-huh. Aunt Ruth did, but her husband passed away in the influenza epidemic of 1918. No children."

Josie opened the bulging screen door on the back porch. Her aunts sat at an old, metal-topped table stemming fresh-picked strawberries. The berries were spilled in a mound between them, the black-green stems heaped on each side of the fruit, the scarlet juice staining their fingers. "Don't leave the door open," Phoebe barked. "I just drove out all those pesky flies."

"Your irises bloomed beautifully," Ruth said. "Wasn't sure they'd do anything, they were so dried out when you planted them last fall."

Phoebe wiped her hands on a stained towel. "Ruthie's fixed fried chicken, stuffed eggs, pickles, and home-baked bread."

"Strawberries, too, Pheeb." She looked at Josie and Elliott. "We even have sugar and some cream to pour over them."

Josie went to help in the kitchen. She scanned the all-too-familiar room. "Everything looks much the same in here." She slipped the neck strap of a faded apron over her head and tied the strings around her waist. "Everything except the pedestal table. Mother always draped it with white damask."

"We like things the way they've always been. No reason to change a thing . . . exceptin' the tablecloth. Handier for Ruth and me to put on a red-and-white-checked oilcloth. Not enough time for all the fineries your mother fooled with."

Beams of fading sunlight showed dust motes dancing across the cracked, worn gray linoleum; the rays playing on the cookstove; the Hoosier cabinet with its built-in, pull-out flour bin; the oak washstand with coatrack hooks above it; and the table with four mismatched chairs. To Josie, the odd bits of furniture always made the room appear shabby. Over the years, she'd dreamed of more for her life than eking out an existence here. Where to go and how to get there were unknowns to her at the time.

Josie, doing the best she could with the chipped and mismatched dishes, arranged the table as properly as possible. The four gathered for their supper, and Ruth prayed the blessing on the food.

Elliott rolled up his shirtsleeves. "Mmm, mmm, mmm." He ate with a healthy appetite.

"Maybe Josie could take you on a tour of the place after you've eaten. Would you like that, young man?" Phoebe asked.

Josie stacked the plates and collected the silverware. "He might not even be interested."

"I am, though." He stood and pushed down his rolled-up sleeves. "Really! I'm ready whenever you are."

She gaped at him, surprised by his answer.

"Better get my sweater off the hook, Josie. Even in May, it'll cool off once the sun's set," Phoebe predicted.

"Of course," Josie said. She grabbed it from the closet and yanked it on. By the door, she glimpsed her reflection in the mirror. The sweater showed a pinched peak in its back from hanging on the hook so long. She shrugged and led the way outside along a path worn bare, past a garden—planted in neat rows with cool-weather crops, now nearly ready to harvest—and past the packing shed.

Elliott slid open the huge barn door on its rolling track, and they went inside the now semi-dark, cavernous building. He stopped in his tracks at the sight of the old Waterloo Boy tractor and emitted a piercing whistle. He made a slow circuit around it. "You ever drive this?"

"A few times. It was more like herding it, though. Aunt Phoebe is pretty possessive of it."

He kept his attention on the farm implement. "I can only imagine the thrill a person would feel with all that power in their control."

She frowned and quirked her mouth. "Thrill? Ho! The engine's roar deafens you and the howl of the gears drown out all the pleasant noises of nature. Come see our apiary."

He nodded. "Okay."

They wandered out of the barn, sliding the door closed. "Aunt Ruth put the beehives between the packing shed and the henhouse 'cause they're sheltered from the north wind there."

"She ever been stung?"

"Hmm. Not that I know about . . . never heard her complain, leastwise. She's happy with her little friends. It only makes sense that stings'd come with the job, though."

"Well, yeah. I'd say it's wise to keep them because of all the nectar from the apple blossoms. How'd she start raising them?"

"I'm not sure. I don't recollect ever hearing how she got started. She probably learned from her mother." Josie stopped near five white boxes. "Better move about slowly," she warned. "Bees don't like abrupt movements. She gets all her supplies from Montgomery Ward."

"Guess a person can order anything through the catalog."

"Uh-huh. We harvest the honey in the fall and leave enough of it for them to survive the winter. Our regular customers say Aunt Ruth's honey is second to none."

Elliott scanned the area. "How many acres are here?"

Josie chuckled. "You sound like a newspaper reporter gathering information for an article. To answer your question: forty. Thirty-three are in apples, pears, and grapes." She pointed to a windmill. "We've a spring over there. We've got some timber for firewood, and course our gardens. We're pretty much self-contained and self-suffi-cient. We lived in an unassuming and frugal way. We didn't have what many of the others here had, but we always had enough to live on." She led him toward a slant-roofed house with a fenced-in yard. "This is the chicken coop. Aunt Ruth has twenty-six laying hens, and they keep us supplied with eggs. She's named all of them and calls them 'her girls.' Does that sound silly to you?" He said nothing, but raised his eyebrows whimsically and tilted his head.

They stepped into the small outbuilding. The chickens fussed, pecking nearer, cocking their sleek heads, and blinking their beady eyes. A rustling hen fluttered down from a straw-packed nest, and Josie caught the Plymouth Rock's gray feather curled and floating in the air. Other hens gabbled over the battered tin feeding pan.

"Kinda flighty, aren't they?" Elliott said, and covered his nose with his hand. "Let's leave."

The light of the late afternoon sun, shining through the trees, cast long, dappled shadows across the lawn. Elliott studied the sky, now turned to lavender. "So peaceful, isn't it? You miss this, don't you?"

"I do love the quietness of rural living. It was all I knew for twenty years, until—"

"Until your mother passed and you went to Terre Haute," he finished.

She nodded. "It's strange to be back. Everything's the same, yet everything's different."

He reached for her hand and grasped it. "Change is inevitable."

"When I look back, I couldn't wait to leave Bradford. If I'd stayed here, I never would have known my father—*and*, never have met you."

"You're happy living in Terre Haute?"

"Oh, my, yes. I did the right thing by going there. For years, I thought it would be fun to be rich and able to sleep as long as I wanted and bathe in a real tub with plenty of bubble bath and have more than one Sunday dress. Then I got them."

"What are you saying?"

"Happiness in life is more than money and comfort. I've learned to connect a sense of purpose for our lives through hard work, accomplishment, and living for others."

They entered the house and went through the kitchen to the parlor, where the two women sat listening to the radio. Phoebe leaned forward and switched off the music. "What'd you think of the place, young man?"

"Quite a spread. I'm impressed. Plenty of work to do."

"Hard work's good for a body and gives meaning to life," Phoebe said. She sat back in the old-fashioned rocker. "We haven't got some of the newfangled conveniences like inside plumbing, but at least we've got electricity and a telephone. And that's more'n some have."

"It's been a long time since we've heard you play the piano, Josie. Would you do us the honors?" Ruth pleaded.

Josie barely had time to sit on the sofa. "Not when Elliott's here. He's a much better player than I am." She looked straight at him. "You play," she ordered.

He stiffened and snapped off a smart salute like a soldier would do to address his commanding officer. "Yes, ma'am." He ran his hand along the top of the old upright. "Nice carpentry work."

"It was Mother's. She played it. I was nine and wanted to take lessons. She scheduled a time for the teacher to come. I couldn't wait. I sat on the front steps staring at the road, but she never came. Mother ended up teaching me. Do you remember that day?" She turned to her aunts.

Elliott straddled the round stool. He swiveled when Josie stopped talking, opened the key cover, and dabbled playing a couple of chords and runs before settling down. "How about this?" He fingered and sang, "The Old Rugged Cross."

His smooth voice rang out clear and strong. "Join me," he called. Before long, their voices rose in an amazing harmony as they sang, "On Jordan's Stormy Banks I Stand," "In the Garden," and "I Love to Tell the Story." Ruth had a high soprano, accurate in pitch; Phoebe a rich, true contralto; Josie a soft mezzo-soprano.

"You're a church-going man, ain't you?" Ruth said.

Elliott spun around to face her. "Yes, ma'am. All my life. My faith in Jesus Christ is very important to me."

Phoebe slapped the arms of the chair. "We always go to church on Sunday mornings. I expect you'll go with us, then. Would you drive us, young man?"

Elliott clasped his hands together between his knees. "Of course, I'd be pleased to do that."

"It's settled." Phoebe turned to Ruth and Josie. "Can't wait to see ole Hester's face when we pull up and pile out of the car, can you?" She snickered and directed her attention back to Elliott. "She's a proverbial news gatherer . . . can't keep her nose out of anything going on. She's no doubt the most dedicated gossip we got in the whole county. Her tongue wags at both ends. How she can put two and two together and come up with ten beats me." They all laughed. Phoebe hoisted herself out of the rocker. "Now, young man, around here, we hit the roost kinda early. You'll have to sleep on the sofa." She yawned and held the back of her hand over her mouth as she walked out of the room.

"Hope you don't mind," Ruth murmured.

"Nope. Not at all. I appreciate your hospitality."

Josie and Ruth found sheets and a pillow, a bath towel, and an extra blanket. They left Elliott to make his own bed.

* * *

"Goodnight, everyone!" Elliott called.

The steeply pitched staircase creaked as Josie ascended to her old sanctuary. The soft sounds of the opening and closing of drawers soon stopped, and the house became still. He lay back, wide awake, his arms locked under his head. A light, warm breeze drifted in through the open windows, stirring the curtains and carrying the sweet scent of the apple blossoms. The quietness and darkness of country life hit him. No streetlights, no automobiles, no noise except for an occasional baying of a dog somewhere in the distance, the hooting of an owl far off in the trees, and the piping of frogs at the spring.

Josie admitted to missing the tranquility of Bradford. He couldn't blame her. "Lord Jesus, stop the nonsense of worrying about the 'ifs.'" He squeezed his eyelids together, but almost immediately, they shot open. *She can't stay here. I don't want to lose her. I'll ask her tomorrow. I've no doubts about it and pray she won't, either.* With that decided, he flung his arm across his forehead and went to sleep, musing with pleasure about the trip home.

* * *

The small procession trooped into the house from church. "It won't take long to put dinner on the table," Ruth said.

"In that case, I'll get the car loaded," Elliott said. "Are your things all packed, Josie?"

She nodded and mounted the stairs to bring her luggage down for him. He crossed the parlor and walked out of the house with it. She went to the kitchen to help.

Ruth tied a limp flour sack backward over Josie's crisp crepe dress. "We think Elliott's lovely, but don't let his attention go to your head."

"Yes, don't be like your mother," Phoebe cautioned. "She was frivolous and reckless and rushed into a relationship without good judgment . . . made up her mind much too quickly. Ruthie and I don't want you running on without looking where you're going. You've not had much opportunity to see men as other girls do, and you haven't known your young man long enough to be sure he's the right one for you. Someday your prince charming will come along."

Josie stiffened. How did her spinster aunt think she knew so much about these things? She said, "Don't worry, I'll never get married unless I'm in love." She placed her index finger over her lips. "Shh, Elliott's coming."

He walked into the kitchen at that point. "I think we've got every-thing. As soon as we finish eating, we'll need to leave."

"We don't do a lot of cooking on Sundays anymore . . . just some-thing easy to prepare after church. Hope that's okay," Ruth said, wistfully.

"Yes, certainly. Your reception and kindness have been truly top-notch, ladies."

Ruth offered the prayer, they ate the light meal, and then it was over.

"We've got to get going soon," Elliott said. "We want to get home before dark."

"Of course," Ruth said. "We were glad you could come here, Elliott, and we're going to miss you, Josie. Hasn't been the same without you."

"I wish you didn't need to go back today," Phoebe said.

Josie stood, untied the sack's knot at her back waist, and smoothed the front of her dress. "Lots of things to do. School, for one."

Ruth extended her hand. "Elliott, be sure to stop in if you're ever this way again."

He pumped her hand. "Goodbye. It's been a privilege and a plea-sure. I've never spent a happier weekend."

They all converged at the car for their final farewells. Josie gave and received kisses and hugs from her aunts and promised them that, before too long, she would come again.

Elliott inserted the key, disengaged the clutch, and the engine growled to life. He waved and shifted the gears, and they pulled away.

Josie twisted about in the seat. "I hate goodbyes," she said. "Part of me wants to stay right here with them." She looked back. They were standing in the same spot at the road's edge, waving and touching their eyes.

"And the other part? Where does it want to be?" Elliott asked.

"Oh, I can't wait to get home to Father . . . and Vertie . . . and Nub." She turned around and composed herself.

Once he pulled onto the highway and headed west, Elliott increased his speed. He gave Josie a sideways glance.

Was he going to say something? Apparently not. "What do you think of my aunts? Do you like them?"

"I do."

"They like you, too. They're so different from Aunt Mae, though. To me, she's the absolute epitome of how an aunt should be."

"Oh? Explain that one."

"She laughs . . . even at herself. She has the gift of seeing the fun side to any situation."

"Ah, but your mother's sisters are dear little ladies."

"You're being kind. The truth is they're middle-aged, dowdy, opinionated, and set in their ways."

"But you love them, anyway." Elliott slowed, veered the car onto the side of the road, and cut the engine. He shifted in the seat to face her. "You're really grand—fine and guileless—an incredible woman."

She shook her head and furrowed her brow. "Actually, I'm very ordinary. You flatter me."

"Hey, that's how I see you. I've seen a number of women, but not one quite like you."

"I'm glad that's how you look at me. I don't to myself."

"Come on. I'm serious. You're not petty or selfish."

"You'll have to rethink your opinion of me. I can be as mean as the worst of them."

He burst out laughing and clutched her hand. "Listen. From the first time we talked . . . remember, at the Trianon? I knew you were different. These past few days helped me figure out what it is. It's accountability. You take it to heart." He paused. "What do you think about marrying a newspaper reporter who's adored you since the first moment he laid eyes on you? I love you, Josie. I want to spend the rest of my life with you."

She gasped. "Oh," she said, a hand going to her lips. "Is this a proposal of marriage?"

He laughed, turned his head, and gave her a slow grin. "Yep. That's what I'm asking. I keep daydreaming that you and I are already married. You know what I mean, don't you?"

"Kind of," Josie whispered.

"I think you love me. You may not realize it yet, but eventually, you will."

She stared at him. "Are you sure you want to do this—now?"

"Absolutely. I want to make some plans for our future together."

She breathed fast. "I'm dumbfounded. I don't know what to say."

"You say yes, that's what you say. Have I been wrong in believing you care for me in the same way I do you?"

She could have answered right away by saying, *You're not wrong, and yes, I'll marry you.* But she said, "Elliott, love is one thing, marriage is another."

"True. But listen, when I first saw you, I knew you were the woman for me. It must have been love at first sight. Don't you think we could be happy together? We'll have a home and a garden and kids. You love me, don't you? Say so if you do."

"Yes, Elliott, I do love you," she said.

"Whew, thank goodness. I was beginning to think you'd never say those words. Say them again, please."

"I love you . . . I've loved you for months and months. But—"

He put his fingers over her lips. "Sh-h! No 'buts.' Just say 'yes.'"

She shook her head. "I need some time."

"How much time?" He lightly stroked the underside of his chin with a knuckle.

"Well, I'm not quite sure right at the moment. One thing I want to do is talk with my father about your intentions. I trust he'll give his consent."

Elliott never took his gaze from her. "He already has."

"What? You've spoken to Father?"

"Yep."

"No kidding?" she asked, appalled. "What'd he say? Did he protest?"

"No. He was surprised, of course. But he gave us his blessing." He bent his head and kissed her on the cheek. With that, Elliott turned the key and started the engine.

"He did? But . . . I'm still in school . . . and what about your mother? I haven't even met her yet."

Elliott looked back over his left shoulder to check for traffic and pulled slowly onto the state road. "Can be taken care of easily enough."

"You won't accept any argument, will you?"

"Nope. My mind's made up. I don't even want to consider the possibility of losing you. The place you belong is with me, Josie. And you know it, too."

Chapter 17

"Listen to this," Josie said. "The management of Columbian Enameling has issued a statement . . . printed right here in *The Terre Haute Tribune.*"

Vertie came over to the kitchen table and sat opposite Josie. "What's it say? Read it." She braced an elbow on the tabletop and folded her knuckles beneath her jaw.

Josie crackled the newspaper, spreading it out before her. "'The Company exceedingly regrets any hardships or community business losses caused by the strike existing since March 23, 1935. Union employees called the strike to force the Company to discharge non-union employees—in other words, to adopt the closed shop. The Company is willing to operate its plant, using former employees, without discrimination against union members and with a change in wages, but only as an open shop without recognition of agreement. The above are the conditions under which the Company has operated continuously for thirty-three years.'"

"Land sakes! Pass me the paper," Vertie said. Josie slid it across to her.

The thump of heavy footfalls thundered from the back porch. Nub came in waving an envelope in the air. "Miss Josie's got some mail."

Josie bounded off her chair. "I do? Let's see." She turned it over curiously. "I don't recognize the handwriting." She studied the handsome monogram, the fine, slanted script. "It's from Elliott's mother." She dropped to the nearest chair. Her hands shook as she ripped open the flap with her forefinger.

Vertie took her time closing the paper and pushing it aside. "Elliott's mother?"

"Yes." Josie showed the return address written in flowing cursive on the back. "Look!"

"What's she want?"

Josie pulled out the beautiful cream-colored stationery and read the large, even writing. "'My dear Joselene, why don't you come over on Saturday, June fifteenth?' . . . She's invited me to Bloomington."

"Watch out," Nub warned. "When a young man takes his girl home to meet the mother, that boy's got something serious on his mind."

Josie creased the letter and fitted it back into the envelope. "What a perfectly charming way to invite me."

Vertie went to peer into the teakettle. She carried it to the sink and turned on the faucet to fill it. "Gotta be more to it than just meeting you, Miss Josie . . . that she'd write you an invitation."

Josie stood, her hands outstretched in front of her, palms up. "Vertie, please. She wanted to be proper. She's just being polite. Plain and simple."

Vertie took the now-filled kettle to the stove and switched on a coil burner. "Seems a might hoity-toity to me."

"How'll you get there?" Nub asked.

"Elliott'll take me, I suppose. It'll be exciting to have this to look forward to, won't it?"

They shrugged. "Maybe."

"You both sound awful. Neither one of you even knows the woman."

* * *

Elliott knocked on the Matthews's front door the Saturday morning of June fifteenth. "Hi," he said when Josie greeted him.

"Good morning. I'm all ready," Josie chirped as she stood in the open doorway.

"Wow! You . . . look—"

She checked her dress and shoes. "Is something wrong?"

"Oh, no . . . believe me."

"What do you think?"

He wiggled his eyebrows and smiled broadly. "*Ve-ry* nice."

"I'm glad you like my outfit." Josie had taken pains in choosing what she wore and had decided on a pink-and-green flowered crepe that boasted a round neckline and cap sleeves. The small green hat was lined with white, and she sported the locket Elliott had given her on Valentine's Day.

"Let's get started. No telling what the traffic will be like." He walked her to the passenger side of the car, opened the door, and stood with his arm bent on the top of the door. "I ought to tell you . . . warn you . . . Mother can be difficult at times. I've no idea about her mood today. She may be my mother, and I love her very much, but honestly, every once in a while, she aggravates me to no end."

Josie laughed. "You make your mother sound like some kind of shrew. She can't be *that* bad."

"You're too sweet . . . always looking for the best in people . . . one of the many reasons I love you." He stepped out of her way. "Climb in."

She got into the car. "Please don't look like a storm cloud all the way there."

At half past nine, they reached the Vinegar Hill district of Bloomington and the Craftsman bungalow with black shutters. Elliott escorted Josie into the house.

Lillian strutted into the room and dramatically looked Josie up and down as Elliott introduced her.

Josie smiled, held out her hand, and said, "Hello." She expected her hostess to at least reciprocate the greeting, but Lillian did not.

Instead, she whirled about to Elliott and asked point-blank, "*This* is the charmer?"

Elliott gave an exaggerated wink at Josie. "Yep. This is Joselene."

"Uh-huh! Come along," Lillian ordered. They followed her, and as they went, Elliott squeezed Josie's hand. His hand was cold to the touch. Was he signaling something? Was she more at ease than he was?

With a grand gesture, Lillian swung open the door to a sunny dining room. "Go on in." She rustled to a chair. "I'll sit here." She pointed—rings flashing on her long fingers—to the other end of the table. "Elliott, down there. Josie, your seat is here, beside me. We need to have ourselves a little chat and get acquainted."

Elliott snorted. "Hold on a minute." He picked up his chair and moved it to the side of the table. He grabbed his place setting and put it on the table across from Josie. "Now we can eat."

Lillian left them, came back with a platter of French toast and set it down, and disappeared again to return with a small white pitcher that she said was melted butter and a larger one of heated maple syrup. On a third trip, she brought out a dish full of sausage links. Then she took her seat.

"Shall we pray? Thank you, Lord, for this food. Bless it, we ask, to the nourishment of our bodies. Amen. I can't tell you how satisfying it is to finally meet you, Joselene . . . and you had a pleasant drive over from Terre Haute?" She poured coffee into their cups without ever looking at either of them.

Josie stirred sugar into the hot drink. "Yes, we did." She lifted her cup and took a sip. Had Lillian even bowed her head and closed her eyes when she prayed? She couldn't have.

Lillian, filling her own cup, was intent on the dark-colored liquid flowing from the steaming spout. "I'm sorry to learn about your mother. Heartbreaking, I know. Elliott told me. One never forgets her mother, does she? You must miss her horribly."

Josie hesitated a moment and swallowed hard. "I . . . do. We were very close. It's sad to lose someone you love dearly and be left to live with only memories." She drizzled syrup onto the French toast. "I'm finding that life rarely is what one thinks it will be."

Lillian put the coffee pot down on the sideboard and glanced away. "Indeed. Some people, when these kinds of unfortunate things happen to them, become bitter and angry. You don't seem to be."

Josie shook her head. "No, it's not my nature."

"Oh," Lillian said, and flattened her lips.

No one said another word, and they ate the rest of the meal in silence. Josie's ears rang with the awkward stillness, broken only by the ticking of an eight-day clock sitting high on a shelf above the buffet.

Lillian pushed her plate to the center and clasped her hands at the table's edge. She glared at Josie. "We have the rest of the morning to talk to some purpose. Let's go into the living room. I want to be comfortable when I hear what you two have in mind for the future. Don't worry about the dishes. I have all the time in the world to wash them and clean up the kitchen." She sprang to her feet, gave a dismissive wave of her hand, and left the table without another glance at either Elliott or Josie, leaving them to trail behind.

A chill ran up Josie's spine and she shuddered. *Lord, give me courage. Yea, though I walk through the valley of the shadow of death, I will fear no evil, for Thou art with me. Thy rod and Thy staff they comfort me.*

Elliott guided Josie to the sofa. He pulled over the leather hassock to sit beside her, and stretched his long legs out in front of him, balancing on his heels, showing his socks.

Lillian sat erect in the wingback chair, like a British aristocrat. "I can imagine how proud you are, Joselene."

"Begging your pardon?"

"Come on, little missy. I'm talking about latching onto Elliott. I had hoped that when the time came he considered marriage, he would choose a girl from here in Bloomington—certainly not one from Terre

Haute, and especially not one with questionable lineage."

Josie flinched. Her face burned, and she cleared her throat. She clamped her icy hands together in her lap to keep them from shaking.

"Mom!" Elliott interjected. "Don't be mean."

Lillian sat stiffly tilted back and jutted out her chin. She said in a voice like stone, "Tell me the plans you've made."

"We haven't made any. We've barely mentioned marriage."

Lillian pinched the bridge of her nose. "Is that the honest-to-goodness truth?"

He rolled his eyes. "Yes, it is."

"Well, fine and dandy, because I need time. Heavens, I don't know what to think right at the moment. I've had you for myself all these years, Elliott. And she's just met you. Nobody should ever come between a mother and her son. Never . . . so, Josie, are you going to begrudge me my little slice of Elliott?"

"Mom, please. I won't have you talk to her like that," he said sharply.

Lillian's face hardened. "Son, what were you thinking? If you go ahead and marry her, she'll expect your loyalties to be to her."

Josie's breath came quick and shallow. She trembled. She shut her eyes as tears threatened. It was more than she could bear. How could she possibly escape this humiliation? She rose unsteadily to her feet and faced Elliott and his mother. "I'm . . . I'm terribly sorry . . . I . . . I need some fresh air."

He clapped his hands to his knees and immediately got to his feet. "I do, too. This is no place for us. A walk sounds just the thing. Let me show you the Indiana University campus. It's quite something to see." He held out his hand for her. She took it, never looking back at Lillian, and together they left the room and the house as quickly as they could. On the sidewalk at the curb, he said, "Don't say anything yet."

She turned to him, almost in tears. Say anything? She couldn't have spoken if she'd wanted to.

"Come this way." Elliott led her across the street and they walked several blocks. "I'm so sorry. You didn't deserve that. Mother will rage and grumble for a while, but in the end, she won't be any more unhappy than she already is."

They turned the corner onto Kirkwood Avenue. He stopped in the middle of the sidewalk, took her hand, and pulled her close to himself.

Was he going to kiss her? No, he didn't. She was disappointed.

Then he took her in his arms. "I love you, Josie. I've been in love with you for a long time."

She let her weight rest against him and relaxed. "I love you, Elliott."

"Then say yes, you'll marry me."

"But . . . what about your mother?"

Elliott frowned. "You're marrying me, not her."

She shook her head. "I wish it were that easy. We don't want to make her too miserable."

"Mother is never happy—about anything. It isn't her nature."

Josie made a face. "Oh, how pitiful."

"You're right."

"Isn't there something I can do or say to please her?"

"Nope. 'Fraid not."

"What are we going to do?"

"Tell you what, for now, let's not hang around here any longer. Let's leave for Terre Haute."

"You mean, just go without saying goodbye to your mother? We can't do that."

He nodded. "Of course we can. It might be better for us to stay away. Just send her a note if you want to. We need to get home." He took her arm, and together they walked slowly back to where he'd left the car.

* * *

Hundreds of strikers—rough men, young and old, jostling and shouting in raucous voices—had created a picket line on the lawn of the Columbian Enameling and Stamping Company. In addition, sympathizers and curious town folks milled about the periphery of the major action. The scene was a beehive of activity, a press photographer snapping picture after picture, capturing the chaos.

Elliott found a safe spot on Beech Street away from the circus of people gathered outside the company's brick offices and listened as a man spoke in a loud voice. He thought the man sounded like Alex Heywood. *Yeah, you probably engineered this uprising, you Benedict Arnold. What better way to endear yourself to the union? You'll get your just dues one day.* Though Elliott strained to hear, he couldn't distinguish all the words as they came and went, but every time the voice peaked, a boom of applause ensued.

Security was tight. Word leaked out the plant had hired armed guards to protect the property from the protestors, and city police restricted people's access to the area.

* * *

A sound jarred Josie to wakefulness. Had the telephone rung? She wasn't sure. The noise had blended into a dream she'd been having. Dazed with sleep, she raised her head a fraction from the pillow. Yes, it was the phone. She bolted upright, her pulse hammering, reached for the wind-up clock on the bedside table, and blinked. Not even five o'clock. Bad news. It always was when a call came that early—and on a Sunday. It jangled again and again.

Her father's bedroom door opened and his shuffling footsteps passed her door and went down the steps and across the hallway to the phone. She swept her legs from under the sheets, slipped off the bed, and put on her robe. What could the call be about? Her stomach churned.

"Hello?" Landon said.

She tiptoed down the stairs. On the bottom step, she sat, drew up her legs, and wrapped her arms around them. From where she sat, the voice on the other end sounded like a metallic rattle.

Landon cupped his palm over the mouthpiece. "Charles Gorby," he whispered to her.

"The plant president?" she mouthed back.

Landon nodded. "What is it?" he asked into the phone. "Yes, I'd been informed a crowd had gathered, but the police were there. They did what? . . . Any damage? . . . Any injuries?" He talked a little more and then said "goodbye." He stared at the receiver for a long moment before slamming it down on its cradle, making it jangle. He put the phone back on the small table and clenched his hands into fists.

Josie clutched at her heart. "What's happened?" She pulled herself up.

Landon gripped her upper arms hard and held her still. "You must stay at the house today. I don't want you going out any farther than the front porch."

Josie shivered and stood stock-still, open-mouthed, and gawked at her father. "What's wrong?"

"Vandalism at the Stamping Mill. Management announced that when the plant reopened, it would be with non-union labor . . . and . . . they increased the number of armed guards as a precaution against retaliation. A mob of strikers and sympathizers formed outside the main building. Police were able to keep things under control until early this morning, when the rioters broke through the barriers and forced entry into the offices. They shattered windows, demolished the telephone exchange, and wrecked the interior of the company's office." He shook his head.

Josie covered her mouth. A sick feeling settled in the pit of her stomach. "Why would grown men destroy the property of the place that hires them?"

"Don't know. Mob hysteria? Last night had a full moon. Maybe it can make a sane person act in strange ways."

Chapter 18

Josie pushed open the back door and burst into the kitchen. "I'm home!" Her raincoat dribbled water onto the floor. She shrugged out of it and threw off the rain cap, draped the wet garments over a chair, and toed off her shoes. "Vertie, where are you?" she called.

The housekeeper marched into the room through the swinging door. "Land sakes. You're soaking wet."

Josie spun around. "I got caught in a downpour. The rain's trickled under the collar of my slicker and run down my back. I'm drenched."

"Get upstairs and out of every stitch of clothing, or you'll catch a death of cold."

Josie shivered. "I won't be long." She pushed open the door and came back into the kitchen. "Why's the table arranged with three place settings? Is Mark coming this evening?"

"No. Mr. Alex Heywood."

"Alex Heywood?" Josie shrilled. "What does *he* want?"

Vertie leaned forward, touched her index finger to her lips, and whispered, "Sh-h. He'll hear you." She indicated with a jerk of her head.

"You mean he's already here?"

She nodded and glanced at the clock. "He arrived . . . oh . . . about ten minutes ago. I sent him to wait in the library."

"Oh, no!"

"Yeah, you'd better go and say a word of greeting and make him welcome before you go upstairs."

But Josie didn't. Instead, she flashed to her room, stripped off her soppy clothes, and got into dry ones. She descended the stairs to the hallway, where the Oriental rug covering the entry muffled the footfalls of her patent leather slippers. She froze in the library's doorway, a wave of nausea storming her stomach. She put her hand to her heart and bit her lower lip, all the while staring at Alex.

He stood at the drop-leaf table, bent over Landon's stack of manila folders. He pulled one out and opened it. He turned over a few pages and read. Shaking his head, he closed the file and slipped it back in its proper place. Then he drew out another one and flipped through the contents.

The distasteful scene made her skin prickle. She shuddered. Elliott's suspicions about the man's lack of integrity were confirmed. Her fists clenched, and her face grew hot. She took a deep breath and let it out, then cleared her throat.

Alex looked up, saw her standing in the opening, slapped shut the folder he'd been reading, and shoved it aside, all in one motion. For several seconds, they glared at each other, then his mouth curved in a smile, while the veins in his neck bulged and pulsated. "There you are."

"What're you doing here?" Her heart beat wildly.

"What do you mean? Your father invited me to dinner tonight." He crossed his arms and stood spraddle-legged. "Didn't he tell you? I was told by your housekeeper to come on in here and make myself comfortable."

Her hands were tightly clamped at her side. "Father might have asked you to dinner, but he never gave you permission to snoop through his folders."

Unruffled, Alex snorted. "I wasn't, as you say, 'snooping.'"

Josie gaped at him. "Excuse me, Alex, but I'm not blind. Those papers are my father's private property."

"No-o-o, they *belong* to the Columbian Enameling and Stamping Company. I work there, too, remember? When I find myself in a position to take advantage of opportunities, I capitalize on it."

"You're despicable—"

"Aw, come on, now. Be nice, Josie. Be nice."

She wanted to move away from the door—away from him. But he took two steps nearer and grabbed hold of her shoulders. The pressure of his fingers was hard against her flesh. "Get your hands off me, Alex!" She flung her arms, breaking his grip, staggered backward and stood, one hand over her heart, the other clinging to the back of a chair. "You're a skunk, Alex. I thought you were my friend—and Father's. He thinks you're working to bring a peaceful resolution to the strike. Here I find you prying into his files. I think you're using his friendship to learn the company's thoughts and plans regarding the labor controversy. Why, Alex, why would you do such a thing?"

He rocked back on his heels, plunged his hands into his pockets, and smirked. "You muddle-headed thing. It's a business matter. I was told to do this. For your information, a peaceful resolution to the issue is subject to interpretation. Can't you see that what I'm doing is to benefit the workers? Common sense says the plant must be unionized."

"No, Alex! How can you think that, let alone say it?"

"Have you forgotten, I'm a union steward? I have to work hard to right a terrible injustice. You're looking at things from the wrong direction."

"You've betrayed many people's trust."

"Ask me if I care."

"Shame on you. Why would you go against the Stamping Mill's policies, treat my father as a friend, and at the same time knife him in the back?"

"Aw, now. I wouldn't put it that way."

"You're incorrigible, Alex. A sneaky, conniving person. The scum of the earth. There're no words low enough to describe you. You're asking honest, hard-working people to break faith with the company that hires them. Are you doing this for money, or because all you care about is advancing yourself? What's the union promising you, anyway, that you would sell out your principles?"

He tapped a knuckle to his chin. "Don't make a scene, Josie. It's unbecoming. You better not think of any crackbrained notions to—"

"To what?"

He ran his tongue under his lower lip. "Maybe tell someone. No one would believe you, even if you told them. Everyone sees you as an illiterate country rube—someone who wouldn't be able to recognize the difference between legal papers and the funny papers."

Josie swallowed hard, did an about-face, and walked out of the room. In the entry, she met her father. "Alex is waiting for you," she snapped.

"Thanks for showing him in," Landon said.

If she'd had her way, she'd be kicking him out the door, pronto. The creep! He gave her the heebie-jeebies. Nothing about him was honorable or decent. Elliott *had* been right about him all along.

Josie charged into the kitchen. "I can't believe Father asked that weasel to eat with us. We've prepared a table for ourselves in the presence of our enemy. Unbelievable!"

Vertie pulled a large, heavy platter of crispy fried chicken from the oven and set it on top of the stove. "Who're you jibber-jabbering about?"

"Alex Heywood. He's just proved to me he's a traitor to the Stamping Mill . . . and father. Anything you want me to help you with?"

"Would you scrape those mashed potatoes into a bowl? I'll finish up this salad and then make some creamy gravy." Vertie poured hot bacon grease and vinegar over the washed leaf lettuce and thinly sliced onions, and tossed the fixings. "Did ya hear the big news story of the day?"

"What is it?"

"On May twenty-seventh, President Roosevelt's NIRA was declared null and void."

The two eyed each other. "Who could do that?"

"The Supreme Court."

Josie licked the potato remains from the pan. "How?"

"Someone sued the government . . . and won." Vertie blended flour into the hot meat drippings and slowly added milk.

Josie tipped her head to one side. "Who on earth'd have enough nerve to do that?"

"Some company in New York called Schechter Poultry Corporation." Vertie filled the gravy boat. "Everything's ready. I think I'll go ahead and leave. I would like to be home before it gets any worse out there. Help me get the food on the dining room table."

The men came to dinner, and the meal took its leisurely course. Alex gave no hint of his earlier conversation with Josie in either words or manner.

Landon busied himself with buttering a slice of bread. "Rumor is, Alex, that you know the reason so many employees feel encouraged to join the union."

"Really? *Me?* I've not been privy to that scuttlebutt, but I'll be truthful and aboveboard with you, Landon. The question as to *why* so many are joining the union has never even come to my mind."

Josie stopped eating and stared at Alex. She rolled her eyes. "I need to be excused." She coughed into her napkin, wiped her mouth, and rose. "All of a sudden I'm sick to my stomach."

Chapter 19

Thursday afternoon, five days after the riot at the Columbian Enameling and Stamping Company, Josie relaxed in the swing on the Matthews's front porch. An oversized book laid open in her lap, and she slowly turned its pages.

"Josie."

Startled, her head snapped up. "Elliott, where did you come from? Golly, don't you ever take any time off?"

He sat beside her. "Not when so much is going on in the city of Terre Haute. What are you reading?"

"Oh, not reading—studying." She fluttered the pages under her thumb. "Art Appreciation class. Paul Cezanne." She closed the book and held it for him to see the front cover, and then reached down and placed it on the floor. "I'm not sure I appreciate his work, though."

"He's a bit of a puzzle, isn't he?" Elliott perched his hat on his knee. "I think he used some Impressionist's techniques. However, if I remember right, most art historians don't identify him with Impressionism. Not to change the subject, but is your father home?"

She shook her head. "He and Mark are at the plant, I think . . . or maybe they're at the office. Anyway, care for some lemonade? I can put ice in it, if you want."

"Sounds mighty refreshing. I'll take it good and cold, please."

Josie hurried to the kitchen and returned in short order with a tall glass. "I made it myself this morning. I figured someone would come along and need something cool to quench his thirst."

Elliott took it from her, jiggled the cubes, and guzzled half of it in what looked like a single mouthful. He gestured with the glass. "Just the way I like it, too. Strong on sugar, short on lemon." He winked at her, rattled the cubes again, and finished off the rest of the drink in one long swig. He smeared the wetness from his lips with the back of a hand, bent over, and put the empty glass on the porch's floor.

Josie leaned forward, poised to stand if necessary. "Want some more? Be glad to get it if you do."

"No, thanks. It did hit the spot, though." He straightened himself, blew out a long breath, and let his gaze shift back to her. "I wonder if Alex Heywood had anything to do with the brawl last Sunday. When I covered the goings-on for the paper, it sounded like he was the one goading the people. You gotta admit he has a natural instinct for leading."

"Yes, but what kind of leader?" She shook her head. "When I caught him red-handed rummaging through Father's files, I didn't want to believe such evil of him. He threatened me if I told anyone about it. He's the awfullest person."

"No kidding? Remember I warned you about him a good while ago."

"Yes, I remember. But at that time, I didn't want to accept the things you were trying to tell me."

"Your father mentioned someone had been pilfering with his papers. Lawyers have a sixth sense about that and can almost smell if someone's been tampering with their stuff."

Her eyebrows drew down in a scowl. "Alex deceived us, and I hate deception. We thought we knew all about him because there seemed so little to know, but I realize now he's not the kind of man one knows."

"He presents himself as a likeable enough guy, I guess."

She leaned toward Elliott. "Course, he did his best to be liked, too. He had a charming façade . . . pleasant and witty."

"He's not the person most people think he is."

She looked into Elliott's face. "You're right. You didn't trust him from the start. I had a gut feeling about him but couldn't put a name to it. Priscilla considered him a friend. I doubt he would have been a loyal one, though, 'cause you couldn't depend on him, although Winnie may argue about that." She shrugged. "I doubt he could ever make a woman happy."

He grinned. "How's that?"

"Because Alex is so narcissistic. He's in love with only one person—himself. He relies a lot on his looks and charisma to get himself out of messes. He's ambitious, but really—"

"He's an opportunist, I'll say that much."

"The vandalism at the plant doesn't make sense."

Elliott was silent for a moment. "It never will, either, because it's about people—people on both sides of the issue who want their way, each pushing their own agenda. The union complains that the company evades paying city taxes." He held up an index finger, and then two fingers. "Second, they believe it exploits the workers." Holding up three fingers, he said, "And probably the biggest complaint is that they believe the plant is antagonistic to a closed shop."

Josie tilted her head. "Hmm, does it pay city taxes?"

He rubbed his eyes with his thumb and forefinger. "No."

"Yet it had county as well as city police officers at the scene after the rampage?"

Elliott nodded, drew the back of his hand across his forehead, and said, "You, Joselene Grace Matthews, sound like a lawyer."

* * *

The next Saturday morning, Elliott opened the kitchen door of his mother's home. "Morning, Mom."

Lillian slowly lowered her coffee cup. There followed a moment of astonished silence. "What a surprise! How is it I'm favored with a visit for the second time in a month?"

"What? Not happy to see me?"

"Of course I am, silly boy. I'm just taken aback a little, that's all. I'm finishing my breakfast. Had any?"

He shook his head. "Not yet. Got up too early. Was in a big hurry to get here."

"Couldn't wait to leave Terre Haute, huh?" She rose and headed to the stove. "Want something?"

He pulled out a chair at the table and sat. "Sure."

"Coffee's ready," Lillian said as she got out the black iron skillet and fried three strips of bacon. "How do you like your eggs? Soft or hard or scrambled?"

"Over easy."

She broke two eggs into the drippings, let them sizzle, gently flipped them, and then slipped them onto a plate. She set the plateful before him. "Eat up," she ordered.

Elliott did. "Thanks, Mom, you're the best," he said between mouthfuls.

Lillian sat at the table across from him and from time to time sipped her coffee. With a teaspoon, she traced lines on the tablecloth with the tip of the handle. "What's the real reason you came? You didn't come just to have breakfast with me."

He gulped some coffee. "Can't fool you, can I? . . . You're right. Now that you've had some time to think about Josie, I came to find out what you thought about her . . . to see if you'd changed your mind." He shoveled another forkful of egg into his mouth.

Lillian glared at him. "Why should I think any differently about her?"

"Listen to you, playing the sly one."

Lillian hooked a finger through the cup's handle, drank the last of her coffee, and focused her attention on the dregs. "She's . . . simple . . . with no outstanding qualities except for a certain degree of attractiveness. She lacks polish."

The room became quiet. Elliott stopped all action of eating. "What—?"

"Son," Lillian reached across the table to pat Elliott's hand with her own, "how can you think you love her, or consider marrying her . . . or that you'll even be happy with her? I've prayed for you every day . . . that God would send a suitable mate for you . . . a woman worthy of the Jacobson name . . . and you bring *her* here. You can't be in love with her."

He brushed her hand away. "Mom, I am." He pushed his plate aside and glowered at her. "It so happens that I'm very happy with her. And, for your information—not that it'll satisfy you—I love her for so many reasons . . . she's wholesome and not pretentious in any way."

Lillian shook her head. "You don't belong with someone like her. How am I supposed to hold my head up when I'm with my friends? Your wife needs to be exceptional, and *that* young woman is anything but. She's no prize, I can tell you. You won't know contentment with her . . . later on."

"You're wrong. Josie's exactly the kind of woman I want as a wife."

"Someday, and I hope it's sooner than later, you'll understand I just want you to be happy."

"But I am. In fact, I'm more than happy."

Lillian got up to refill their coffee cups. "You need someone who's more our type. It's been an uphill battle for *me* to think of an appropriate match for *you*, and Josie isn't the kind of woman I'd choose for you."

"Mom, the choice is not yours to make, but mine."

She poured the steaming and fragrant coffee, came back to the table, and sat. "How hard would it be for you to . . ." She fell silent, swallowed, and began again. "Would you do something for me?"

He patted her arm. "Do you think there's anything I wouldn't do?"

"Remember, I'm asking for your sake."

He brought his cup to his lips and peeked over its rim. "What is it?"

Lillian's hands trembled. She picked up a morsel of toast and began to pulverize it between her fingers and thumb. "Will you break off with her?"

"What?" He smacked his cup down so hard that some of the liquid splashed out. "You have no right to ask that."

"I think I do, because you can do better, Elliott. Perhaps you haven't reflected adequately upon the unsuitability of her."

"Ish kabibble, Mom. Josie's completely befitting." He shook his head and thumped the table with his fist. "No, I won't give her up."

"Why? I only ask because . . . because you're so very dear to me. I don't want to see you make a huge mistake and throw away any chances for success in this life. It seems to me the two of you are moving too fast. Give yourselves more time. Surely you're aware of how her background goes against all the rules of our code."

"Yours, not mine."

"If you marry her, you'll regret it as long as you live. The things that may not matter to you now will be so much more important in a few years. All I can say is, she better be a decent person."

"Mom, I wouldn't be serious about her if she weren't."

"Well, look at her parents. I wouldn't be surprised if Josie's morals were rather loose. That kind of behavior often runs in families. You deserve a girl who's got . . . social status . . . and sophistication . . . and money. The Jacobson family has always maintained a high level of respectability. Frankly, she would not make a proper Jacobson wife. Just decide to wait for someone else to come along."

"You're talking nonsense. Josie's a fine Christian woman—beautiful inside and out. No one can be any better than she is. She brings out the best in me. With her by my side, I believe I can do anything. I'm fortunate to have met her. So, you're telling me to give her up? Unthinkable!"

"It's just that I'm not able to sit back and watch you make a mess of your life." Lillian sucked in her breath sharply. "You've not listened to one solitary reason I've given. Okay, then, have it your way. Go ahead and make your plans with her. I think you're being foolish, Elliott. Keep everything low key, because I guarantee you'll be sorry later on. I don't want people prying with a lot of questions about what happened. Josie's still got her schooling to finish. And, you never know . . . things can be different. Just you wait and see."

"Here I came all this way hoping you'd give us your blessing."

"Come now, you couldn't expect me to do that if you turn your back on me—the one who raised you, your own mother? If you can settle it with your conscience to ignore what I want for you, and if you think you can support a wife, well and good. But I don't think so."

Elliott got to his feet and glowered at her. "Spare me any more of your comments. I'm sick and tired of your carping about her." He turned, let out a sigh, and left her without saying another word, closing the door behind him.

In the past, her look would've been enough for him to rethink the issue. Not this time. In the past, she would've accused him of abandoning her, and he knew her habit was to load on the guilt and leave him with the impression he'd committed some unspeakable crime by not wanting to please her. Not today.

How much time had he wasted acquiescing to her wishes? He admitted that part of the reason he took the reporter's job in Terre Haute was to escape her incessant demands. The time was ripe for him to refuse to give in to her.

Chapter 20

July arrived, indescribably hot and muggy. The whole Farrington's Grove neighborhood on South Sixth Street smelled of summer.

Mae had driven over from Indianapolis and showed up at the Matthews's home late in the morning on Independence Day. She now clattered alongside Josie in the kitchen. "The heat is so oppressive in here. I'm glad that oscillating fan is going." It rattled away on the counter's top.

Josie took a loaf of American cheese out of the refrigerator, set it on the table, and sliced through it. "It doesn't seem like it's cooling anything, though . . . just pushing around the same old steamy air."

"What're the plans for today?" Mae stood at the table smearing softened butter on slices of bread for grilled sandwiches.

"Priscilla, Mark, Elliott, and I are going swimming this afternoon."

"Which place?" Mae went to the dish cabinet to collect the table service.

"Izaak Walton Beach."

"All the way over in West Terre Haute? Isn't she worried about contracting polio from an old lake? Why not go to the Fairbanks Park municipal pool?"

"It's closed . . . developed a crack. Somebody said the earth moved— whatever that means. Later we're to join you, Clarinda, and Father for a picnic at Deming Park, and then go to Memorial Stadium for the city's annual fireworks display. We've already got the tickets."

Mae layered the buttered bread and cheese on a heated cast iron griddle. "We'll be busy, for sure. Is there a picnic basket we can use?"

"Yes, Vertie found one . . ." Josie removed a metal tray from the freezing compartment in the refrigerator, manhandled the ice cubes out of it, and emptied them onto a kitchen towel. "Out in the garage . . . the neatest thing . . . shaped like a basket, and looks like one, too, with a lithographed wicker design. The thing's really made of tin. Neat, huh? I think Nub stored some of his tools there. Vertie's scrubbed it clean." She pounded the ice cubes with a mallet, scooping up the chips into two tall tumblers. "What d'you want to drink?"

"Coca-Cola, if there is any." Mae's attention was on the sandwiches. She lifted a corner of one. "Crispy enough for you?" Not waiting for a response, she flipped them both.

Josie went to the pantry, returned with two glass bottles, and opened them. She poured the carbonated beverage into the ice-filled glasses and waited for the foam to subside.

Mae brought over the grilled cheese. She sat and jiggled the glass before she took a gulp of the cola. "Mmm, so refreshing." She set the glass down. "Now, tell me about your visit to Bloomington. What's Elliott's mother like? Is she nice?"

"Umm, no-o-o. She's awfully self-centered and utterly selfish, and, well, basically an unreasonable person with a very sharp tongue. The way she looked at me was plum scary. Honestly, she's about as lovable as a timber rattlesnake."

Mae, cutting her sandwich in two, stopped in the act. "Huh, that sounds frightening." She picked up a half and took a bite. "She may be a lot different when you know her."

"I feel sorry for Elliott. She makes life terribly trying for him. Her smiles seemed fake . . . plastered on. I decided a cheerful expression's physically impossible for her. This is gonna sound awful, but . . . well, it seemed her lips were pursed so hard . . . as though someone had sewn around her mouth and pulled the threads too tight. Truthfully, I think she's a vinegar-tongued, soulless ogre who sits up all night because she's too mean to sleep." Josie shut her eyes and shuddered.

Mae furrowed her brow. "That's horrifying!"

"I know. May God forgive me for even saying it. Lillian isn't capable of being happy, only of being less disgruntled. Those words are Elliott's, not mine. To be totally honest, I was absolutely humiliated by her."

"My gracious, and what does the dreadful woman look like?"

Josie jammed the bits of cheesy crusts into her mouth, and with her cheeks still bulging, said, "It was weird, but there was something familiar about her . . . the eyes or mouth . . . something reminded me of Vertie." She finished drinking her cola, got up, and took her dishes to the sink. After she rinsed them, she spun around to face her aunt. "Only in a way, mind you. Maybe I'm just imagining things. Who knows? Golly, I better get ready." She headed toward the swing door.

"Wait an hour after you eat so you won't suffer with stomach cramps!" Mae yelled.

In her room, Josie pulled on a green-and-blue striped bathing suit, lowered a multi-colored cotton dress over it, and crammed her bare feet into a pair of espadrilles.

She moseyed over to the Van Allens's and knocked. Mark opened the door. "We're all ready."

The four piled into his Buick and started for the lake. Twenty minutes later, they crossed the Wabash River and pulled into the lot of the Izaak Walton Beach. They took off their shoes at the car and walked gingerly on the hot, loose, dirty sand, shuffling their way to the water's edge.

Elliott rushed off. "I'm gonna jump in." His voice died away as he plunged into the water and swam across the silky expanse.

Josie's gaze fixed on his broad back, the sheen of the mid-afternoon water behind him. He was everything she'd wanted in a husband: strong, educated, and handsome—but most important of all, he was a Christian who could share her faith in God. *You've blessed me, Lord, by sending Elliott into my life. He'll comfort and cherish me all his life.*

He came up out of the small waves as smoothly as a seal, his dark hair flung back like a mane. "Come on!" he shouted. "Feels great!"

Josie wet her feet in the shifting, sinking, watery sand and waded out until she stood knee-deep in the water. She proceeded farther out until she was submerged to her chin. The deeper water took her breath away, it was so cold. She took in a big gulp of air, slid under the surface, and pushed off from the bottom, propelling herself through the water.

At half past four, the swimmers emerged, flushed, tired, and sunburned. With towels hung about their shoulders, they climbed into Mark's car. He drove east on Ohio Boulevard toward Deming Park and cruised around until they found Landon, Clarinda, and Mae Anise waving for him to stop. He eased the car onto the grass and shut off the motor.

"Why don't you guys move another table over here?" Clarinda suggested. "We need more room. It's simply too hot to be so scrunched up." They did, and she covered the two with a too-short flower-print oilcloth.

Mark, Elliott, and Josie carried the sliced ham, potato and bean salads, sweet pickles, tomato wedges, and stuffed eggs from Landon's Chrysler. Priscilla carried the chocolate cake, licking her fingers free of the too-soft frosting. Plates, metal tumblers, and silverware were taken out of the tin basket and arranged on the tables by Clarinda and Mae Anise.

Casually, Elliott and Josie eased away from the others and ambled toward Mark's car to get a blanket. He caught her hand and held it as they walked.

"I love you so much," he said. "Do you love me?"

"A nice time for you to find out."

"Are you going to marry me?"

She grinned at him and nodded. "Yes. Did you forget?"

He stopped and turned her around to face him. "Course not. No regrets?"

"No regrets."

"Happy?"

"I'm goofy with happiness . . . it's enough to scare a person. In fact, 'happy' doesn't correctly express how I feel. *Ecstatic* is a better word."

He quirked his eyebrows and gazed at her with that special gleam in his eyes. "What did I ever do to attract a woman like you?"

Josie's heart beat faster. "Apparently the right thing."

"That's good . . . because I have no idea what I'd do without you."

She nudged him. "They're waiting for us."

"Oh, yeah. The very first time I saw you, I said, 'Self, there's a gal you want to know.'"

She chuckled. "You say so now."

"Hey, I said it then, too. Not that I was in love with you. But I had been praying for a wife, and there you were . . . right in front of me . . . at your father's door."

They reached Mark's car. Elliott opened the trunk, turned to Josie, and looked into her eyes. "I'd like to announce our engagement before we eat. Is that all right with you?"

"I feel only pleasure and pride that you want to do that. What do you think they'll say?"

He shrugged. "We'll soon find out." He reached for the blanket, took it out of the trunk's cavity, and slammed the lid.

"Father certainly was agreeable. I'm relieved about that. Your mother's reaction was disappointing. I was so hoping she'd like me. Our news could have been exciting."

"Honey, it *is* exciting," he said. "We're going to be married. I'm sorry I can't afford to give you a diamond right now."

"Elliott, I know what your intentions are, and so will everyone else in a little while."

"You're my girl. I love you and always will, Josie. Josie? Yoo-hoo. Joselene Grace. Where are you?"

"Huh? Oh, sorry. I got lost in a dream world for a minute."

"I could tell by the look in your eyes. Where were you? You were smiling."

She touched his arm. "I'm too embarrassed to tell."

"Aww, don't be. I'm your future husband."

"I imagined I was already Mrs. Elliott Randolph Jacobson—loved, cared for, and kept happy as no other woman has been in this world before. We owned a cute little house with a garden, and a yard where our babies could play and make mud pies."

"Wow! All that in a few moments?"

She smiled. "Uh-huh."

"Amazing. One day it won't be a daydream, but a reality." He bent and kissed her gently.

"Hurry up, you two!" Priscilla called. "We want to sit down. You're taking forever. What're you two talking about?"

Elliott and Josie reached the others, unfolded the cover, and spread it on the grass under a sycamore tree. "You'll soon find out." He took a table knife and tapped its handle against the green-glass juice jar full of tea. *Tink-tink-tink.* He raised his hands for silence. The others stopped talking and gave him their attention. "Ladies and gentlemen," he said, in an announcer's voice. "I'd like to make an announcement." Josie came to stand by his side. He put his arm about her and drew her close. She glanced up at him, and he winked at her. "I have asked this beautiful, wonderful young woman to be my wife."

"What did she say?" Priscilla asked.

Elliott lifted a hand and scratched his eyebrow with a thumb. "The marvelous thing is, she's said yes. I'm pretty pumped, I confess. We just wanted to share this news with you."

The others exploded with cheers and gathered around the two, shaking Elliott's hand and patting his back and hugging Josie. With the notice duly given and the food blessed, the holiday outdoor meal began.

Landon loaded up his plate and sat on the attached bench of the rustic table. "I haven't eaten outdoors in a long time." After the meal, he rubbed his hands together. "Anyone want some ice cream?" He looked around at everyone's face.

Priscilla's head went up. "Where? Is someone selling it here?"

"I'm not talking about *buying*. I'm talking about *making*. Everything we need is in my car."

"We're going to make it?"

"Yes, Priscilla, we sure are. Mae has concocted the custard base, and there's a huge block of ice in my trunk under a heavy rug."

"And how long will it take us?" she grumbled.

"Oh, about a half-hour to three-quarters of one. Depends on us," Landon said.

"Sounds like fun," offered Elliott.

"It'd be a perfect way to cool off on a hot afternoon," Mark said. He and Elliott went to the Chrysler and carted everything back.

Mae dumped the thick, soupy mixture into the gleaming metal freezer can, dropped the dasher in place, and fitted the almost-filled canister into the wooden bucket. "Good. Just the right amount," she said. "It needs to have plenty of room to freeze, or it'll be grainy."

Elliott began cracking the block of ice with a ball-peen hammer. Mark shoveled handfuls of chips all around it.

"I'll go first," Priscilla said. "It'll be easy enough." She knelt at the freezer and cranked furiously.

"Whoa. Slow down," Landon said. "Tell you what. Let's lift the bucket up to the table. Gets too hard on the legs as well as the back if we squat very long."

They all stood in a semicircle, added ice and salt when necessary, and took turns with the crank. The spinning canister grinding in the icy water was the only sound. When the concoction hardened and the cranking became more difficult, Mark finished up.

Mae Anise sat at the opposite end of the table and Josie joined her. "I can tell you're happy. Women in love always show it in their faces. And you have an aura of such joy about you, you simply glow." She smiled and patted Josie's arm.

Elliott chipped off a chunk of ice and plunked it into his glass of tea. "Does anyone else want some for a glass before I sit down?" No one responded. He took a big swig before he sat.

Priscilla dug out the bowls and spoons. "Hasn't there been enough time for the ice cream to ripen?"

"Hardly," said Landon. However, he unpacked the freezer and scooped up the ice cream.

Clarinda cut generous portions of the cake and placed a wedge inside each bowl. They ate until the container was empty. Clarinda collected the odds and ends of the meal. Mae shook out the tablecloth and blanket, folded them, and stuffed them into the car.

Landon, carrying the picnic basket to the car, tilted his head back and surveyed the curve of the western horizon. Armadas of creamy white clouds had given way to dark ones, now gathering and advancing. "Don't like the granite coloring of the sky over there," he indicated with a jerk of his head. "A storm's brewing."

A low rumble of thunder sounded in the distance. "Maybe a shower will bring us some relief from the heat and humidity," Mae said.

The two younger couples reached the sanctuary of Mark's car as the rain lashed down. They frantically rolled up the windows, the downpour battering the roof, pelting the windshield, spattering and splashing the glass, and spiraling downward in streaming rivulets that obscured their vision.

Mark inserted the key and the engine churned to life. He switched on the wipers and drove out of the park. As they made their way west on Ohio Boulevard and then north onto Brown Avenue, the sky lightened, the rain slackened, turned to a drizzle, and then stopped—all in a matter of minutes and a few blocks.

They rolled down the windows and a blast of cooler air emitting the scent of steamy cement filled the car. Grateful for the breeze, Josie allowed it to rush across her sweaty face and blow through her hair.

With the cars parked at the stadium, the small procession trailed to the entrance marked for ticket holders. Priscilla pointed to a long line of people at the main gate. "Omigosh. Look at that. They probably waited until the cloudburst stopped, and now they're all scrambling to get in. Thank goodness we've already got our tickets."

Elliott looked at his watch. "Ten minutes or so 'til the pre-dusk show starts . . . fifteen minutes at the most. The storm probably caused some delay."

Josie laughed softly. "How can there be anything in the daylight?"

"Always are. They're always spectacular, too."

The group made their way into the grandstand. "We'll have a parade and a color guard, too," Elliott said. "This year the drill's by the New Albany drum and bugle corps. Then 'The Star-Spangled Banner.'"

"I get goosebumps whenever I sing our national anthem," Josie said.

They found a large enough seating area to accommodate all of them.

Twilight came, then darkness. Volleys of fireworks burst above their heads in a red, white, and blue dahlia of light. The crowd emitted ecstatic "oooh's and aahh's." When the show was over, the announcer's voice urged everyone to drive home safely.

The party of seven made their way to the cars. Priscilla snagged Josie's arm. "I'm excited for you and Elliott. And I don't want to sound picayunish, but I always thought if an engagement was announced, a diamond's been involved. You know, as a sign of intent."

Josie scowled. "I know what Elliott's intentions are, and we are engaged. What difference would a ring make?"

Priscilla hurriedly said, "Oh, none."

"What are you saying, then?"

Priscilla flapped her hand. "Oh, nothing."

"You meant *something*, or you wouldn't have said anything. Why make a mystery of it?"

"Just went through my mind . . . that without a ring . . . you can't say you're officially engaged."

Josie glared at Priscilla, took in a great breath through her nose, and gritted her teeth, but said nothing.

Chapter 21

The first two weeks of July followed the same pattern as the last two weeks of June for the Columbian Enameling and Stamping Company—weeks filled with tension, days packed with accusations, threats, and growing resentment between the union and management. The company remained on strike without any communication between the two sides that resembled meaningful dialogue.

On Wednesday, July seventeenth, a private security force of fifty men armed with shotguns and submachine guns entered the plant. Hostilities mounted. Four days later, on Sunday, union people and sympathizers organized a citywide labor holiday to begin Monday morning at one o'clock.

Josie awoke before the night sky lightened. She lay in bed, suspended between waking and sleeping, but the aroma of coffee wafted her way and proved too tempting.

She tossed her rumpled pillow aside, got up, and put on her dressing gown. Shoving her feet into bedroom slippers, she headed downstairs for the kitchen, where her father sat at the table, the remains of his breakfast surrounding him.

"You're up early," she said, coming toward him. "Gracious, but you look as though you're carrying the weight of the world on your shoulders."

"I feel like I do."

"Didn't sleep well?"

He drew a breath. "I haven't been to bed . . . yet."

"I've never seen you so tired. Are you sick?"

"Yes, but not in the way you think."

"Golly, your eyes look hollow to me." A shiver ran through her and she stared at him, her hand going instinctively to her heart. "It's happened, hasn't it? I should've known. The unions banded together, didn't they? What are we going to do?"

"The only thing we can do is go about our business as best we can. Won't be easy, though." He rubbed both palms across the growth of stubble that shadowed his chin. "Mark and I feared this'd happen. Not a matter of if, but when. Been brewing a long time. We'd failed to prevent it once negotiations stopped. Nothing more we could've done to stave off the walkout."

She got a cup out of the cabinet. "What happened with the reps the company hired to visit the workers in their homes?"

"Weren't able to convince them to abandon the union. Failure there, too. We'll just have to wait and see what happens."

Josie went to her father and put her hand on his shoulder. "Waiting's the worse. This is all so horrible . . . like a bad dream, only turned into a . . . a fantastic nightmare. I hate it." Landon covered her hand with his own, squeezing hard. She looked at him, relishing his caress, mindful of how far he'd come in accepting her since her arrival. A tear rolled down her cheek. "I think we've got to leave this matter in God's hands and trust Him to straighten it out."

"Terre Haute will seem abandoned today, a dead zone. And because the local newspapers have had limited publicity about the unions' threats, the general strike will come as a surprise to the majority of the city's non-labor people . . . Hungry?"

"Not much of an appetite anymore. This kind of news drains a person of any interest in food." She pulled out a chair, but never sat.

Landon got to his feet and moved toward the stove. "Better eat something. Otherwise, you'll have a long morning." He lifted the coffee pot, peered inside, and put it back down on the burner. "Anything sound appetizing to you?"

"Um . . . I'll try an egg . . . fried hard. I don't want any of the white to be runny. I can fix it."

"Go ahead and pour your coffee." He pointed to the canister. "There's plenty of sugar for you . . . any toast?"

"Yes, but I can make that." She put a slice of bread into the toaster. "Where're Vertie and Nub?"

He went to the refrigerator, opened the door, and got the egg out of a bowl. "Don't come until five-thirty or six. Hope they don't run into any trouble. Without question, some hooligans'll be out there enforcing the walkout."

Josie stirred her coffee clinking the bowl of the spoon against the cup's rim. "What will the people do?"

He cracked the shell against the skillet's edge. The egg sizzled as he topped off his coffee. "Be inconvenienced at best."

Josie ate in silence. Deliverance came when Vertie and Nub burst in on them.

Vertie slipped a fresh red gingham apron over her head. "Land sakes. What're you two doing up at this hour of the morning—and already had breakfast?"

Landon ran his fingers through his uncombed hair. "Well, Vertie, I've been up all night."

"What!?" She began clearing the table of the dirty dishes. "You'd better go to bed and get some proper rest, Mr. Matthews. You look used up to me . . . your eyes look bruised . . . ringed with dark shadows."

"I won't be able to sleep with the city in such chaos."

She carried the stack to the sink, turned, and shook her finger at him. "Can't do nobody no good by being too tired to think. Right now, a good snooze is the best thing for you."

"Can't say I'll not be able to think, but I won't go to bed until I see a solid plan for resolving this crisis."

Around nine o'clock, the telephone rang. Josie, in the library, walked out to the entry. "Don't bother, Vertie. I'll get it," she called, as she went. She lifted the receiver. "Hello?"

"Morning, Josie."

"Elliott?" She shuddered. "What's wrong?"

"I'm calling to check on Landon. How's he doing?"

"He was up all night. I'm anxious about him. What about yourself?"

"All I can say is that I'm on the job—taking a break right now, hanging in there. Course, the rain hasn't helped in any of this. I think a cold's coming on. I've developed a dry tickle at the back of my throat."

"Better grease up with Vicks salve tonight before you go to bed."

"Yeah, I'll do that. Listen, you stay put today, you hear? . . . Vigilante groups are out on the streets. Squads of strikers are cruising around the city checking on unionized plants and businesses and threatening those not complying with the walkout."

Her hand went involuntarily to her mouth. A shiver shot up her spine. Her knees trembled. "Oh, Elliott, I can't stand it. The news is becoming grimmer as the day goes on."

"'Fraid so. Rode in a squad car earlier when the officers were called to an auto service station where over a hundred sympathizers were gathered and intimidating the employees to join the walkout. The cops were able to disperse the crowd. I tell you, though, skirmishes are breaking out like firecrackers on a string." Elliott paused to cough. "Hey, just left a lady who owns a grocery on Tenth. She's having to defend her store entrance with a revolver in order to keep it open."

Josie cringed. "This is absolute craziness. Just because they're angry doesn't justify violence . . . Can you stop by this evening?"

"Will try to, but don't know yet. I gotta go now."

"Love you," she said, and replaced the phone's earpiece in its cradle.

Elliott, getting to the Matthews's home late that evening, loosened his tie, pulled on its knot, and unfastened the collar button under it. "Don't come too close to me, Josie. I'm not only full of ugly germs, I'm nasty. Hair's plastered to my forehead. Shirt's soaked and clinging to my back. Collar's sticking to my neck. I'm worse than this morning, completely drained of strength and energy, and I don't want to pass on any flu bugs to you."

"Your eyes are glazed over." She ignored his warning and touched her fingers to his cheeks. "You're feverish. You're definitely ill. You need to go home, grease up with Vicks salve, and climb into bed."

"Yeah. I wish I could kiss you, though."

"I do, too, but I don't want your cold."

"Better not, then. Wanted you and your father to be aware that Mayor Beecher and other city officials have telegraphed Governor McNutt and requested that he declare a state of emergency and deploy National Guard troops here to quell the upheaval."

Josie tensed. "Gracious."

"They think the city's police force is insufficient to curb the mob intimidation."

"Elliott, we'll be a city under military rule."

"True, to a certain extent. But, hey, this is only the third general strike in the history of the United States of America. We don't know how to grapple with situations like this." He stopped and struggled to take in a breath. "I'm bushed and haveta be up early tomorrow to cover a conference between city and county authorities and the management of the Stamping Mill, so I better say goodnight."

He went to the door and stood in the opening at the same time as a car with flashing red lights sped past on South Sixth Street.

Josie gripped his arm with both hands and gasped. "That siren's sound pierces the eardrums." She pulled away from him slowly, her heart hammering against her ribs.

At noon the next day, Elliott telephoned her. "Called as soon as possible. The meeting lasted four hours. The union's gained nothing, and the company's conceded nothing. They're at an impasse."

"How're you doing?"

The line went silent for a moment. Finally, Elliott said, "Honestly? . . . I feel rotten. Got a splitting headache . . . my sore throat's returned with a vengeance . . . my nose is stuffed up . . . and I'm bone-tired and achy."

"Where are you?"

"In my office. Do you want me to come over?"

"No!" she said, abruptly. "Not with that cold. You shouldn't even be working. You ought to be home in bed. Just call it a day."

He let out a wheezy breath. "Yeah. Now that the militia has come and the city has pretty well quieted down, I'm going to take a few days off, go to my mom's, and see if I can recover from whatever this is. I'll call you from there."

"All right. I'll be praying for you."

"Thanks. Love you, Josie."

"I love you, too, Elliott. Let me know when you get there."

"I will. I promise."

* * *

When Landon arrived home, he came through the kitchen to the swing door and called out, "Josie, you home?"

"Yes, I'm in my room."

"Can you come down?"

"Be there in a minute," she hollered back, and that's about all the time it took when she walked into the room. "What is it?"

He put his briefcase on the table. "Got some incredible information out of all this."

"Great! I want to hear something that's encouraging. What is it?" She faced her father, wide-eyed.

"Alex Heywood has left his position at the plant. He's gone."

Silence reigned, except for Josie's quickly drawn, shocked breath. "You mean he's gone, for real? How could he?"

"An old, cynical observation says every man has his price.

Management asked Alex what his price was, he named it, they paid it, and he's out."

"Where'd he go?"

"Don't know. Don't want to, either. Good riddance to him, I say. With his disloyalty to the company, he's caused a lot of trouble there."

"But what'll happen to him? He's always bragged about sitting pretty with the union."

"I'm sure he's lost all credibility and proved he's not trustworthy with them or the company. He's sold out, so he's on his own now."

"Well, at least Alex is no longer a menace with the Stamping Mill, and I'll be able to relax a little more when the National Guard leaves. It was a relief to see them come establish law and order, but the tramping of their boots and the rumbling of their troop trucks unnerve me. I want it all to be over." She went to the refrigerator, opened the door, and reached for a quart of milk.

"You don't want the militia to go too soon, though. We still need them right now. Today, they had to use tear gas and their rifle butts on two separate occasions outside the plant. Ended with the arrest of a hundred eighty-five people."

Josie shuddered. "No! Why?"

Landon's chest rose and fell on a considerable sigh. "The people refused to disband."

"I'll be glad when Terre Haute is back to normal."

"That may never become a reality. The general strike hasn't been only about anger toward a union, it's also been about the disruption of an entire community. People have chosen sides, drawn thick lines, and hardened their positions. Families and friends have been torn asunder. I suspect our city will never recover from what's happened."

* * *

Saturday afternoon, Josie sat curled up in Landon's leather chair, reading the Bible. A voice called from the open door.

"Hey."

Her head snapped up. "Mark! I'm sorry, I didn't hear you come in."

"How's it going?" he asked.

"I'm gathering strength and solace, both at the same time. Listen to this. I'm reading from the book of Isaiah, Chapter 43. 'But now thus saith the Lord that created thee, O Jacob, and he that formed thee, O Israel, Fear not: for I have redeemed thee, I have called thee by thy name; thou art mine. When thou passest through the waters, I will be with thee; and through the rivers, they shall not overflow thee; when thou walkest through the fire, thou shalt not be burned; neither shall the flame kindle upon thee. For I am the Lord thy God, the Holy One of Israel, thy Saviour.'" She shut her Bible.

He pulled the rocking chair beside her and sat. "Nice. Does give comfort, doesn't it? Heard anything from Elliott?"

She frowned. "No, nothing since he left Terre Haute last Wednesday. He was sick, but he told me he'd call when he got to his mother's. Do you think something's wrong?"

"I doubt it. Somebody would have contacted you if that were true. Have you called his mother's?"

"Twice. No answer . . . written him two letters. No word yet, of course. I miss him more than ever."

"I suspect you do. But it sounds like you're doing all you can. He'll probably contact you soon. Why not come to the movies with Priscilla and me? We're going to the Indiana Theater."

"I've never been there before."

"New bill. *Shanghai*'s playing. Charles Boyer and Loretta Young. Romance. Touching dramatic climax. Come on, say you'll go," he coaxed. "It'll give you something different to do."

Josie twisted her mouth. "Shouldn't we consult with Priscilla?"

Mark grinned. "No, we'll take our chances. I'm sure she won't mind."

"The last thing I need to do is sit at home and stew. All right, I'll go."

* * *

Mark parked his car on Ohio Boulevard. The three climbed out and made their way to the corner marble ticket booth.

"I can't wait to see this place," Josie said.

"You've never been inside the Indiana Theater?" Priscilla asked. "I can't believe that. After all these months in Terre Haute?"

"No. No reason to."

"Didn't you go to the movies with Alex and Elliott?"

"Yes."

"Where did you go?"

"The Orpheum."

"Their lobby is so ho-hum compared to the one at this movie house. Just you wait and see."

When Josie strolled into the spacious rotunda with its sweeping staircases, she stood rooted to the floor, her eyes wide, her mouth opened, forming an "O" but never sounding a word. She slowly turned around and around, taking in the elegance of the beautiful domed foyer with its marble terrazzo floors, the huge ornate crystal chandeliers glittering like giant tiers of brilliant diamonds, and the heavily ornamented ceiling of the lobby.

Even though the auditorium was still lit up, a young man with a flashlight conducted them to their seats. Josie edged her way into the row, then Mark and Priscilla.

"This is an amazing place, like a fairyland," Josie whispered to him, "and we've been transported to another reality. The way these ceiling lights are, it's as if we're outside under a starry host."

"The designer is world-famous for his movie palaces. His name's John Eberson. He also designed the Hippodrome. This is called Spanish Baroque."

"Very impressive," she said.

The lights dimmed. The screen came to life and the enchantment began. Josie sat engrossed in the story of the beautiful American woman who searched throughout China for the man she loved.

The picture show ended and the three went out into the cooler summer night. "What'd you gals think?" Mark asked.

"I enjoyed it," Josie said. "Barbara Howard reminded me of *me*—looking for her man."

Priscilla slipped her hand through the crook in Josie's arm as they approached Mark's car. "Where *is* Elliott? Yuh don't suppose he's played a lousy trick on you and skipped out? Yuh oughta question if a man like Elliott could really fall in love with you."

Josie flinched and pushed Priscilla's hand away. "Elliott does love me."

"You think so, huh? Well, he's gone, isn't he? And he hasn't gotten in contact with you, has he? I'd be suspicious of him. Maybe he was using you to get his newspaper scoops about the Stamping Mill. It sure looks like it to me now that the strike's been called, and he's done with you. He's simply disappeared."

Josie glared at Priscilla, released a snort, and stopped short. She grabbed Priscilla's arm with a ferocity that caused her to halt immediately, swinging Priscilla about to face her. "Elliott was quite ill when he left Terre Haute, or don't you remember?" she said, through gritted teeth.

Priscilla jerked her arm free from Josie's grasp. "You have no idea where he is, do you? I think you did need a ring."

That was mean. Josie swallowed hard. She wanted Elliott to come back and put his arms about her and tell her how much he missed her. Were her aunts in Bradford right—that he wasn't the marrying type? Had she done a foolish thing by falling in love with the first man who showed an attraction to her? Now Priscilla was making these snide comments.

Josie went over and over in her mind what he'd promised. "I'll call from Mother's." But he hadn't called. The ugly idea that he might have regretted their engagement crossed her mind. She suppressed it as being unworthy of him. But it persisted, all the same, to torment her in an unguarded moment.

Once back home, she wandered into the living room and sat at the piano. She put her head down on her arms and began to sob. A host of memories rushed through her mind. She'd never met anyone like Elliott. The man—his charm, his sense of humor, his kisses—and his mother—had captured her every thought. "Where are you, Elliott? What's happened to you?"

* * *

Lillian stood at one side of Elliott's high hospital bed. "He's trying to speak."

Wilma James, middle-aged and pleasantly dowdy, wearing a smart little cap nestled at the back of her head, was the nurse in charge. Her white starched uniform crackled in the darkened room, which reeked of disinfectants. "Mr. Jacobson. Elliott. Open your eyes," she urged. She reached into the bedside table, took out a small pan, and set it under the sink's faucet, partially filling it with warm water. She dipped a washcloth into the water and wiped his face with it.

"Josie," Elliott mumbled.

Lillian, who had moved away as Wilma tended to her patient, now came closer. "Didn't he say something?"

"Yes, but I couldn't really understand him," Wilma said, as she tipped the pan and the water ran down the drain. "It sounded like he was saying 'Josie.' Does that name mean anything to you?"

"No, I'm afraid not. His fever must've made him sort of delirious."

The nurse straightened the top sheet and cover and tucked them in. "He's drowsy now, but he'll recognize you when he wakes up," she said, and left the room.

Elliott opened his eyes. "Josie?"

Lillian stood helpless by his side. "It's your mother."

He rested in the nest of pillows, his eyes closed, his breathing labored. "So drained. What's happened to me?"

"You've got . . . pneumonia."

He worked his dry and chapped lips to moisten them. "Where am I?"

"Methodist Hospital in Indianapolis."

He did not open his eyes. "Does Josie know?"

"Yes, yes, she's been phoned several times. You don't need visitors yet. If you only knew how relieved I am to have you wake up. You've had a narrow escape from death." Lillian brushed the wave of dark hair off his forehead. "It's given me quite a scare."

He sighed. "Has she been here?"

"No . . . she hasn't bothered to come."

He opened his eyes to a slit. "Is there something you're not telling me?"

"What an accusation. I've told you everything. You surely don't think—"

"Maybe she doesn't want to see me."

Wilma walked in with a medicine tray holding a small glass. "Mr. Jacobson, I want you to drink this."

He looked warily at her. "What is it?"

"Orange juice. Lots of Vitamin C." She held the glass for him. "Take your time, now." She waited patiently until he drank all of it.

He looked at her. "Will I be well enough someday and have the strength to hold my own drinking glass?"

"Of course. You've made great progress in your four days here. We've already removed your oxygen tent." She jotted some notes on the chart hung at the foot of the bed.

"I came here four days ago? I don't remember a thing."

She came around to the side of the bed and pressed her fingers against his wrist. "You were very ill." She made more notations and left the room.

Elliott fidgeted in the bed, making three pillows drop to the floor. Lillian gathered them up, fluffed them, and rearranged them for him. She perched herself on the side of the bed, causing him to move his feet under the sheet to accommodate her. "It's all right if you can't remember."

"How did I get sick?"

"I don't know *how*, but you came home aching and having a hard time catching your breath. You looked white as a ghost, exhausted after having reported on that general strike in Terre Haute. Your resistance was undoubtedly lowered due to inadequate rest. It rained the whole blessed time, if I remember right. You came home and crawled into bed, achy, you said. It was while you were driving to Bloomington that you had a shaking chill, because you wanted a hot water bottle when you came in. After the way you looked and coughed so deeply, I brought you here. It's a good thing I did, too. The doctors are trying a new medication. They call it sulfa, and consider it a miracle drug."

"I remember I went from feeling bad to worse. All that seems a long time ago."

"I'm sure that's true. Now that you're on the mend, don't worry about it."

"I won't. I won't even think about it. I will think about Josie, though. Call her, okay?"

Lillian patted his hand. "Yes, yes. Now lie back and rest. You've had a hard fight . . . and thank goodness . . . you've won it." She exhaled a puff of air while a sense of peace ran through her from her head to her feet, and she relaxed.

Chapter 22

"This is absolutely perfect for eating *alfresco*, Clarinda," Josie said, stepping onto the flagstone floor of the Van Allens's outdoor room.

"It's been so hot and muggy today. Course, it is the middle of summer, isn't it? I figured the grape arbor with its shade would provide us some relief," Clarinda said. "Besides, this space is quite pleasant after dark and the candles are lit."

"I agree with you. Anything I can do to help?" Josie asked.

"I think we're pretty well done here." Clarinda straightened the red linen tablecloth and fiddled with the silverware. "Thank you for offering, though." She turned, walked away, and disappeared into the house.

Priscilla approached with a cut-glass pitcher of iced tea. She put it next to the vivid red ironstone dinnerware and cloth napkins, backed up, and scrutinized the table. "I hope the men hurry up. I'm starving."

Clarinda came near holding a sprawling bouquet of freshly cut zinnias arranged in a blue Ball quart canning jar. "Come now, Priscilla. You can't be hungry."

"I am, too. I worked up an appetite moving the old library table out here and setting it up as a buffet table."

"Your vine-covered patio is a magical place of beauty," Josie said. "We can watch the moon rise and whitewash this whole area with its light."

Priscilla flapped her hand. "You're so poetical. Well, for your information, it isn't full tonight. Sorry. Look, this table wobbles. Help me prop it up." She handed over a thick-handled table knife. "Put the handle under one of the legs. If Mother'll hold the pitcher, I'll raise the table a smidgen for you."

"The stones are so irregular and uneven. It may take something more than this." Josie got down on her hands and knees and wedged the flatware under the table leg.

"See?" Priscilla said. "I was right. It did the trick."

At six, the usual five gathered for the meal. "We've got corn on the cob, spare ribs, sliced tomatoes, and cucumbers . . . and a peach cobbler still in the oven," Clarinda said. "Mark, would you offer the blessing on the food, please?"

He did. They filled their plates and found a chair to their liking. Conversation flowed easily.

Mark laid aside a gnawed-on rib bone, got up, and set his plate on the seat. He went to refill his glass with tea. On his way back, he dropped to a squat right beside Josie. "Heard from Elliott?" he whispered.

She looked away for a moment, and with unwelcomed tears thickening her throat, said, "No. If I don't hear anything soon, then . . . well . . . I'm not sure what I'll do. I feel . . . hurt would be the best way to describe it."

"Confused by it all?" he offered.

"Yes, and disappointed. I have written to his mother's address, but he hasn't responded." Where was Elliott? What was he doing? Who was he with? Did he even think of her anymore?

"Well, if Elliott's the kind of man I think he is, he'd never up and leave you."

"You're right. He's a man of integrity, and that's one of the reasons I love him."

The hostesses excused themselves, and soon sounds of dishes clinking and clacking came from the kitchen. Clarinda appeared carrying a tray holding a straight-from-the-oven peach cobbler bubbling and oozing its pink-amber juice, smelling scrumptious, and looking so tempting. She put it down on the table.

Priscilla trailed her, bearing a white creamer and a coffee pot. "You can pour cream over your slice to cool it down. And I brought coffee. No one may want anything hot to drink, but here it is just the same."

Clarinda scooped up generous servings, and they dug into the hot dessert.

Josie poured the thick, sweet cream over her peaches and crust. "Mm-mmm," she said. "This was a fabulous summer supper." She scraped her bowl and licked her spoon, relishing the last morsel of it.

Landon breathed a long sigh and reclined in his Adirondack chair. "Clarinda, it was a most savory meal."

"Let's clear the table so the bugs don't bother us," Priscilla said.

Josie and Mark never objected to the chore. They stacked the dishes and carried them to the kitchen. They took away the bones and corn cobs gnawed clean, the coffee cups, the creamer, and the pie pan.

Josie returned to the pergola and moved the rocking chair to the shadows. It creaked when she lowered herself into it. She closed her eyes and slowly rocked, listening to the cicadas—invisible among the branches, droning their interminable cadences—and to the rattling and hissing sound of the lawn sprinkler next door, which was spewing forth its punctual jets of water over the grass. A delicate breeze ruffled the grape leaves above her.

Priscilla came out of the house. "Where'd you go off to, Josie?"

"Over here. Enjoying the evening."

Priscilla ambled over. "Mark wants to play croquet."

"I'm terrible at it. You both'll be upset if I do."

"Can't be any worse than me." She grasped Josie's hands to pull her out of the rocker.

Mark placed the nine wickets in the proper layout on a shadowy stretch of the yard now bathed in the orange light of sunset. "Take a mallet, Josie. Grab the black one."

She complied. "All right, but you'll be sorry."

"Priscilla's awful, too," he said in a low tone.

Priscilla shot first, Josie last. Mark took his time with each turn and caused the game to linger.

The sun dipped closer to the horizon, its apricot color giving way to twilight. "You take too long," Priscilla whined. "Quit holding us up. Just hit the ball. At this rate, we won't finish until midnight."

Josie, her red-gold hair plastered against her neck, leaned on her mallet as Mark lined up a tricky stroke. "I'm sorry, but I've developed a throbbing headache. I can't continue." She massaged her temples.

She walked back to the arbor. "Is it all right if I join you two?" she asked Landon and Clarinda.

"Sit down, dear. Probably the heat . . . Now, Landon, how is the situation at the Stamping Mill? Have things settled down?"

"Somewhat." Landon raked his fingers through his hair. "We resumed operations August first—with scab labor, of course. So far, there're no discussions planned with union representatives, federal mediators, the press, or anyone else who're hoping for a policy revision."

"Since you mentioned change, I'm fearful of this new Social Security thing that'll become law in a few days. Aren't we getting close to taking the mark of the beast?" Clarinda asked.

Landon made a snorting noise. "What're you talking about?"

"In the Bible, the book of Revelation. A person must have a number in order to do any business transactions."

"I don't know anything about that, but don't get me started on the issue of Social Security. It's nothing but an entitlement, plain and simple."

"Oh, no, you're mistaken, Landon. They call it an insurance

program. People pay into it. A trust fund's been established for the contributions."

"Hogwash. President Roosevelt intended to make it look like people contributed to a fund, but the fact is, the government spends the money as soon as it comes in. It's a pyramid scheme designed to addict the American people to welfare. Think about it, people will draw out a whole lot more money than they'll ever pay into it. The problems with this political plan will be immense down the road, believe me."

Josie stopped rocking. "Why would our own President authorize such a shady program?"

"Power—and to make the people dependent on good ole Uncle Sam."

"I worry for you young people today, Josie," Clarinda said. "The government's intruding more and more into our lives. I can see we're losing more and more of our freedoms, bit by bit. I hate to think about all the rules and regulations you'll contend with when you and Priscilla are my age . . . Mercy me, Landon, isn't it hard to believe we're not the young ones? It jolts me when I see our daughters. Goodness, the years passed by so quickly."

She reached across the space and rested her hand on Josie's arm. "You've been good for Priscilla. I had worried she might associate with girls who do silly and daring things. I'm sure you're aware of the sort I'm talking about. Girls who aren't . . . well, reputable. Perhaps I shouldn't ask, and you can tell me to mind my own business, but I haven't seen Elliott around for quite a while. What's going on between you two?"

"Nothing at the moment," Josie said. "He went home to his mother's after the general strike—sick with a bad cold. Not seen or heard from him since."

"How odd. You two didn't quarrel, did you? Quick words, or an argument and blame? Sometimes things are said that aren't meant, and then later regretted."

"No, we've not quarreled."

"I don't know Elliott all that well, but it doesn't sound like him. Something's not right."

"That's what I say, too."

"Could there be another woman?"

How dare Clarinda think a thing like that about Elliott, let alone say it. Josie wanted to jump up and scream at the woman.

"Not Elliott's style," Landon said, before Josie could respond.

She clasped her hands at her chest. Her father had defended Elliott. He must believe Elliott an honorable man and didn't like how Clarinda was talking about him.

Landon slapped the wooden chair arm. "Wait a minute. I just had a thought. Elliott's mother is a controlling woman. Maybe *she's* the other woman."

Josie planted her feet and sat up straight. Perhaps her father was right that *Lillian* was the reason Elliott hadn't called. After all, she did say no one, not even a wife, should come between a mother and her son—ever. It could be that Lillian convinced him to drop her. No, he loved her. He wasn't shallow. He'd proved himself trustworthy. Josie's head throbbed more.

"You mean she's made trouble already?" Clarinda asked.

"Yes," Josie said.

"No sense to it, either," Landon added. "She has strong ideas about the kind of girl she's looking for—"

"And I don't fit the bill," Josie chimed in.

"Remember, he's her only child. It makes a difference to a mother—"

"Don't make excuses for her," Landon interrupted. "I've got some work to do. I'm going on home. I'll leave the front porch light on for you, Josie. Mark and Priscilla can walk you over when you're ready. Thanks for a delicious meal and a nice evening, Clarinda." The soft scuffing sound of his footsteps faded across the yard.

Clarinda got to her feet and moved methodically from one candle to another, blowing out each small, wavering flame. Josie stood, and without speaking, took the flowers to the kitchen. Clarinda followed her with the tablecloth and napkins.

"My headache's made my eyes hurt, and I feel queasy."

"Would you like for me to get you an ice pack . . . or some aspirin?"

"No, thank you," Josie said. "I just want to lie down. Will you tell Mark and Priscilla? Your dinner was wonderful. Goodnight."

Josie, plodding home, lifted her face to the night sky. The moon was large but not quite full above the treetops, and the stars sprinkled about were white and twinkling. "O God, give me wisdom and understanding in this matter with Elliott. Your Word says to stop worrying. Calm my troubled mind with Your peace."

She mounted the porch steps, opened and closed the front door, and stood for a minute in the middle of the entry, pressing her palms against the sides of her head. She paused with one foot on the bottom step, intending to make her way upstairs to the bedroom. Instead, she slumped down on the third stair, braced her shoulder against the wall, and cradled her face in her trembling hands. Holding back nothing, she let loose her suppressed emotions and wept, not a gentle flow, but a flood of tears, and uncontrollable sobs with them, her whole body quaking.

"I'll call," he'd promised. She believed him—no reason not to. But no call came. No letter, either. No harsh words, no disagreements had happened between them. Yet the days slipped by, empty of any communication. He loved her. But being distanced from her, and being with his mother, maybe he became consumed with doubts and had second thoughts about their relationship. Maybe her aunts were right, or Priscilla. Maybe she did need a ring to be properly engaged.

Landon made his way down the stairwell. "Josie?"

She froze halfway through a gut-heaving sob. She straightened and turned, pushing her hair off her face, and fixed her gaze on him, unable to speak, tears streaming unheeded down her cheeks.

He sat beside her and put a bracing arm about her. "What is it?"

She buried her face against his shoulder. Wiping her runny nose on the back of her hand, she raised her head. "Do you have a handkerchief?" Not too many months ago, it was the same question she'd asked when Elliott gave her one.

Landon reached into a pocket, pulled out a clean, heavily monogrammed one, and pressed it into her shaking hands. "Tell me."

She took it, mopped her eyes, dabbed at her face, buried her nose in it, and blew. "My head hurts terribly." She took a long sobbing breath. "I miss Elliott so much I could burst. My heart burns in me like a blaze, consuming me, like I'm being burned alive. I can't eat or sleep. I write him every day. He hasn't responded, even once, so I'm not sure where he is or how he is or what he's feeling. I call his mother's house every other day. No answer. I'm scared." She grabbed hold of his arm. "Do you think he may regret our engagement?"

Landon covered her hand with his. "Elliott's not the type to leave you without any kind of word. My guess is something's happened."

"Do you suppose he's been in an accident? Surely Lillian would have contacted me if that had taken place. Don't you think?"

"Maybe. Then again, she might not want you to know. Lillian hasn't been too keen on your engagement."

"It seems like he's just vanished. I'm not coping very well, am I?"

"On the contrary, I consider it a miracle you've held up as long as you have, Joselene. There's practically no limit to what a brave person can bear, and you're certainly *that*."

"You think I'm courageous?"

"Yes, I do."

"I wish there were something we could do."

Landon heaved himself up. He took hold of Josie's hands and helped her stand. "We can do several things. In the morning, we'll go to the *Star*'s office and inquire there. We can check at his rooming house. We'll make sure you have the right telephone number for his mother." He brushed her disheveled hair back from her face. "Right now, you need to find the aspirins and go to bed."

She nodded. "I'll shut off all the lights."

He turned and climbed the stairs. "Goodnight."

Josie came out of the pantry with two aspirins, took a drinking glass out of the cabinet, and turned on the sink faucet. Startled by frantic tapping on the backdoor window, she stood rooted where she was, her heart pounding, the water rushing over the glass's rim. She peeked over her shoulder to see a face with hands cupped to its sides peering inside.

"Vertie!"

Josie rushed to open the door. "What's wrong?" She pulled out a chair from the kitchen table. "Sit down and catch your breath. Is something wrong with Nub?"

Vertie's shoulders drooped forward. She panted laboriously, shook her head, and pulled in a hefty gulp of air, catching enough breath to say, "Mr. Jacobson."

"Elliott? What's happened?"

Vertie puffed breathlessly. "He's . . . been . . . really sick."

A knot formed in Josie's stomach. Her heart banged in her chest. Her knees shook. "Elliott? Why wouldn't he tell me?"

"Because . . . he . . . couldn't. Elliott's at . . . the Methodist Hospital in Indianapolis." She pushed herself off the chair. "He's been . . . there . . . two weeks."

Josie took hold of Vertie's arms in a viselike grip. "Is it the Spanish influenza? Aunt Ruth's husband died of that. Elliott's not going to die, is he?" She released her grasp on Vertie and sank, stricken, onto the chair's edge.

"They've had quite a . . . a time . . . with him. He's been . . . bad, Miss Josie."

Josie glared at Vertie. "I don't understand. Who told you this?"

"His cold went into pneumonia."

"Elliott's been ill all this time?" She shivered, her hands cold and clammy, her arms dangling at her side. "I must go there." She questioned Vertie again. "But how did you find out?"

"I went to the newspaper office and asked about him. I wouldn't fib to you about Elliott. Why should I?"

"I'm not saying you're lying. I'm just wondering why you'd even care what happened to him. Why should he concern you?"

"He's . . . important to me . . . because . . . Elliott's my grandson."

"What?" Josie gasped, fell back against the chair, and locked her hands on top of her head. "Your what?"

Vertie nodded. "My grandson."

Josie gaped at the woman. "How come he's never said anything?"

"'Cause he doesn't know."

Josie leaped up immediately. "You mean he's been coming here all this time and has no idea who you are?"

"Yes, that's exactly what I'm saying."

"But . . . that means . . . Lillian is your daughter." Her conclusion explained how the two reminded her of one another. The puzzle made sense. "I thought your daughter's name was Elizabeth?"

"She's one and the same. When Elizabeth ran away from home, she changed her name to Lillian Rose Randolph."

Josie flopped into the chair, shook her head, and expelled a breath through puffed-out cheeks. "But . . . I thought she left Terre Haute years ago and had nothing to do with you and Nub."

"That much is true, but Nub and I kept track of her and Elliott over the years."

How had Vertie managed to keep such a secret? "Isn't it sad that both my mother and Elliott's majored in deception? Did they never stop to think the truth would win out someday?"

The kitchen door swung open. Landon entered wearing his dressing robe. "What's going on down here, Vertie? Josie?" He looked at one and then the other.

"Elliott's at Methodist Hospital." Josie hoisted herself up and faced him. "I must go to him first thing tomorrow." She told her father the whole story. "Will you let me have your car?"

"You sure you can drive, as anxious as you are?"

"Yes, quite. I have to go to him. I know he needs me."

"You can take the car. I'll phone Mae Anise and explain everything."

"What if she's not there or has plans or won't want me to stay with her?"

"Nonsense. She'll be delighted to welcome you. I'll give you money for essentials. Are you sure you don't want me to go with you?"

She shook her head. "No, I gotta do this on my own." She looked from Landon to Vertie. "I guess this shows how despicable Lillian is."

"She obviously didn't want you to know about him," Landon said. "We can only speculate about her motives. Josie, you have a long day ahead of you. Better get some rest."

"You may be gone by the time I come in the morning," Vertie said. "I'll sure keep you in my prayers, as well as Elliott's recovery." She embraced Josie. "Sorry this is the way things turned out, but he'll get well with you there. Goodnight." She left and closed the kitchen door.

Josie walked over to lock it. "I doubt I'll be able to sleep a wink tonight," she said to Landon.

In her room, she undressed and put on her nightgown. Before getting into bed, she knelt and prayed. "Lord God, You know all the people involved in this. Our foibles and our hearts. I cannot change any one of them. I can only open my life to You, and leave the outcome to You, believing You will do what is right and what is best for all of us. Give me safe travel and wisdom and courage and grace. Amen."

She slid between the coolness of the sheets and sank back on the pillows. What on earth would she say to Lillian? Something subtle, nothing spectacular. The clock downstairs struck one before she figured out *what* she must say, and by the time the clock struck two, she decided *how* to say it. Then she turned on her side, wriggled into a comfortable position, closed her eyes, and slept.

Chapter 23

Tiptoeing into the dimly lit, iodoform-and-carbolic-scented hospital room, Josie staggered backward at the sight of Elliott in the bed and grabbed at her chest. He looked shockingly thin.

He lay with his eyes closed, covered to his shoulders with a thin sheet. His head, with hair tousled into a dark, disorderly mop, rested deep in the white linen pillow. Elliott, scarcely recognizable, had not been shaved for days, and had rough stubble covering his chin.

Josie went to his bedside, took his hand, and held it. "Holy God," she prayed, "giver of all good things. I'm asking that You touch Elliott and make him well."

He slowly opened his eyes, now sunken pockets with darkness under them. He tried to speak, but the words came out in a hoarse whisper. "Josie, you've come. What a swell thing for you to do. You're here—at exactly the moment I wanted you most. Or am I dreaming? It *is* you, isn't it?" Elliott reached up and touched a wave of red-gold hair that showed under her close-set hat.

She put her finger to his dry lips. "Sh-h-h. Yes, it's me. I'm here." She smoothed back his dark hair.

"I'm crazy to see you . . . missed you so much. Beginning to think you'd forgotten about me." He closed his eyes and let go with a huge sigh. "I needed to see your face and hear your voice. It's so wonderful to be talking to you again. I'll be all right now."

"I'd have come days ago, but didn't find out until last night that you were ill. I promise I won't leave until you're well."

He nodded and then coughed. "I don't understand. Mother said she called you every day."

The nurse came noiselessly into the room. Elliott scowled at her and shifted his gaze to Josie, who said, "Sh-h-h. We won't talk about it now." She slipped away from his bedside.

The nurse stuck a thermometer under his tongue and lifted up his wrist to take his pulse. She wrote the numbers on the chart and left the room.

Josie came near, bent over him, and kissed his forehead, failing to notice the woman standing in the doorway.

A shrill voice cut through the air. "What's going on here?"

Startled, both of them turned sharply and saw Elliott's mother, her eyes like two coals on fire.

"What're you doing here?" She glowered at Josie. A moment of uncomfortable silence followed.

"Isn't it an answer to prayer that Josie came, Mother?"

Lillian, erect and unflinching, glared at Elliott. "How long has she been here? All visits are limited to ten minutes."

Josie shivered with a cold chill. She cleared her throat, and straightened her spine. "I haven't been here that long."

"One of us has to leave, and it's not going to be me," Lillian said. "After all, he is my son." She came close to Josie. "Get out of here," she ordered.

A nurse came back with a stethoscope slung around her neck. She went to Elliott, listened to his chest, tapped around on it, then listened again. She also took his blood pressure. After writing the numbers on a chart, she said, "Only one visitor at a time, please."

"Yes, I'm just now going," Josie said. "I'll be in the waiting room and come back in a short while." She wagged her little finger at Elliott. "Now, you be good and get well."

*   *   *

Josie rose from the sofa when Lillian strutted into the waiting room. "I thought you'd stay a little while longer."

Lillian smirked, lowering herself to a chair, rigid like a reigning sovereign. "Only ten minutes per visit. Remember? You'd already usurped the time. Besides, I came in here to talk to *you*." She signed for Josie to sit opposite her. "You think you're clever, don't you? Coming here. Listen to me, little missy, I don't want Elliott to be in too big a hurry to leave here. I want him fully recovered. Do you understand?"

Josie nodded slowly, licking her lips.

"How long are you planning on staying?"

"Until he's well enough to go home. He'll be growing stronger every day now since I'm here. The only things wrong with him are weakness and wanting me."

"Let's get something settled right here and now. The best thing you can do for him is to give him up."

Josie narrowed her eyes and looked at Lillian for a long moment of silence. Then . . . "Excuse me, but I couldn't do anything like that."

"I'll never give my blessing for the two of you to marry. Do you understand?"

"I do . . . completely. Why didn't you telephone or write me about his illness? All these days and weeks, you never informed me that he was so ill. I had a right to know."

"It wasn't life or death. If it had been, of course, I would have contacted you. I believe Elliott wants you out of his life."

Josie shook her head. "No. You're wrong there. He loves me. He's asked me to be his wife, and I will. I love him very much."

"Love! What does someone of your caliber know about love?"

Josie flinched and blinked her eyes. "You might not be aware how often I called, but surely when you got home, you found all my letters to him . . . and read them, too, I suspect." Her tone was sharp. "Which of us did you want to see suffer the most? Elliott, or me? I think you're like those mothers who would rather their children were unhappy than have them be made happy by someone else."

Lillian's face twitched. "How dare you! Any mother would've done what I did. I will not allow my son to marry beneath the Jacobson name. Can't you imagine how humiliating it'll be when his wife is discussed as you probably will be?"

"No one will even be concerned about it unless you start the discussion. Which, by the way, won't worry me, because over the years, I've heard people say everything about me they could think of."

"You intend to win, then."

"What do you mean? This isn't a contest. I'm sure Elliott and I will be very happy in our marriage."

Lillian sneered. "Don't be ridiculous!"

"You think I am?"

"Absolutely. You obviously don't understand the differences in social status. By the way, how did you even find out he was here?"

"My father's housekeeper. She told me last night."

Lillian pulled in a deep breath through her nose, gripped the arms of the chair as she pushed herself up, and struggled to stand. Towering over Josie, looking down at her, she said, "This impasse has got to stop somewhere. You have no idea what it takes to be a Jacobson. As his mother, I'm going to make sure—"

"Of what?" Josie exclaimed, louder than she'd intended.

Lillian glared at her. "That my son won't marry the wrong girl." She flapped her arms and stamped her foot. "I want him to be happy. I believe he's throwing away any chances for happiness in this life if he marries a girl who's . . . who's nothing but a walking mortal sin. I won't permit you to besmirch the Jacobsons' honored name."

Josie sighed and said, "I also want Elliott to be happy. His wife's one prayer should be to make his life and home peaceful and loving. I pray every night for God to make me the helpmate Elliott needs."

Lillian laughed with a grating sound. "You're being absurd." She moved stiffly toward the door to leave.

"Is that right, Elizabeth Delphine?"

Lillian stopped in the threshold, mid-stride, and glanced back at Josie. Her complexion paled. "Wha-what did you call me?"

"Elizabeth Delphine. That's your *real* name, isn't it?"

"My *name* is Lillian Rose Randolph Jacobson."

"Seems strange two people in Terre Haute think you're their daughter who ran away from home. Came to Indianapolis, married and moved to Bloomington, and started a new life."

Lillian made a little gesture with her hands. "How in the world are you acquainted with Abner and LaVerta Engle?"

"I find it interesting you mentioned the Engles, because I never said who the two people were. But, since you asked, I told you before, they work for my father. I found out who you really are."

Lillian looked down at the floor instead of at Josie and touched her lips with her fingertips. "I expect you're going to tell Elliott?"

"Yes, when he's well and strong . . . no idea how, but I'm sure it'll happen. He deserves to know the truth. I did, too, about my father. I wish somebody would have intervened for me just as I'm going to do for Elliott."

Lillian brushed the skirt of her dress, arranged her handbag on her wrist, and put on her white gloves. "I must go now," she murmured. She rubbed her forehead. "A horrible headache." She went out of the room without bothering to say goodbye.

Josie watched her go. Trembling, she remained seated.

* * *

"What are you asking?" Josie sat in the chair by Elliott's bed.

He was propped against heaped pillows, his left arm crooked

behind his head. He was clean-shaven, but still hollow-eyed. "What you and Mother talked about."

She clasped her hands in her lap. "What does it matter now? Everything's all right between your mother and me."

"Oh, yeah. Yesterday you came in here, and my mother would hardly look at you. The two of you leave my room, talk, and now she's eating out of your hand, as they say. Something prompted her change of heart to knuckle under to you as she has."

Josie got up from the chair to pull the window shade, hesitated in the action, and glanced back over her shoulder at him. "Are you accusing me of putting the bite on her?"

"Yes. I think you did."

She shrugged. "What can I say?"

Elliott half raised himself up on his elbows. "You had to've said something. She's no longer opposed to our marrying."

Her gaze caught his. "Why don't you ask her?"

"I would . . . except there won't be a straightforward answer. In almost everything she says, there's something true *and* . . . untrue."

For a long moment, she studied him. His lips were chapped, and his cheeks gaunt. "Are you saying your mother speaks falsehoods?"

He sank back against the pillows. "Not exactly. I'm saying she tries to protect me from unpleasantness."

She stood nearby now. "Is that what you call it? Hah! For goodness sake, Elliott, she manipulates you. I can visualize all the little old ladies as they huddle around each other and talk about the nice, widowed Lillian who dotes on her son because he does everything she asks him to do."

He motioned to her and patted the sheet at his side. "Come here." He held out his hand, caught hers, and drew her down to sit on the bed beside him. "Don't tell me you're jealous of Mother."

"Gracious, no."

He stroked her cheek with the back of his hand. "Sounds like it to me."

She twisted her head to the side. "You're mistaken," she snapped. "I honestly believe your mother didn't want me to know what had happened to you."

"Why wouldn't she? She says I nearly died."

"I had written you every day for weeks. I called your mother's house every two or three days. She never once let me know you were here."

He shook his head. "Mother told me you couldn't come."

Josie rolled her eyes upward. "For goodness sake. Didn't you think it was strange I wouldn't? Don't you think your mother was quite capable of never telling you anything about my letters?"

"I . . . believed her."

"Your mother is a very determined lady. She had great ambitions for you, and frankly, I didn't match her vision for you."

"How *did* you find out I was here?"

"Vertie."

He tilted his head and wrinkled his brow. "What would it matter to your housekeeper where I was?"

Josie said in a slow and deliberate manner, "Vertie cares a lot about you, Elliott, because . . . she's your grandmother. It was your mother's mother who told me."

He folded his arms across his chest. "You're crazy!"

Josie jumped to her feet, a hand pressed against her breastbone, her heart pounding. "I beg your pardon!"

"Look, I'm sorry I said what I did."

"Well, you should be, because it's the truth."

"Vertie's given you some cockamamie story, though, because neither of my grandmothers is alive."

Josie held up her hand. "Not true. Your mother's mother is Vertie. Nub is your grandfather. Ask your mother."

"I will. So, go ahead. Tell me Vertie's version."

"Elliott, you can believe your mother or . . . me. The choice is yours, but I wouldn't lie to you. Vertie wouldn't, either. She and Nub worked hard to give their daughter, whose name was Elizabeth Delphine, as much as they could afford while she was growing up. They had a son, too. George Henry. He had epilepsy—a lick on the head triggered seizures. His medicine cost a lot of money, which they didn't have. Lizzydelle—that was her nickname—became embittered and embarrassed about their poverty. She wanted to achieve what she called a certain station in life. When she turned eighteen, she moved out—left home the week after high school graduation. Came to Indianapolis, changed her name to Lillian Rose Randolph, and made a new life for herself. Somewhere along the way, she met Parker Jacobson, and they married. Anyway, after a while, Nub and Vertie went to see her . . . your mother and father lived in Bloomington by that time . . . to let her know her brother had passed away from seizures, one after another. Nothing could be done for him. His body simply wore out, and his heart stopped. He was sixteen."

"Let me guess. Mother sent them away."

Josie nodded. "They wrote to her. Your mother answered that she would come, but she never did. I think she just decided to move on with her life. She had her friends and enjoyed a different lifestyle. And to her, they didn't fit in."

"Hey, I've got to hand it to you, it could be true."

Josie stiffened. "It *is*. Why should it not be? I wouldn't invent such a story." She glared at him. "What kind of person do you take me for, Elliott? . . . You do believe me, don't you?"

"Only because of the person you are," he said. "I just want to check things out, that's all. This comes as quite a shock. When did you hear this?"

"The night before I came to Indianapolis."

He pulled the sheet up to his armpits. "Still doesn't explain how Vertie found out I was here."

Josie fluffed and rearranged the pillows behind his head. "She went to the *Star*'s office and inquired about you. She said she was your grandmother. They told her your mother had notified them that you were hospitalized and would be laid up for some time. Vertie knew I didn't know. She came to the house and confessed everything. I was stunned, of course."

"You told all of this to my mother?"

Josie nodded. "It's awful to be deceived . . . and deprived of the truth . . . and a relationship. I'm fed up with lies and secrets after living with both for twenty years. I deserved to know my father, just as you deserve to know your grandparents. We mustn't continue this legacy of deceit."

"Agreed, but it's still knocked the breath out of me."

"I wasn't sure how to tell you."

"Mother told me her mother passed away when I was a little boy."

Josie shook her head. "She let you believe that, but did she ever say it in so many words?"

"Hmm. I'll have to think about that. Probably wouldn't make any difference. Do you realize we might have broken up because of Mother's conniving? I wonder how many other couples who would've been tremendously happy break up because of their parents' wishes?"

"I thank Vertie . . . and God . . . every day for you and for all the tomorrows we'll share from now on. Your mother learned the harsh lesson that no mother can ever make up to a man for his future wife. I prayed earnestly about what to say to her, and then thought long and hard about how to say it. But when I had my chance, there was no reason to get even. She has nothing compared to what we have."

On Tuesday, when Josie arrived, she found Elliott standing at the window, his shoulder propped against the casement, and looking out.

"Hello," she whispered.

He turned abruptly and flashed a smile at her.

"What're you doing up?"

"Watching the traffic sweep back and forth on Capitol Avenue. Guess what? Good news. I'm being released from this place tomorrow. Come over here." He flung out an arm and she snuggled against him, tucking her forehead under his chin. "Ah-h-h, this feels so right."

She leaned back her head to look into his face, her hands resting on his chest. "Elliott?"

"Hm?"

"When I came in, you had such a sober expression on your face. What was it you were so deep in thought about?"

"Us . . ." One corner of his mouth curled into the lopsided grin, "and how fortunate we were to find each other in the first place, for me to get sick, *and then* for things to work out this way. I couldn't have recovered so quickly if it hadn't been for you." He dipped his head and kissed her. "Been aching to do that for days. You're a remarkable woman."

"I love it when you say so. Now, here we are, and nobody will be able to separate us again—ever."

"Let's set a wedding date."

"All right. I've been thinking about that, too."

"Yeah? Well then, why should we wait? Long engagements are terrible. The first wild excitement of passion isn't meant to last indefinitely. Wouldn't it be the limit if we eloped? We could."

She shook her head. "We can't behave like people in novels."

"Why not? Let's get married tomorrow. Nothing's preventing us. I want you for my wife, Josie." He cinched her tighter around the waist and rubbed his cheek against her hair. "You belong with me. I begrudge every moment we're apart."

"Funny thing . . . only a year ago, I was a poor country girl. Now, I've a wealthy father and a comely sweetheart who's going to marry me. Life is awesome, isn't it?"

"Yep," he said. "I remember you once told me you thought about your father and what he'd be like. What did you think your husband would be like?"

"Mmm. The usual. Tall, dark, and handsome. Umm . . . smart and witty."

"Well, aren't you a lucky gal? I fill that bill perfectly."

She puckered her lips, wiggled her eyebrows whimsically, and gave

her head a little shake. "Another thing, I knew he'd be a humble man."
She laughed, and he did, too.

"Josie, with what we've been through, I don't want to lose any more
time. I'm serious. Two months at the most. I don't want to put it off."

"All right. Let's say the third week of October. That's a little over two
months, though. The college will be closed for Teacher's Institute from
Wednesday evening through Sunday evening."

"That'll be perfect. You promise, now? No backing out?"

Chapter 24

Josie awakened before sunrise. She pulled the sheet up to her nose and turned over in bed with a great flouncing to face the window. She vowed to stay there until daylight came, but the aroma of something delicious in the oven teased her nose. Had Vertie already come? She threw back the bedcover and pulled on a dressing gown. She cleaned her teeth and washed her face. She brushed out her red-gold hair, pinned it up carelessly, and hurried down the stairs to the kitchen.

"You're here early!"

"Couldn't wait to put my hands at work making these biscuits so's they'd be ready for everyone on time," Vertie said. "They've got to be the best for my grandson's wedding." She gave a little jerk of her head toward the stove. "Coffee's perked."

Josie shook her head. "Hot tea for me this morning. I'm too jittery for coffee." She took the kettle to the sink, filled it, and put it on the coil burner to boil. Then she went to the back door and looked out. "I absolutely love this season. The chilly mornings, warm afternoons, and brisk nights, sun-shiny days and drier air, clear blue skies, crimson and ocher leaves. M-m-m." She wrapped her arms about herself.

"It's a perfect day for a wedding, isn't it?" She spun away from the door, came back, and sat at the table. "The weather has been surprisingly beautiful, hasn't it? Not too cold, a slight breeze. To me, it not only smells like fall—it tastes like it."

"Um-hum." Vertie never looked up but measured flour into a big yellow bowl and cut lard into it until the mixture resembled cornmeal. With slow, careful gestures, she mixed in the correct amount of milk, lightly kneaded the pliable dough, and rolled it out until it was about a half-inch thick. Using a tin cutter, she cut out little hearts, twist by twist, and placed them on the metal baking sheets.

Steam rose from the kettle. Josie waited until Vertie slid the pans in the oven to bake before she made her cup of tea—strong and syrupy sweet.

"Better eat something substantial, Josie. You don't wanna keel over at the groom's feet." Vertie whanged a spoon against the inside of the emptied bowl, scraping out all traces of the remaining batter. "Now, then, when those come out, I'll give you some to sample."

She opened the refrigerator door and stabbed several thin slices of ham with a knifepoint. In no time, the little hearts were done. Vertie lifted three off the hot sheet, cut each biscuit in half, and made sandwiches. She stood by while Josie tasted them.

"M-m-m. They're scrumptious." Josie sat with one leg tucked under her and munched on her breakfast. "The great white canopy is set up by the garden. It'll be the perfect place for our reception. I'm glad Nub and I worked hard on the yard this past spring, getting things in shape. Little did we even suspect how crucial that would turn out to be." She glanced at Vertie, who transferred more biscuits to a dish towel spread out on the counter.

"Your wedding and reception are gonna be breathtaking—nothing short of a dream. Girls will want their own to be like yours."

"To be honest, I pictured something small in size . . . quiet and simple . . . but oh no, Priscilla had something else in mind. She's more of a pro at planning shindigs and such, so I let her say what she thought because I didn't want to hear her complain about it."

Vertie raised an eyebrow. She touched Josie's arm. "It's a fact Miss Priscilla'd be able to whine the feathers off a chicken. She's never had any trouble having a say about anything or anybody. But this is your day, not hers. You got the right to do things the way you want."

Josie leaned back in her chair, sipping her tea. "I know. Priscilla said weddings take months to organize. We've certainly had our work cut out for us what with classes to attend, invitations to order and send, a gown to buy, and a reception to plan with only a little over seven weeks to get everything done. It's been hectic, but it hasn't been impossible. We've survived."

Vertie said nothing. She went to the sink and rinsed out the bowl.

Josie rattled on. "I'm pleased Mark and Elliott got the furniture moved out of the living room and arranged the folding chairs. Isn't it funny we rented them from a funeral parlor?" She chuckled. "A professional photographer is coming who'll take pictures for us. We'll have a write-up with a picture put in the newspaper's society column. I told Priscilla that Aunt Mae and I'd be over at about eight to help them cut flowers from their beds. The Indian summer weather is absolute perfection for today . . . no rain. And because a killing frost's held off—thank God for His goodness—we'll have plenty of blooms. It would've cost a fortune for the amount we need if we'd had to buy them from a florist. Clarinda and Priscilla were very generous to offer all we needed, as well as their silver candelabra with white candles to use on the fireplace mantel. Yikes, look at the time! Aunt Mae better wake up, and I better put some clothes on. We've got work to do."

* * *

Josie snipped the stems of the freshly-cut flowers to the right length, all the while imagining what it would be like to be married to a man who was a gentle, unpretentious companion.

"Josie? Yoo-hoo. Earth to Josie. Come ba-ack. Can you hear me?"

She came out of her reverie and turned quickly to face Priscilla, "Sorry, I was lost in another world."

"I could tell. A pleasant one, though, wasn't it? You had a smile on your face. Ready to become Mrs. Elliott Randolph Jacobson?"

"The name has a definite ring to it, doesn't it?"

"Come on. Time to dress. Leave this job for others to handle," Priscilla urged. She left the back porch and entered the house.

"Guess I've got to go," Josie said to Mae. "Can you finish up what's left to do?" She went in, passed through the kitchen, and made her way across the front hallway when a knock sounded at the front door. She turned aside and flung it open. "Aunt Phoebe and Aunt Ruth!" Josie hugged them. "You had to leave Bradford in the wee hours this morning to arrive here at this hour."

"We did," Ruth announced. "It never occurred to us to miss this day." She made a stirring motion with her hand. "Turn around. Let's look at you." She stepped back. "You're glowing."

Josie laughed. "You're kidding, aren't you? I'm wearing an old cotton dress and not cleaned up. Haven't even touched my hair, yet."

"Doesn't matter. Is there anything we can do to help?" Phoebe asked.

"Yes, there is. Follow me." Josie took them to Mae Anise, introduced them, and instructed them where to place the flower baskets at the appropriate intervals along the bride's path. Then she went upstairs to take a bath.

While the water ran into the tub, Josie turned her attention to the bridal gown hanging on the wardrobe's door. Her hands stroked the soft, satiny folds.

Priscilla came up behind her. "Mae outdid herself. You'll look ravishing in this."

"Breathtaking, isn't it?"

"I'll say. The most gorgeous thing I've ever seen. You better hurry and get into the tub so you'll be able to put it on . . . or else you'll marry Elliott wearing an old housedress. I'm going into the next room. Holler if you need help. I'll leave the door open a little so I can hear you."

Josie smiled. She went into the bathroom, looked out the window upon the scene taking place in the side yard, and shivered. Vertie and Nub were making their way to where Lillian sat. "Lord, only You know the degree of pain in each of them. May reconciliation take place as much as possible for their own sakes, as well as for Elliott's."

* * *

Lillian arrived at the Matthews's house earlier in the day than she'd intended. She steered clear of the flurry of activity happening on the back porch, where people were cutting and arranging flowers in baskets, as well as the commotion going on inside the kitchen and dining room, where people were setting up for the brunch. She went outside and sat on a wooden chair at a little table under the great canopy. She hadn't been to Terre Haute for twenty-five years.

Nub and Vertie came out the back door, down the steps, and toward her. She had not considered her parents for years.

"Hello, Mother." She nodded to Nub. "Dad."

He remained standing and cleared his throat. "How was your trip from Bloomington?"

"Uneventful. Say what you came out here to say and get it over with," she snapped. "We haven't a lot of time before others will be arriving."

Vertie sat across from her daughter. "Eliza . . . uh, Lillian, why did you cut us out of your life?"

"Yeah, how could you resent your mama and me so much?"

"Oh, for heaven's sake. To this day, I'm haunted by the memories of my growing-up years and how you treated me."

"Whatever do you mean?"

"You always favored George Henry and gave him the best, and me the leftovers. I never felt loved."

"Your ideas of what love is are all messed up, then," Nub said.

"Maybe we weren't as affectionate as what you wanted us to be, but don't say we didn't love you."

Lillian bristled. "I never once heard you tell me you did."

"Land sakes, we didn't think we had to in so many words."

"Your mother's right. We provided for you and thought that was enough. You can't really, in your heart, believe we didn't love you."

"See?" She exploded. "Don't tell me what I think or don't. What did you care?" She sprang to her feet and glared at him. "You were always gone."

He took a deep breath. "Sit down, daughter. You're not running away this time. Now, listen to my side of the story. I was away much of the time because I was working to provide for you."

Vertie held up a hand. "Your father's right. We sacrificed to make certain you had the things you needed."

"Oh, sure," Lillian said, icy-voiced. "Take his part. I had to wear hand-me-down clothes and—"

Vertie interrupted. "Stop it, right there. You sound like a spoiled, self-centered child. Those clothes were nice . . . and clean. Our family finances were always under pressure, that's true. But we got by. There's no disgrace in being poor, Lillian."

"I couldn't have friends over to spend the night," she shrieked.

"Land sakes, don't you realize George Henry's grand mal attacks would've scared the living daylights out of them?"

For a moment, Lillian sat glowering at her mother. "I hated every minute at home—the futility of life you both accepted and resigned yourselves to. Not me! I wanted a different life—a better one. I knew I wouldn't be able to find it if I'd stayed with you . . . and in Terre Haute."

"Don't be ungrateful, Lillian. The Good Book warns against wishing for more. Did you find what you were looking for?" Vertie asked.

"I'm not finished," Lillian shouted. "I endured ridicule by my classmates because I went without new books and . . . bought candy and . . . patent-leather shoes. I was never invited to their parties and left out of—" she flapped her arms—"out of everything. I lived with a sense of inferiority."

Nub shook his head. "Only because you compared yourself with them and what they had. It made you miserable, too, didn't it? Envy rots a person's bones."

"What a thing to say."

"Your life wasn't so terrible, daughter. Somehow, though, you're convinced that your memory is correct."

"I decided what was essential to me and jumped at the opportunity to achieve it. I figured there was more out there than what was here in Terre Haute."

"You've brought a lot of unhappiness on yourself . . . and others . . . and on us."

"As if you cared!" Lillian hissed the words.

"Land sakes, we sure did. More than you'll ever realize," Vertie said. "Give us a little credit."

"Daughter, life is not easy—for anyone. Only you can hate longer and more intense and . . . meaner than anybody else."

Lillian scooted back from the little table, pushed up off the chair, and lashed out at them. "You two know you're in the wrong, but won't admit it."

"Looky here," Nub said. "We all make our lives what they are. You found your kind of success by strength of will and hardness of heart . . . and a haughty spirit. You now have the money you always coveted, but you made a pretty general failure of happiness in life."

Lillian huffed something under her breath and stomped away, turning her back on her parents—again. She'd bared her soul to them, and what did it get her? Their pity. She didn't want that. She wanted them to see the truth.

What was that, anyway? Over the years, could her facts have become twisted and replaced with a completely erroneous scenario? Strange how time had magnified her hurt feelings and misunderstandings instead of lessening them. The confrontation with her parents today was long overdue, and the delay had been her own fault. They reached out to her, but she cut them off.

Why had she picked at the emotional wounds so long and allowed her anger and bitterness to fester? What could she do now to restore peace and heal the breach in her relationship with them? She mulled these things over while pacing up and down the front sidewalk.

Chapter 25

From her room, Josie heard the front door open and close and shuffling in the entry hall. Before long, the air rang with the screaks and squeals of violins being tuned. The musicians had arrived—and on time. She put on the finishing touches of her makeup.

Mae tapped on the bedroom door and poked her head in. "Yoo-hoo! How's it going? Could you use another pair of hands?"

"Yes. Come in."

"Where's Priscilla? Shouldn't she be in here helping you?"

"She's next door getting dressed herself. Will you help me slip into my wedding gown? I don't want to mess up my face and hair."

"Of course." Mae lifted the smooth satin over her niece's head.

Josie turned to the mirror. The long skirt, cut on the bias, draped her slim figure in a most becoming way. The Juliet sleeves ended in deep points on the tops of her hands and buttoned at the wrists, and both the front and back of the bodice were "V" shaped.

"You're stunning," Mae said, standing beside her niece.

"Aunt Mae, I can't thank you enough for all you've done. This gown is divine, and I'm amazed how unbelievably well it fits me. How did you manage that?"

"Remember, honey, I got the one you wore at Christmas. I had all your measurements."

"Oh, yeah. You mean this was made specifically for me?"

"I do. Now turn around and let me attach the train." It hooked to the back of her waist and flowed in folds. "Are you wearing the emerald necklace your father gave you?"

"No, the locket Elliott gave me for Valentine's Day. It accentuates the neckline."

"Nice. Get it and I'll fasten it for you."

Josie stood gazing at her reflection. She sighed. "I wish Mother were here. I miss her so much. She died over a year ago, and still an emptiness remains in my spirit." Tears hovered in her eyes. "Am I being maudlin, or is it the music downstairs affecting me? She loved music—especially the violin." The strains of "Love Dreams," "At Dawning," "Sanctuary of the Heart," "Oh, Promise Me," and "I Love You, Truly" drifted up to the two. "Priscilla was right. The string ensemble is quite accomplished."

"My heart aches for you. I know something of how you're feeling, and even though it's the happiest day of your life, you'll never be able to forget your grief."

"Mother loved colorful flowers, too." Josie could no longer see her reflection in the mirror clearly.

"You look exquisite, Josie. It's time I need to get dressed myself." Mae went to the door, paused, and looked back at her niece. "Priscilla can help you with your veil."

"Thanks for being with me this morning."

"It was my pleasure." She left and in a matter of minutes . . .

Priscilla appeared in the doorway. "Josie? Why are you crying? Stop, you don't want to ruin your makeup . . . or get any stains on your gown."

"No, you're right. I'm thinking how Mother would have been overjoyed to participate in this day." She took Priscilla's hands. "You understand?"

Priscilla wobbled her head. "Not completely. I can only guess how horrible you feel, though." She rubbed across Josie's shoulders. "So-o-o, what do you think? Will I do as your maid of honor?" She turned a full circle for the bride's inspection.

Josie put a hand to her mouth. "You look fabulous. That blue matches your eyes perfectly. Aunt Mae did an incredible job selecting our gowns, didn't she?"

Priscilla fiddled with the pearl buttons of her dyed-to-match gloves. "A fantastic job. Oh, Josie, you're gorgeous. Aren't you simply overflowing with joy?"

"Very much so."

"That's all that matters. Now, what do you need help with?"

"My fingertip veil."

Priscilla held up the white tulle attached to a halo of pearls and orange blossoms and posited it on Josie's head.

"Is it secure enough? There're some combs we can twist a little if we need to. Are you nervous?"

"Isn't it obvious?"

"How can you be? You're marrying the man of your dreams."

"I know. God has richly blessed me."

The two made their way to the stairway and stopped. "I'm not poetical like you," Priscilla said. "No elegant words about love and marriage come to my mind, but I'm ecstatic things have worked out this way for you. I hope you'll always be as happy as you are now. You deserve it." She lightly squeezed Josie's arms, then she slowly descended to the front hall, where Landon handed her a single long-stemmed calla lily before she proceeded into the living room.

Josie followed moments later, taking her time, careful not to trip on the hem, holding it up as she took each step. Her father stood at the base of the stairs. He extended his hand to her when she stepped off. "You're loveliness personified."

Then . . . Landon pulled her to him and surrounded her with an embrace—a big bear hug. "I've always wanted a daughter with my color of hair and eyes . . . and you came into my life. You've made me proud to be your father, Joselene. I'm so sorry . . . about the past."

Josie, struck dumb by the awareness at what just happened, blinked and swallowed. Her wish had finally come true. She'd waited a long time for this, dreamed of it, lived for it. She clung to him and didn't want to let go. He held on to her, too. At last, she knew she'd won a place in his heart. She now had a father who loved her for who she was. And he was giving her away to a terrific man who'd asked her to be his wife. She pulled away, stared at him, and caught her breath.

"Something wrong?"

"No, it's just that I am the happiest woman in the whole world. Let me see if I got any makeup on your suit." She checked his lapel and his sleeves, and found no smudges.

Landon reached into his pocket and pulled out a penny. "Here."

"What's this for?"

"An old English superstition . . . it symbolizes good health and wealth for the couple. The bride is given a coin by her father, and she puts it in her shoe."

"That's a new one on me, but okay." She removed her white patent leather slipper, dropped the penny into it, and put her foot back in.

Priscilla had by this time reached her designated spot. At once the musicians began the strains of "Jesu, Joy of Man's Desiring."

Landon straightened his tie. "This is our song."

Josie carefully lowered the veil over her face, and Landon gave her a white calla lily. "Ready?" He brought her free hand through the crook of his bent arm, then covered it with his own fingers. Together, daughter and father made their grand entrance into the living room.

The officiant, Judge Kramer, Landon's long-time friend, imposing in his long black robe, announced in his deep voice, "All rise."

Everyone did and turned as Josie and Landon, measuring their steps with the music, progressed along the walkway amidst a soft ripple of whispers. Josie's gaze fixed upon Elliott standing in front of the fireplace, handsome in his black three-piece suit. She smiled at him all the way down the aisle. *I'm going to be his wife and have the responsibility for his meals, his clothes, his comfort, his home, his children. With God's help, I'll strive to be the best helpmate any man ever had in the whole world. Lord God, I love him so much. Bless our marriage.*

When they got to where Elliott stood, Landon squeezed Josie's hand. Soon the music stopped, and everyone sat. Josie stood with her father and Elliott—the two men she loved more than anything in the world.

"Who gives this woman to be wedded to this man?" the judge asked in a clear voice.

"I do," Landon said. "And proudly," he whispered to Josie. He relinquished her hand to Elliott, kissed her on one cheek, and took a seat beside Mae Anise.

The ceremony began. "Elliott Randolph, do you take Joselene Grace . . ." The spell of the moment spread through the room.

Josie held tightly to Elliott's hand and closed her eyes. She heard the words, but the judge reading them and Elliott's declaration seemed a million miles away. Then it was her turn. The two promised each other to share all that was to come, for better or worse, for richer or poorer, in sickness, and in health. They vowed to give and receive, to speak and listen, to inspire and respond, and to love and cherish.

Mark read the scripture from Ecclesiastes, Chapter 4. "'Two are better than one . . . For if they fall, the one will lift up his fellow; but woe to him that is alone when he falleth; for he hath not another to help him up. Again, if two lie together, then they have heat; but can one be warm alone? And if one prevails against him, two shall withstand him; and a threefold cord is not quickly broken.'"

Priscilla sang "The Lord's Prayer." Her soprano voice rose high and sweet. With the piano and the string quartet, it was a beautiful rendition.

The judge said, "May I have the ring, please?" Mark deposited it in the man's opened palm. "Let this ring signify to all the uniting of Elliott and Joselene in holy matrimony."

He presented it to Elliott who held Joselene's left hand and slipped the plain gold band partially over her knuckle.

She pushed it all the way down her fourth finger, looked at it, and drew a long breath, glancing up into his face. He winked at her.

The judge concluded, "Now, by the power vested in me by the State of Indiana, I pronounce that you are husband and wife." He looked at Elliott, "You may kiss your bride."

Elliott took his time in lifting Josie's veil. He pulled her into his arms, dipped down, and murmured into her hair. "Hello, Mrs. Elliott Randolph Jacobson." Then he kissed her on the lips with a gentleness almost amounting to reverence.

The nuptials finished, the bride and groom walked back up the aisle, her left hand tucked into his arm. They stopped at the base of the stairs.

"Where shall we stand to greet everyone?" Elliott glanced around, let his gaze return to her.

"Why not here?" she said. "That'll keep them pretty much corralled, and we can move into the dining room for breakfast."

Wedding guests pressed against the couple from all sides, hugging and kissing, and congratulating them. As they went away one by one, Josie and Elliott became separated, leaving Josie alone with her aunts.

Ruth latched hold of Josie's hand. "It was so beautiful . . . like a coronation . . . or the Academy Awards."

"You two make an extraordinarily attractive couple," Phoebe said. "We wouldn't have missed this for anything."

"I'm glad you came to celebrate with us. I know this is a busy time at the orchard. I appreciate that you made the sacrifice by being here. This day wouldn't have been as glorious if you two hadn't come."

Lillian joined the three. "A simple little service. But it was properly done, anyway. I suppose I'm to kiss you."

"If you like." Josie leaned forward to accept Lillian's congratulations. But their cheeks barely touched. Josie glanced around for Elliott. Where did he get off to? She spied him at the other end of the room with her father and the judge.

Ruth faced Lillian. "Your son sure is lucky."

Phoebe added, "I hope he realizes what he's got. Josie's a right smart girl."

Elliott strolled across the space to Josie's side at that very moment. He put an arm around his wife's waist and pulled her close, nuzzling her ear. "I'll go along with that remark. I don't know what I'd do without this wonderful woman. This is the happiest day of my life."

Lillian stomped off. Ruth and Phoebe stared at the woman who was now their niece's new mother-in-law. They, too, left the couple, and Elliott took Josie's hands. "Honey, we're never going to change Mother. She is who she is."

"You're right."

"And, for the record, this really is the happiest day of my life. So, we're not going to let her ruin our wedding day, are we?"

She looked into his face. "Absolutely not."

The photographer came up. "I'm set to take pictures of the wedding party."

"Let's eat first. Picture taking can wait."

"Whatever you say," he said, toying with his camera.

"May I have everyone's attention?" Elliott said, and waited for the talking to tone down. "Let's all go to the dining room and be entertained with food. Table's full, ready for us to come and devour."

They sat down to the brunch at ten forty-five. On the menu were Vertie's little heart-shaped biscuits with ham slices, Quiche Lorraine, cream puffs, and mixed fresh fruit with honey dressing as the main items. Coffee and tea completed the fare.

After the meal, the wedding party went to the living room to pose for the official photographs. The guests meandered in and out as the photographer did his thing.

Nub and Vertie were the last to have their official photograph taken with the couple. Josie kissed each on the cheek. "Thank you both for all you've done."

"Yes," Elliott said, "I can never be grateful enough for all your help, Grandmother."

She placed her hands on each side of his face and planted a kiss on his forehead. "I love to hear you call me that. I've waited a mighty long time."

"Well, *Grandmother*, from the moment I saw this young woman, I wanted her to be a part of my life, and now look, I got my wish."

Vertie's eyes got watery. "I got mine, too." She patted Elliott on his forearm. "For years, I prayed you'd get the opportunity to know your grandfather and me. Couldn't imagine how it'd happen, or when, but never gave up hoping and praying—and look here." She beamed. "I'm happier than I can speak of. You coming here, Josie. You, Elliott, meeting her . . . and now you're married. You both've survived your mothers' mistakes of choosing to practice deception. I presume both of them thought they were doing what was best." She shook her head. "You've learned how honesty is vital to relationships. Josie, I'm gratified you had the courage to keep another woman from coming between you and Elliott—even if the other woman was my daughter. Isn't it astonishing to see how God has a way of righting wrongs? If we're patient, His blessings do come. He'll work things out at the right time and in the right way. Reminds me of my favorite passage in the Good Book. It goes something like this: In all things—not just some, but all—God works for the good of those who love Him. I believe God's got something special in store for the two of you. Think about it: He brought you together in a miraculous way, wouldn't you say? Today was meant to be."

"No doubt about it," agreed Elliott. He kissed Vertie and hugged Nub, and he and Josie left to go outside.

The backyard looked sumptuous with a lavish white canopy that contrasted with the red, yellow, and russet leaves blazing in their autumn colors. Josie's well-groomed garden, along with the canopy's supports entwined with ivy, captured the elegance of the occasion. Small tables with white damask tablecloths and chairs with white pillow covers over their backs were arranged around the periphery of the reception area.

"What a perfect Indian summer day, isn't it? Rich October-blue sky—God's blessing, for sure."

"Yep," said Elliott. "All those foreboding clouds of yesterday blew away during the night. Fortunately, the air isn't cold."

The bride's table, handsomely appointed with a white lace cloth, held the five-tier wedding cake, which boasted white and cream-colored spun sugar roses cascading down its side like a fountain.

At one o'clock, Josie and Elliott took their place, and with his hand over hers, they plunged the knife into the bottom tier and sliced through the triple layer. Each broke off a morsel and fed the other from the same slice. Everyone cheered and clapped. The photographer snapped the activity.

At three, they prepared to leave for the French Lick Springs Resort. Many of the guests rushed to the front yard, stood around Elliott's Studebaker, and dilly-dallied until the newlyweds arrived. The couple posed for some final pictures.

Elliott stooped to whisper in Josie's ear, "Did you ever dream of happiness like this?"

She shook her head. "Never. I can't believe it yet. I feel like the princess in a fairy tale who lived happily ever after."

"Our future, Mrs. Elliott Randolph Jacobson, is what we make it, and I intend to make it better than either you or I ever dreamed possible."

She smiled and held her hand up to twiddle her ring. "Uh-huh. I like that idea, and so far, I like being married to you."

He licked his lips, his eyes ticking back and forth. "Realize what that means?"

She nodded. "Uh-huh."

He put his arms around her. "Scared?"

She shook her head. "Uh-uh."

Elliott opened the car door for her and shut it after she climbed in.

He went around to slide in his place by her side. "Ah, Josie my love, my darling wife, this is when the real adventure of life begins—from this day forward. This is the place you belong—right here with me." Then his lips were on hers, and she knew he was right.

Acknowledgments

Dreams can and do come true. My dream of writing a book started many years ago. Through encouragement from family and friends, and perseverance, *The Place You Belong* has become reality. The story is a product of my imagination, although it centers around a historical event. Within the pages, fictional characters interact with famous political figures.

I was blessed to have numerous readers. The very first reader was my daughter, Valerie. Her suggestions about the characters and storyline were greatly appreciated. My sisters, Judy Deuel and Lois Hartman, were also first readers. I offer my special thanks to them for their attention to detail and getting the words right.

Carol Helderman, a sister in Christ, and Phil Meyer, an attorney extraordinaire, gave me great advice on how to make a more compelling story. I'm grateful for the readers of the final draft: Cornelia Ahrens, Sharron Cline, and Jane Clary. They are sisters in Christ who gave their encouragement and excitement in getting the story published.

For several members of my family, I say thank you, thank you, thank you, for the technological support each of you gave me: my son, Chip, and his wife, my daughter-in-law, Paula; my son-in-law, Larry Stice; and my brother-in-law, Will Deuel (who was also an early reader). Thank you for your patience with me.

I thank my brother-in-law, Paul Hartman, and my sister-in-law, Bonnie Noe, for filling the role of proofreaders. I thank many other friends for their interest in this story.

Almost most of all, I'm grateful for my best friend and husband, Roy, who provided immense support to me. I thank him for his unfailing love and patience and thank God for giving him the ability to come up with just the right word when I got stuck or needed to test an idea. Thank you, my beloved, for always believing in me.

Above all, I praise our Lord and Savior Jesus Christ for this opportunity to fulfill my dream.